The Adventures of

OPAL AND CUPID

The Adventures of
OPAL AND CUPID

A story by
THOMAS TRYON
WITH CLIVE WILSON

VIKING

VIKING
Published by the Penguin Group
Penguin Books USA Inc., 375 Hudson Street, New York, New York 10014, U.S.A.
Penguin Books Ltd, 27 Wrights Lane, London W8 5TZ, England
Penguin Books Australia Ltd, Ringwood, Victoria, Australia
Penguin Books Canada Ltd, 10 Alcorn Avenue, Toronto, Ontario, Canada M4V 3B2
Penguin Books (N.Z.) Ltd, 182–190 Wairau Road, Auckland 10, New Zealand

Penguin Books Ltd, Registered Offices: Harmondsworth, Middlesex, England

First published in 1992 by Viking, a division of Penguin Books USA Inc.

1   3   5   7   9   10   8   6   4   2

LIBRARY OF CONGRESS CATALOGING-IN-PUBLICATION DATA
Tryon, Thomas. The adventures of Opal and Cupid / by Thomas
Tryon.   p.   cm.
Summary: Young Opal Thigpen meets Cupid, an elephant in a traveling
show, and the two have a series of adventures as they rise to stardom.
ISBN 0-670-82239-6 [1. Friendship—Fiction. 2. Elephants—Fiction.] I. Title.
PZ7.T976Ad   1992   [Fic]—dc20   90-33139 CIP AC

Printed in U.S.A.
Set in 11 pt. Weiss

Drawings by Rachel Isadora

CONTENTS

The Adventures of

OPAL AND CUPID

Chapter One

Gunshot!

THE ROOSTER HAD CROWED AT SIX, TELLING THE folks of Peavine Hollow that it was time to rise and shine. The pearly dawn was parting the darkened sky, stroking the summer-green fields with long, golden fingers of light, promising a day of surpassing fineness. But on this particular morning Opal Thigpen decided to linger a while in bed. It was Sunday, and old Granny Bid was still fast asleep in the adjoining room of the little house they shared by the river. Opal stretched luxuriously under the covers, dreaming of what might lie in store for her on so glorious a morning. Would it be a day filled with all good things—or perhaps even bad ones—for who knew after all what the future held for anyone? Time alone would tell. The fact was, it would shortly prove an exceptional day in her young life, combining both the good and the bad, which was pretty much the way things went on planet Earth.

Ever since she was born, Opal Thigpen had been sleeping in

that same old bed, which creaked and squeaked every time she rolled over. She stretched again, yawned, and wriggled her toes, which stuck out from under a crazy quilt of brightly colored gingham patches. After a moment she peeked under the blanket, as a small furry creature nestled its way along her side. It was her pet rabbit, Lola. The animal felt warm from having slept all night under the covers, and Opal sat the downy white form on her chest and hugged it so that the soft pink ears tickled her nose.

"Lola, honey," she whispered, "time to stir our stumps, I reckon." In her thirteen years' worth of experience, Opal had found that most animals were better company than most humans. Animals even had a better sense of humor and were better listeners. Lucerne, the holstein cow, always appreciated a good joke, and Zephyr, the Poland brood sow that lived in the Cumberpatches' pigpen, never tired of hearing you talk. Frankly, when you came down to it, Opal found most four-legged creatures a lot more comforting than people.

Without warning, a loud shot rang out, shattering the Sabbath stillness. Opal sprang from her bed and leaned out across the low windowsill to fasten her eyes on the jerk-kneed, scarecrowlike figure of her neighbor, Old Man Cumberpatch, brandishing a smoking shotgun in the doorway of his old ramshackle house.

"What's happenin' yonder?" an alarmed Granny Bid called from the next room.

"It's that mean old Grampaw Cumberpatch!" cried Opal. "He's been shooting critters again." She leaned farther out for a better view.

"Durn tootin' I have!" crowed the old man happily as he clattered off his porch and hobbled over to the kitchen garden.

Opal watched in speechless horror as he picked up a furry brown object and held it aloft like a trophy. "Got the plaguey beast plumb thoo the eyeballs!" he boasted, hopping around like an old jackanapes among the crooked rows of his cabbage bed.

"Lord a'mercy, he shot Brownie!" cried the stricken Opal. "Granny, do you hear? Grampaw Cumberpatch took his shotgun and he shot Lola's daddy!" Without waiting for a response and clutching little Lola in her arms, she dashed out of the cabin, her petticoat flapping loosely around her legs.

"You shot my rabbit!" she wailed as she rushed up to Grampaw Cumberpatch, who tipped back his straw hat and rubbed the end of his red nose.

"Gol-danged right I shot him, girl," he declared. "And I'll shoot any other animules that is dang-fooled enough to eat of my early cabbages!" He gave his murdered victim a good shake, then cupped his hand and called inside. "Come lookee here, Eee-toyle, see how yore daddy gotcha rabbit stew for supper! Count on it!"

In a flash Etoile Cumberpatch appeared barefooted on the porch, her hair in bedspring curlers under a sky-blue net.

"Shot him good, didja, Grampaw? Plumb thoo the head? There's a good one for you! Serves you'uns right," she screeched at Opal. "That'll teach you t'keep yer durn critters proper penned up! Any more of your long-ears come eatin' of our garden, Grampaw'll blast the whole lot. Us'ns'll be feasting fer a month a' Sundays."

There was nothing Opal disliked more than listening to the screechings of Etoile Cumberpatch. Sobbing, she tore her eyes from the bloody sight and ran away to the rabbit hutch, cradling Lola against her chest, that sweet little girl-child of Brownie's, whose heart was beating like a trip hammer.

As Opal had suspected, the first thing her eye fell on was the place in the pen where the chicken wire had been deliberately pried loose. She knew full well whose mischief this was: Henhouse Cumberpatch. Henhouse had been a touch "tetched" ever since his fourth birthday, when Iota the mule had kicked him in the head. Fixing it for Brownie to get out so Grampaw could shoot him dead and they could all plunk themselves down to a nice rabbit stew at supper was just like Henhouse.

Fighting back her tears, Opal opened the hutch and slipped Lola amid the clean straw with her brothers and sisters. Then, leaving the door slightly ajar, she kept very still, allowing the little rabbits to hop all around her hands, picking them up and fondling them, whispering into their pink ears and gently stroking their backs. She hated so to be the bearer of bad tidings. How could she tell these sweet furry creatures that they were fatherless now, that their daddy was going to end up in a ragout? Opal didn't have the heart; she was fatherless, too—motherless as well—and she knew only too clearly just how that felt.

Her own daddy, Jimmy-Jack Thigpen, had been the only boy of Granny Bid's only boy, and she had cared for him and raised him like a son. After Jimmy-Jack married Opal's momma, they had all gone on living together in Bid's little house right there in the Hollow, and when Opal was born she had immediately become the apple of her daddy's eye. From what she could remember of her early childhood years, they were the happiest of times. Jimmy-Jack had been the limberest tap dancer in the whole of Cotton County, and his daughter had taken right after him, dancing with him since she was in rompers. Oh, how she loved it!

Then one day her momma took sick. The poor soul, she wasted away for all of June through October, and when the frost was on the pumpkins she upped and died, leaving Opal and her daddy brokenhearted. One morning Jimmy-Jack had hopped the seven o'clock train, leaving Opal in Granny Bid's safe care and vowing to seek his fame and fortune in "the show biz" in New York City. He promised to send for Opal as soon as he'd hit the Big Time, but so far Opal was still living there in the Hollow with her only

4

other kin, who at one hundred and two years last New Year's was the absolute oldest person in the county. But, even though she was an ancient and had been written up in the *Peavine Daily Clarion*, that mind of Granny Bid's was often sharp as a tack.

Safely stowing Lola among her brothers and sisters, Opal secured the hutch and left the rabbits contentedly nibbling some rhubarb tops while she went on to her regular morning chore. In the cow shed it was cool and dark, and she could be alone while she milked. She took her pail and the three-legged stool, and while she drained the cow's udders she had a morning's worth of conversation with her, for that was exactly how long the job took.

"Maybe you didn't see what happened, Lucerne," she began, "but that wicked old Grampaw Cumberpatch shot Brownie. How do you like that?" Lucerne mooed and shook her blunted horns to indicate her concern, but, being a cow, there was very little Lucerne could do. Besides, the Cumberpatches were a rowdy lot, always shooting off things—either their weapons or their mouths. Certainly they were the poorest and trashiest of all the poor white trash living in the Hollow. And who could do anything about their orneriness? Not Opal, not in a lifetime.

For as long as anyone could remember here in Peavine Hollow, the Cumberpatches had been tenant farmers on a good piece of bottom land that had been held in fief by the Primroses up on the hill for more than two centuries. They managed to scratch only the barest living from the earth, depending entirely on a few paltry acres of cotton to feed, clothe, and shelter a family as large as that of the Old Woman Who Lived in a Shoe. While the Primroses were one of the most distinguished and cream-of-the-cream families in the county, the Cumberpatches were a clan of ne'er-do-wells with branches reaching like the tangled twigs of a bramblebush all over that corner of the state. Some folks liked to say the Cumberpatch tribe was one of the Lost Tribes of Israel. Sister Eclipse, Granny Bid's friend, declared they were more likely one of the plagues of Egypt, like the locusts or the fiery rain.

As Opal continued her milking, she turned her mind to more gratifying thoughts about her daddy so far away up north, picturing a time they would be together again. If only she could go and visit him in New York City and see all the sights that she knew about only from his picture postcards. Why, maybe they could dream up an act dancing together—they might even hit the Big Time Daddy still talked about sometimes when he wrote her.

Maybe such a grand and wonderful fate was what Sister Eclipse had meant when she told Opal's fortune with her pack of cards. "The cards never lie," she had said as she predicted how a great fiery ball was going to come rolling down the Old Cotton Road, straight for Opal's door stoop.

But Opal found room for doubt. Here she was, stuck in Peavine Hollow, just a "no-account chile," which was what Etoile Cumberpatch always called her. And if such wondrous things had been ordained for her by fate, where were they? And how would a girl like Opal recognize them when they showed up? Of course, a ball of fire was a ball of fire, anyone could see that, but this wasn't Bible times. This was 1936, and Mr. Roosevelt was in the White House. She bet Mr. Roosevelt hadn't ever seen any fiery balls.

These thoughts were interrupted by the sudden noise of a bang-'em-up machine coming along the road, a sound she recognized instantly as that of Sister Eclipse's "contraption." It being Sunday, Sister was coming to sit with Granny Bid, which would allow Opal to attend church service. Finishing up quickly, she hung her milking stool on its peg, fitted the bar across Lucerne's chest, and went out to meet her visitor.

The Dented Dragon, as Sister Eclipse called it because it had so many dents and holes in it and because it steamed and smoked like a scaly monster in a fairy tale, was just pulling into the dooryard. With a superabundance of screeching gears and the fierce protesting of thinly shoed brakes, the faithful truck ground to a halt. Sister Eclipse switched off the engine, fiddled with the magneto some, and finally extracted her considerable weight from the oilcloth seat, like a large, fat cork popping out of a bottle.

"Happy Sunday, honeychile," she called out in her firm, resolute voice. Sister Eclipse was short and roly-poly, with a button nose, bright twinkling eyes, and a broad smile that lit up her plump, brown face. Today she wore a fresh-washed calico dress and a straw hat in the general shape of a flowerpot, with a bold red flower stuck on it, and her shoes had X's cut in them to let her corns "breathe." Clutched in one hand was an old carpetbag, which chinked when she set it on the ground, suggesting glass containers of a medicinal nature.

When Opal disclosed the unhappy news about the death of Brownie, Sister shaded her eyes against the rising sun and scowled over at the Cumberpatch place. Henhouse Cumberpatch and his younger brother Yclept were chasing the pullets helter-skelter across the yard and kicking up considerable ruckus.

"I'll teach that mean old crawdad to shoot other folks' rabbits," Sister muttered, grimly jutting out her bottom lip (always a sign of stormy weather). As they watched, Henhouse picked up a bed slat and winged it at his brother, whereupon Yclept set to caterwaulin', causing their mother Etoile to appear on the porch and attempt to screech the boy into silence. When their sister Miss'sipp stuck her oversized head out the upper-story window and began hollerin', too, it sounded like somebody had shaken up a bag full of wet cats.

Picking up her carpetbag, Sister took Opal by the elbow and urged her toward the cabin. From inside Bid's room came the sound of her feeble cough and the creak of her bed as she stirred. Sister Eclipse tiptoed in, leaving Opal to carry her pail of milk into the country room and set it on the pantry shelf. There she lit a fire in the wood stove and popped the kettle on the plate to heat up some water. After she'd shaken herself into her old raggedy dress and pinafore that said BURDEAL'S CORNMEAL FLOUR on the front and offered a printed recipe for monkey biscuits on the back, she went back into the kitchen and fixed Bid her morning cup of chicory. Before taking it in, she added exactly twenty drops of Sister Eclipse's root-squeeze 'lixir, the tonic that Sister swore kept Granny alive and hale. When she'd stirred the cup a-plenty, she carried it in on a saucer that had had a large crack in it all of Opal's life but had never broke yet.

"How're you feeling, Biddy, dear?" Sister was asking at the old lady's bedside. She bent down and gave her bony shoulder a gentle shake. "Mornin', hon, rise and shine. Sheep's in the meadow, cow's in the corn. Here's Opie with a nice cup of your chic'ry."

She took the steaming cup from Opal and passed it to Bid, who accepted it gratefully, appreciative of its warmth in her pale, withered hands. As she sipped, she moved her head about against her pillow, squinting against the light. Her skin was wrinkled, almost the same color as her pale, well-worn bedsheet, and her eyes were all shriveled up. There was so little of her that her body hardly made an outline under the coverlet.

She didn't empty the cup, drinking only partway, just enough to satisfy Sister's persnickety standards of health. Then the drink was set aside. Granny Bid made a nasty monkey-face.

"You put in some o'Sister's 'lixir, didn't you?" she accused Opal.

"Of course she did," said Sister, "twenny drops of Sister Eclipse's 'Lixir of Life every day, and you're bound to live another fifty years."

"I don't care to live another fifty years!" exclaimed the old lady with a sudden show of spirit. "Matter of fact I don't care to live one more year."

" 'Course you do! Now go on, honeychile," Sister coaxed, "try another lick. It'll give you good where you needs it the mostest, I promise."

Bid made a face. "Lord, how I hate the taste of that godacious stuff. I can hardly think what poison y'all must put in it."

Sister laid a finger alongside her nose. "That for me to know and you to find out, hon. Sister Eclipse don't tell none of her secrets to nobody. Most folks simply dotes on my 'lixir. They say it gives 'em plenny of vim, plenny of vigor."

This much was true. In that neck of the woods, Sister Eclipse was famous for her root-squeeze tonic, whose recipe she said had been handed down to her from an old Choctaw Indian woman, a concoction good for anything from rickets in the young to baldness in the aged. Sister made a good living at her work, traveling from house to house along the Old Cotton Road in the Dented Dragon, selling her bottles with their bright, fancy labels proclaiming the slogan, "Shuts Off the Moon, Turns On the Sun." Anybody walking the back roads of Peavine knew about Sister's extravagant claim from the large-type advertisements to that effect tacked up on telegraph poles and barn sidings.

Yet Sister often joked that her best advertisement was Bid herself. While Sister and her elixir had become a legend for keeping people going, Granny Bid was a legend for keeping going period. With such a mutual interest, it was only natural that the two would have become tried and true friends.

Sister turned to Opal—and to a more pleasant subject than

9

old Bid's health. "I stopped by the postbox last evening, honey-chile. Brought you a piece of mail. Bet you can guess what 'tis." She was holding a picture postcard in her hand.

Opal's heart skipped a beat. Yes, it was from Daddy. Another addition to her collection. This one showed a handsome aerial view of Central Park, with a lake and boats, and ducks—a big green park right in the middle of the city! Why, it was as if they'd taken the whole of Peavine Hollow and plunked it down among all those tall buildings. Turning the card over, Opal read:

> Dear Opie,
> I am fine and hoping you are the same. We have had a fine spring and look forward to a fine summer, too. I am a dancing fool, tapping my feet off every chance I get. But I still haven't had a dancing partner good as you. Love to Granny Bid. Love to you, too.
>
> > Your daddy,
> > Jimmy-Jack Thigpen.

"Now, isn't that nice?" said Sister Eclipse, who had taken the liberty of reading the message. "Wid all dem fine folks up there in the big city he still 'preciates yo' dancin' talents."

Opal's smile was a mile wide as she showed her granny the postcard, and because Bid's eyesight was bad, she described the tinted photo of Central Park to her. At the thought of her grandson so far away, tears started down both sides of the old woman's nose.

"Never goin' to see my Jimmy-Jack again," she complained in a quavering voice.

"Hush, now!" Sister Eclipse said sternly. "We won't have no such doleful talk on such a glorious day." She set down her carpetbag and looked 'round at the chair by the window, wondering if its spindly legs would support her weight. "Now," she said, seating herself with utmost delicacy, "we'll just set here in this nice sunshine God gave us streaming in, while Opie rustles us up some vittles—won't you, Opie?" she prompted.

Opal left Sister conversing with Bid, and went about seeing to breakfast—bits of fatback fried up in the black iron spider, and some fried mush. While they ate off china plates at Bid's bedside, Sister Eclipse reported the latest news. Very little went on in the Hollow without Sister knowing about it, and though Bid felt poorly much of the time, she was never so bad off she couldn't listen to a bit of gossip.

"Here's a choice piece of news for you, Biddy, dear!" Sister announced cheerfully. "Comp'ny's comin'." Bid's eyes widened. "Not comp'ny to you, honey," Sister went on, "but comp'ny to the Primroses up yonder to the Palace."

The Palace was what Sister Eclipse jokingly called the Primrose mansion, the large white-columned plantation house belonging to Colonel and Augusta Primrose, the last of the famous line of Southern aristocracy that went all the way back to the days when the state was first being settled after the Indians had been kicked out. Getting the jump on Palace gossip was a major event indeed.

"When's he comin', this company?" piped Bid.

"Not *he*. *She*. She's a-comin' from Savannah and she's a-comin' terday. And Jekyll, he's gonna fetch her in the Rolls after church."

Jekyll was the Primroses' man-of-all-work, butler, chauffeur, and chief cook and bottle washer; the Rolls was the fabled English motor vehicle that the Colonel had driven around in for years and that was a noted landmark in that part of the state. Jekyll kept the chrome grille so shiny you could see it nearly half a mile off.

Granny Bid folded her arms over her spare chest and jutted her lip. "If this comp'ny's a friend of 'Gusta Primrose, she can't be of much account."

"Why do you say that, Biddy, dear?" inquired Sister, for Augusta was known for both the quality and breadth of her acquaintanceship.

" 'Cause it's true, that's why," grumbled the old lady. A deep furrow dug in between her thin brows. "No friend of 'Gusta Primrose is worth the powder t'blow 'em up with. That stuck-up woman's never been t'see me once since I took sick."

Opal felt a pang; Granny was right. Bid had been working for the Primrose family clear back to the Civil War, as loyal and devoted a servant to them as Opal's momma was later on (which was how she'd met Opal's daddy), and now even as Opal herself was—at least after school and on Saturdays, except during the summer when she would work mornings, then have the rest of the day to herself. But though Miss Augusta sometimes inquired after Granny's health when she bumped into Opal in the kitchen and one day had sent her home with a basket of red turnips for Bid from the garden, Miss Augusta hadn't ever bothered to stop by to see for herself how her former employee was doing.

"I've known that woman since she and the Colonel got hitched," Bid went on, "and I know her for what she is."

"Now, Biddy, dear, don'tcha go gettin' yourself in a swivet," said Sister Eclipse soothingly. "You know the doctor don't like you gettin' upset. It's bad for your heart."

As always, Opal's breakfast was tasty, and after the plates were empty and there wasn't any more to eat, she did up the dishes and dried them, then spread the small towel on a snowball bush under the window. Back in her room, she changed out of her raggedy dress into her yellow organza (the only "good dress" in

12

her closet), combed out her soft, brown curls, dusted off her old shoes (the only ones, period), located her cracked patent leather change purse, and was ready for church. All she needed was to get a nickel from the sugar bowl for the weekly offering. As she walked into the kitchen she could hear Granny and Sister still talking.

"That poor child," said Bid softly. "She's got such a heavy load to carry on her two narrow shoulders."

"Strong shoulders, Biddie!" declared Sister Eclipse affirmatively. "She's ox-strong, Opie is, a reg'lar Atlas. Ain't I tole you, how she be marked for great things? Didn't I see it plain, a big ball of fire rollin' right down that road there, straight to Opie's door? That girl is marked fo' fame an' forchune, she sholy is. She got a big white light all the way 'round her, head to toe. See if it isn't so."

Opal, however much she might have desired to, was unable to remain and listen, for it was time for her to leave the Hollow if she was to be at church on time. The way was long, requiring over an hour on foot in each direction, and the day was already growing warm.

When she went in to show off how she looked to Granny, Sister Eclipse had a parting word. "I want you t'be partick'lar careful today, Opie," she declared. "I done looked at your cards before I come out today, and you must give partick'lar care to strangers."

"Strangers?" repeated Opal blankly.

"Well, one stranger, it 'pears like. He's in your cards, jack of spades. A dark man—dark like me. Mayhap he looks like a scarecrow."

A *scarecrow?* What an odd thing for her to say. Opal was going to church, not to romp around in a cornfield. What would she be doing with a scarecrow?

"Yes'm," she said meekly, having been raised to listen to her elders. Then, after kissing Bid's pale, papery cheek and promising faithfully to hurry home right after church, she set out on her way, never dreaming what things lay in store for her in the matter of talkative strangers on this fine, warm, summer Sunday in June.

Chapter Two

"Just Call Me Banjo"

THE CHURCH OF GILEAD'S BALM, WHERE OPAL attended service each Sunday, lay five miles east of Peavine, a goodly distance by anyone's yardstick. She would have to walk the whole way unless somebody chanced by to give her a ride. Today, although there was a deal of traffic along the road, no one troubled to stop, and so she continued walking. To save on shoe leather, she carried her Sunday shoes by their straps, like a lunch basket. Going barefoot didn't hurt her feet any; she was used to it.

Up ahead along the Peavine Road, she spotted an odd sight: A man in patched pants and an old brown hat with holes in it was standing on a short ladder by the side of the road nailing up a poster on a telegraph pole, while a small dog looked up at him with keen alertness. The poster was printed in several colors, and as she approached, Opal saw that it was an advertisement for Beebee's Bantam Wonder Show.

Instantly she felt a pang of excitement. The traveling show came to town once a year, and she longed to go but never had. She always heard about it though, usually from Etoile Cumberpatch, who went every year and then talked all summer about the fat lady with the wart and the dead baby in the bottle. This year, according to the advertisement, a troupe of performing elephants was included. This detail heightened Opal's interest, for to her way of thinking there was nothing in the world like an elephant, that most curious-looking of Mother Nature's assortment of beasts, the single great and gentle monster in the world's menagerie.

"Hidy, li'l bug," said the coffee-colored man, tipping his hat with a gallant flourish and smiling a bright, friendly smile.

Opal ducked her head and didn't reply, remembering what Sister Eclipse had just said about strangers. Even so, Opal found the poster man to have a coaxing manner, and she rather liked the way he called her li'l bug. Nobody had ever called her anything but Opie until now.

Displaying an unusual warmth of feeling and affability, the man hopped nimbly down from his ladder and pushed his hat back on his head. At his feet lay a sizable stack of placards, and between his teeth he clenched a row of silver-headed tacks. As Opal watched, his little dog got up on its hind legs and footed a fancy circle around her in the roadway, cocking its head alluringly and hanging out its pink, sugary tongue.

"That's Pickles," the man said, pointing at the clever little dog. "Pickles is jest tellin' you she cottons to you." He waited a moment or two, then, when Opal still refused to speak, he went on. "Fine day for churchgoing," he remarked, and Opal marveled at the clever way he managed to talk around the tacks in his mouth without swallowing them. He had such a jaunty air about him, and he looked so spritely and full of congenial talk that she felt the urge to stay where she was and hear what he had to say, especially about the traveling show. But this became a virtual impossibility as an automobile came roaring along the road toward them.

Opal recognized the vehicle right away, the famous Rolls-Royce belonging to the Primroses. Before it engulfed them in a heavy cloud of dust she was able to make out its occupants: at the wheel, Jekyll, in full livery, and next to him, Cousin Blossom, the poor relation who wasn't allowed to ride in the back, where the Colonel and his wife sat. As the car continued down the road and the dust settled Opal could make out the rigid index finger of Miss Augusta shaking a warning through the back window, admonishing her not to dillydally with strangers on the way to church.

The Primroses were traveling to their own church, twice as fancy and not half so far away as Opal's, but Augusta would never in her life think of offering Opal a ride. She had never learned about showing consideration for others, even for her employees—never mind that Opal only did scullery work in her kitchen, and part time at that. Miss Blossom, on the other hand, was always very considerate to Opal when she was working up at the mansion and might easily have stopped to pick Opal up, had it been her Rolls-Royce. Miss Blossie was one of those people who always practiced the Golden Rule: "Do unto others as you would have others do unto you." Ever since Opal had first learned about that in school, it seemed to her that it was a very handy rule in life and that the world would be a far nicer place if more people practiced it.

Hearing the church bells ringing across the field, and knowing it could only mean trouble to listen any further to the stranger from the traveling show, no matter how interesting, Opal quickened her step again, leaving him to his labors.

She arrived at the Church of Gilead's Balm just in time for the sermon. This Sunday, like every Sunday, it was hellfire and brimstone pouring from the preacher's lips, loud enough to bring any sinner in Peavine Hills to righteousness. As Opal listened, it became something of an embarrassment to her to remind herself that her own daddy, Jimmy-Jack Thigpen, fell into that category of sinners. It was hard to think of someone as a sinner when you loved him so much—though not so hard to love him even if he was a sinner. As a younger man, Opal's daddy hadn't ever been much of a churchgoer. He was more interested in a shady bend in the Cotton River where the catfish were sure to bite or in riding the rods to Countytown to show off his fancy footwork at the Dime-a-Dance. And of course there was always the chance to roll some bones, for Jimmy-Jack Thigpen was a gamblin' man. He wasn't out of rompers before he could roll boxcars or Little Joe from Kokomo or an Eighter from Decatur, and since then dice had become his favorite playthings. Sundays were always filled with all sorts of things Jimmy-Jack wanted to do and only one thing he didn't want to do: go to church.

The sermon grew longer, the room warmer; as it often did, Opal's attention wavered, and her thoughts drifted northward on the map again, clear across the Mason-Dixon Line to New York City, where her daddy was. He'd been gone so long now, and even though he sent a postal order on the tenth of every month, which helped to keep body and soul alive, when would he send for Opal? When Granny Bid passed through those Pearly Gates she longed to see, wouldn't Opal's daddy send for her? Wouldn't she at last get to see Rockefeller Center and the Empire State Building and the Statue of Liberty, and all the other places in the postal cards? *Please, God,* she prayed, *make it so. . . .*

Opal didn't know just where her daddy lived, but she knew

where he worked, and sometimes Miss Blossom would drop him a line for Opal and let him know that she and Granny Bid were doing all right. He said he was tapping with the chorus at a big theater in New York; it was called the Radio City Music Hall. Once he'd sent a snapshot taken of him in his dancing costume, a flashy red suit with shiny brass buttons and gold braid and stripes down the sides of his pants. Boy, he looked snazzy! She was so proud, she treasured that photograph and each one of his cards, which she kept tacked up on the wall by her bed, so she could lie at night dreaming of New York and the Tallest Building in the World and riding the Cyclone at Coney Island. And someday, she fervently prayed, Daddy would hit the Big Time and would send for her and then, and then—she scarcely dared think what that might be like. But when that day finally came it would be dreams come true for Opal Thigpen.

Almost before she knew it, she had her shoes off again and was walking her dusty way back home. People passed her in their automobiles, but still nobody offered to help her out with a ride. By now the sun was noon-high, the day hotter than hell's hinge, and she felt the perspiration popping out on her skin, adding damp wrinkles to her dress.

After a while Opal noticed that on every tenth telegraph pole or so there was another traveling show poster. The poster man had done his work well, except for the fact that on each pole where he'd tacked up one of his own advertisements he'd taken down one of Sister Eclipse's. Not seeing all those cards with Sister's smiling face and catchy slogan lining the roadside didn't seem right, somehow, considering all the trouble Sister had gone to in putting them up.

Shading her eyes to look ahead, Opal saw the very man sitting on a fence rail beside the road. Again he tipped his hat at her, the way any gentleman would, and hopped down from the fence, while Pickles, the little dog, followed him.

"Good mornin' again, li'l bug," the man greeted her, sweeping his hat across his chest and bowing in a gallant fashion. His hat, all crushed out of shape, was every bit as disreputable as he himself appeared to be.

Opal mumbled a polite good morning, shyly dropping her head and keeping well to her side of the road. He wasn't any less a stranger at twelve o'clock than he had been at ten.

"No need to be afraid, li'l bug, no one's going to hurt you," he reassured her. Then, half-wanting to stay on and talk some more, but knowing she must be on her way, she said a prim good-bye and set out again. She was surprised when the man took up his bundle on its stick, picked up his little foot ladder and tool box, slung his banjo across his back, and without so much as a by-your-leave stepped right along beside her.

"What's your name, anyhow?" he asked friendly-like.

Opal gave her name.

"Opal!" exclaimed the tramp approvingly. "Now there's an artful moniker! I expect you got it 'cause your momma thought you was a jewel."

Opal looked away to hide her smile and shook her head, and the tramp hitched a foot to get in step with her.

"Just call me Banjo, that's m'name—Banjo B. Bailey, at your service." And he tipped his hat again and flashed his shiny grin.

Just ahead of them the little dog began dancing around on its hind legs again. Her sweet, pointed face seemed to have traces of a smile, as if she was a very good-natured dog, indeed, and capable of all sorts of clever tricks.

"Why do you call her Pickles?" Opal asked. Banjo chuckled.

" 'Cause she loves 'em. Pickles, I mean. That there dog goes

20

for any pickle made by the hand of man. Or woman. Sweet
pickles, watermelon pickles, cucumber pickles, mustard pickles,
butter pickles, piccalilli, pickle relish, pickled peppers—name
'em, she likes 'em. But her favorites is dill. She'll do away with
a dill pickle in a trice, believe you me. Lookee here, see what
she'll do for this."

He had pulled a dill pickle from one of his pockets and as he
held it out the little dog went crazy, running in circles and madly
barking.

"All right, that's enough of that sorta stuff, girlie," said her
master. "Now you just show this li'l bug what you can do. C'mon,
show us, quick!"

With that the dog sprang into the air, turned a complete circle
and landed on her four feet again.

"Now sit you down," Banjo told her, and the dog sat obediently
and didn't move a hair. Banjo tossed the pickle into the air and,
at a sign from him, Pickles caught and downed it at a gulp before
it could hit the ground.

"Goodness, won't that give her a colic?" Opal asked.

"Naw, that's just how she does. Crazy over pickles." He patted
the dog affectionately.

Opal was impressed, and she suspected that the little creature
with the big, brown eyes, so bright and clever-looking, had a
few more surprising stunts up her sleeve.

"Which way are you heading?" she inquired, forgetting by now
all about Sister Eclipse's admonition regarding strangers.

"My work's 'bout done, so I'm headin' over Peavine way," he
said, holding out the last showcard so Opal could have a good
look.

"That there's Colonel Beebee's pet pachyderm," he said
proudly, pointing to the picture of the elephant. "Cupid—Queen
of the Tanbark, that's her. Ain't she a li'l beauty, though? Clever'n

all gosh 'n' get-out, too. Why, that ol' elephant can multiply."

Opal had never heard of an animal who could do arithmetic.

"Multiply—like rabbits," said Banjo with a hearty guffaw. Opal could tell he liked a good joke. She looked more closely at the picture of Cupid, the Queen of the Tanbark, which, as Banjo explained, was what they called the wood chips with which they covered the floor of the circus ring. The elephant certainly had a pleasant face—there was something about the eyes, a sincere, even knowing look, and the curve of the mouth gave her such a winning smile. How many elephants did you know that smiled? Opal felt immediately attracted. What a strange-looking creature she was, how unlike any others on the planet, so massive and powerful, yet somehow graceful. Banjo described Cupid as being of the African variety as opposed to the Indian kind, which had much smaller ears and were not as easily trained. It was nothing, he went on, to see a momma elephant spank her naughty baby with a broken-off shrub or branch. Opal was amazed at this fact, and thought, *Well, elephants had to bring up their children just like humans did, as best they could. . . .*

Next to Cupid on the showcard stood a fierce-looking man, all got up like a Great White Hunter.

"Who's that?" asked Opal.

"He's the one got the trained elephants," Banjo replied. "Nate Seeger of Nate Seeger's Wild African Elephant Bazaar. But you don't want to truck with him. He's a real bad apple, Nate, and you know what bad apples do."

Opal knew, all right. One bad apple spoiled the whole barrel. She didn't think she'd like this Nate person very much.

After Banjo nailed up the last poster, he drew from his pocket a large watch on a gold chain. "My, my, gettin' on fo' lunch time, ain't that a fact," he observed, sighting at the sun as though to measure it against his watch face. "And I is *so* thirsty, I reckon, my tongue is spittin' cotton. A wonder they don't have a well hereabouts. You might care to have a look at my watch." He held it so it turned and twisted on its chain, glinting in the sunlight. Opal thought that spinning gold watch was one of the prettiest sights she'd ever seen.

Then it disappeared as Banjo jammed his hand deep in his pocket. Continuing along, Opal stole glances at him. His old hat was tipped as far back on his black, woolly head of hair as it would go without slipping off, and there were deep furrows across his broad, dark forehead. When he spoke, it was in a deep rumbling sort of voice, something like the preacher's voice today. Even though he was only a trampy-looking fellow with patches on his knees, no laces in his shoes, and his shirt cuffs all frayed, Opal thought him a most sympathetic individual. His talk was so cheerful and so filled with amusing and interesting topics that she found herself listening attentively to every word and not thinking a thing about the fact that she was walking along and talking her head off with a perfect stranger!

She looked away, ashamed to think what Sister or Granny Bid would have to say, and began counting the telegraph posts; they always told her how far from home she was. She couldn't help but notice the traveling show placards again.

Observing her, Banjo announced proudly, "I works for that show, you know. They pays my bread and board, Colonel Beebe does. He be the owner of the enterprise," he added parenthetically. "Why, but for me the whole shebang would be closed long ago." He was bragging, but somehow Opal didn't mind it. Suddenly he stopped walking, and he spread his arms out in front of her as though on display. "I stand before you," he went on, "the logical product of the show business. I confess it, I am the

23

descendant of a theatrical family with a long and venerable history. And there was a day when I myself was in the limelight, struttin' my stuff."

"You were?"

" 'Deed I was. Why, I first trod the boards as a mere toddler."

Opal felt heady with pleasure and delight. Why, she thought, here's a man who's known the show business all his life! Maybe he'd give her a pointer or two, something she could dazzle her daddy with one day. But first there was the matter of Sister's posters to address. She turned her gaze to the 'Lixir of Life advertisement lying by the roadside. "Sister's not going to like that, you know," she said with a frown. "She won't like it at all."

"What won't yer sister like?" Banjo inquired.

"Oh, she's not my sister," Opal corrected. "That's just what folks call her. Sister Eclipse. I don't have a sister. Nor brother, either. Nor mother or father."

"By golly, you must be some kind of orphan."

"Practically. I got Granny Bid—She's my great-granny—but I won't have her long." She gave a bulletin concerning Bid's age and the state of her health.

"A hunnert and two?" Banjo whistled his surprise. "Does she keep her faculties?"

"She's bright as a penny most of the time."

"Then that's too bad about her bad ticker. But I guess if she's that old, I reckon it's about time for her to start catching up."

"Catching up with who?"

"With the Good Lord, I expect. Ain't that who we all wants to catch up with? But tell me," he went on, "what won't she like, this Sister Eclipse?"

"She won't like the fact that you've been taking down her 'lixir cards and putting up your own."

"I has to," Banjo protested. "Them's the Colonel's orders. Mr.

Beebee, he don't want no other cards distracting the eye of the passer-bys. 'Sides, that 'lixir, it's just barrel dregs, it don't do nobody no good."

"Yes, it does," said Opal loyally, speaking more sharply than she was used to doing. "My great-granny's been taking it for years and look how old she is. Anyhow, Sister's got a healthy brand of temper," she added, "so you'd better not let her catch you monkeying 'round with her 'lixir cards."

"A healthy brand of temper, you don't say. . . ."

"Yes, sir, she does. She crowned our neighbor Tulaine Cumberpatch with the rotating parts of a Hoover vacuum cleaner one time. Twenty-eight stitches they took."

Banjo's look was rueful, and he tugged on his lip thoughtfully. "Too late to put all them posters back up again, I reckon. Maybe she'd like it if I was to slip her some free passes to the travelin' show."

"Oh, I'm sure she'd enjoy that!" Opal said with enthusiasm. "She's kindly partial to a show. Time was, she was in the show business herself."

Banjo picked up one of the cards and took a closer look at Sister. "In the show business? You don't say. I wonder . . . would she be by way of bein' a married lady?"

Opal dropped her eyes modestly. "Sister's a widow lady."

"*You don't say!* Well, well, think of that." Obviously Banjo *was* thinking of "that," and very hard, too. "And . . . is she by way of making much money with this here 'lixir?"

Opal nodded. "She's nesting her money all right. I heard her say to Granny Bid she's got more'n a thousand dollars in the Farmer's Rutabaga."

"Farmer's rutabaga what?"

"Farmer's Rutabaga Bank."

Banjo's face brightened further. "Oh? She got over one

thousand *dollars*—in a *bank?* Why, good for her. A most enterprising woman, I judge her to be. And where'd you say she lives,
this 'lixir lady?"

"She lives in the Hollow, over yonder where Moccasin Creek
runs into the Cotton River. She's got herself a little houseboat
called the *Bouncing Bett.*"

Banjo was further illuminated and he made close note of this
information. "Moccasin Creek, eh? Little boat, you say? *Bouncin'
Bett?*"

"Yessir, but this morning she's visiting with Granny in the
Hollow. So I could go to Sunday service."

Banjo nodded encouragingly. "Highly commendable. Every
right-thinking girl should attend Sunday service."

They walked along some more, conversing back and forth,
and pretty soon they came upon another cornfield, and among
the tall green rows stood a scarecrow wearing a tall hat. For a
head, the scarecrow had a bag of straw with a painted-on face,
a wide grin showing lots of crooked teeth, two dots for a nose,
and X's for eyes. Opal noticed how Banjo dragged his step and
kept glancing curiously at the scarecrow as they passed by. When
she'd thought about the matter she guessed the reason for his
attraction to the straw figure.

"Were you thinking of trading garments?" she asked.

Banjo shot her a look of profound appreciation. "Well, if you
ain't the trickiest li'l bug in God's green world!" he exclaimed,
smacking his palms together. "I admit it, such a thought had
crossed my mind." He glanced slyly in both directions. "Do you
think anyone would object? I pretty well fancy that weskit of
domineering plaid—I saw its like in a recent magazine issue—
while the jacket looks to be of a far better quality than the garment
I have on my back. I wonder if a switch might not be in order."

"By all means, run quick and switch," said Opal, "before some-body passes along and spies you."

In the wink of an eye Banjo was over the fence and into the cornfield, shucking off his patched coat as he marched along the row to the scarecrow. Opal watched with interest. First the black hat disappeared from view, next the jacket, and there was a good deal of hopping around in the stand of corn, while overhead some crows objected noisily. Presently Banjo reappeared, trotting jaun-tily along the row, grinning as he jumped over the fence and landed in front of her.

"Now, say, little lady, how do I look? Does I pass mustard?" He put on the tall beaver hat which he'd exchanged for his own and displayed himself before her, turning front and back. Opal had to admit it, he was done up to the nines—Banjo looked just fine, truly a man of parts.

Just then she heard a car motor approaching, and when she turned around to look she saw the shiny chrome grille of the Primroses' Rolls-Royce headed straight in their direction.

Oh, dear, she thought, *now I'm bound to catch it.* This was what came of ignoring smart advice and stopping to talk to strangers. She felt herself shrink up as the car drove by and all the faces stared out of the windows at her. But this time there was an extra face—one Opal had never seen before. She felt sure it must belong to the Primroses' guest from Savannah, whom Sister Eclipse said they'd planned to pick up at the railroad station in Tilley after church. And so, apparently, they had.

But if Opal thought she was going to see Augusta Primrose shaking her finger at her, she was in error. That lady passed in queenly fashion, straight-backed and showing only her haughty profile, never turning a hair to take notice of the girl.

The wheels raised another cloud of dust across the road, into which the Rolls-Royce was swallowed as if through some cunning feat of magic. By the time the dust had settled once again, Banjo had made profitable use of his hitching thumb by flagging down a truck that came along carrying a load of bananas. The driver let them climb on board—he was going past Peavine Hollow and would gladly drop them—and so they rode the rest of the way together and together had the pleasure of eating a banana each into the bargain.

Chapter Three

Banjo Meets His Match and Miss Blossom Comes to Call

WHEN THEY ARRIVED TO THE HOLLOW, THE FRIENDLY truck driver stopped just long enough for his passengers to get down, then he ground his gears strenuously and chugged off on his way. Opal crossed the road, followed by Banjo, and they walked along the grassy patch by the fence. Over at the Cumberpatches' place the folks were all sitting out on the porch, strung out like so many crows on a wire: Old Man Cumberpatch and his wife, the gaunt and witchy-looking Melissande, looking like a covered-wagon lady in the wilted sunbonnet that she wore so often people said she slept in it; the boys, Renfrew, Tulaine, Buster, Billy Rondo, Beaudine, Yclept, Four Dice, and Henhouse; Tulaine's wife, Etoile; the Cumberpatch girls, Desiree, Miss'sipp, and Sally Dawn, with Fayette cranking the ice-cream churn in a bucket of rock salt; while Etoile's infant, Precious One, tumbled in the dirt where the chickens scratched. Even Sad Man, the Cumberpatches' hound, was there, lackadaisically drooping on

29

the warped and knotty floorboards. The sight of Opal approaching with Banjo got all those crows' feathers ruffled fast.

"Opal Thigpen, whatchou doin' bringin' that reckless-lookin' desperado 'round here for anyways?" demanded Tulaine Cumberpatch as he came flying off the porch, leaping clear over a heap of rubber tires with no treads on them. Tulaine was fat, with a big, soft stomach and hard little eyes that never missed a trick. He had a red, wet face and no neck to speak of, and he hung his thumbs in his suspenders as he stood glaring at Opal.

Fayette had sauntered up for a closer look, tossing her head with a mess of tin and rubber curlers in her hair. "Looks t'me," she began, "like he b'long in jail 'stead a'runnin' 'round loose."

"His name's Banjo," Opal began politely, only to be cut off by the shrill voice of Etoile.

"You don't dast set foot on our proppity, you dirty old tramp, you! Shoo! Shoo!" she cried, flapping her skirts as if she was shooing hens into a coop. "Take yourself along afore I set the hounds on you."

Banjo merely shrugged, grinned good-naturedly, and tipped his hat over his brow, sniffing the hole in his lapel where there might be a boutonniere, but wasn't. "Calm down, missus, you're turnin' beet red all over your face."

"Don't you give me no sass, you nasty old tramp!" cried Etoile. "Look at you, if you ain't a sight to cause despair." Her eyes popped in her head as she took in his appearance. "Why—! I b'lieve I've seen them clothes before! Where'd you come by them?"

When Opal explained about the scarecrow and the informal exchange of garments, Etoile's face grew redder.

"Mean t'tell me you done robbed a poor *scarecrow* of its clothes? Why, a scarecrow ain't got nuthin' *but* its clothes. Don't you know you could be put in jail for such a trespass!"

"It was tit-for-tat. I left him my own duds," Banjo explained in

30

a carefree tone, offering the benefit of his smile and removing his tall beaver hat to smooth its nap with his elbow.

"Well, if you ain't got some nerve!" exclaimed Etoile. "I'd just like to see you come 'round and rob *our* scarecrow, that's what I'd like to see! You just step along now, like I said, or for sure pap'll send t'town for the constable. Officer Belter, he's a dangerous varmint, and he packs a gun. Now you just skeedaddle afore he turns up here under your nose!"

Banjo set his hat back on his head and responded in a dignified tone. "Very well, miss. I was brought up never to go where I wasn't wanted. I'll just mosey on over t'Peavine, some. 'Day, l'il bug. 'Day to you, miss."

But before he could start off, leaving Etoile gaping, his little dog Pickles perked up and growled. Sister Eclipse, who'd been listening from the porch with Granny Bid, had decided it was time to stop listening and start moving.

"Lord love a duck, Opal Thigpen!" Sister cried, her generous flesh bouncing and rolling as she came toward them on her small, dainty feet. "I vow you ain't got the sense God gave a goat! Didn't I tell you to pick up your feet and march right home again? Didn't I say no loitering or lallygagging along the way? What on earth possesses you, girl? You got a head full a'unginned cotton in that skull of yours?"

Opal didn't bother answering because she knew from experience it paid little to answer back to folks, especially bossy ones like Sister Eclipse. It fell to Mr. Banjo Bailey to spread oil on troubled waters.

"May I presume upon what is obviously a very short acquaintance to greet you two ladies," he began, tipping his hat, first for Sister, then for Granny Bid still rocking on her porch, and speaking in a smooth-as-molasses voice quite unknown to Opal, "and to offer my sincerest apologies for the tardiness of this here young lady, whose fault it was not. The truth is, her being late was the fact of her being engaged in a charitable act, and all on behalf of this poor specimen of humanity you see standing before you."

He jerked a little bow as if he were on stage and was about to add to his remarks when Sister Eclipse opened her mouth.

"What d'you mean with this talk of charitable acts of business?" she demanded, fairly bursting with suspicion and ill will.

"This young lady has played the part of the Good Samaritan to this humble wayfarer," continued Banjo in his deep, brown-sugary voice. "And without her assistance I fear the present moment would find me in far worse condition than I am."

Sister jammed her hands onto her hips. "Well, what happened? Say—ain't I seen you hereabouts before?"

"I think not, gracious lady, since to have gazed upon you but once would have engraved your image upon both brain and heart, never to be erased."

Opal stared open-mouthed, unable to believe the honeyed words that were dripping from Banjo's lips. "No, dear lady, we have not met," he went on, "until this very moment, which I shall treasure evermore, safeguarding it within the tabernacle of my heart."

"Oh, brother. Keep your tabernacles, man," retorted Sister Eclipse. "Stop all this sniffin' 'round like a bear at a honeypot and tell us what Opal did to be so late."

"As I say, madame, her tardiness is to be laid entirely at my door—if I *had* a door, which, alas, I do not. In sooth, had she not come along when she did to succor me, the slender thread of my life might well have been severed right then and there along the Peavine Road."

"Well, what did she do?"

"Yes, what?" piped up old Granny, whose hearing was better than anyone thought and whose little gray eyes swiveled back and forth between the two protagonists of the drama, neither of whom looked ready to back down. Banjo toyed with the pearly buttons on his recently appropriated vest and went on.

"Look how this poor, poor man, he come walkin' 'long of the Cotton Road, a-thirstin' like to die and about to expire from sunstroke."

"What, a man like you?" cried Sister loudly. "You look sound as an oak and nowhere close to dyin' of heat exhaustion."

Banjo's eye sparked at her words. "It gladdens this heart to hear you say so, dear lady. But I promise you, my step was failing and my work not yet done—"

"Work! What work? Dollars t'donuts, you never done a honest lick of work in your life."

Banjo shook his head sadly. "Then you woulda lost your bet, madame, for I engage in honorable employment each and every day of my life."

"Izzat so! Like what?"

Opal picked that moment to step in with a helpful word, explaining that Banjo was in the show business.

"What—him?" Sister scoffed. "In show business? I'll eat that hat of his if he is."

Banjo raised a placating hand.

"Tut-tut, madame, if you are suffering the pangs of hunger, I feel sure we can find tastier fare for you than my unworthy head-gear. The fact remains, however, that I am engaged in work among the brotherhood of artists, roustabouts, and mendicants we loosely call the members of the show business. I am employed by Colonel Beebee as what is known as the advance man, charged with the task of letting the folks know that our show is available for viewing."

Sister Eclipse had calmed herself somewhat and was listening carefully to what Banjo had to say.

33

"Yes, I seen a batch of them Beebee posters tacked up all over the place."

"To be sure. And you is lookin' at that man who is responsible for placing them before your eyes."

Sister's entire form expanded as she drew in an angry breath, and her eyes came close to popping out of her head. "You mean to say you're the vandal who's been rippin' down my 'lixir posters and puttin' up those cheap show cards?" She advanced threateningly on Banjo. "Why, you buzzard, I said if I ever caught that yellow hound dog who was yankin' down my adverts, I'd have his flesh!"

"Madame, I assure you," Banjo said entreatingly, placing his hat over his heart, "had I the least inklin' that those there cards belonged t'your enterprise, believe me, I would have staved off all the legions of ancient Rome to keep them undisturbed by mortal man. For who has not heard of Sister Eclipse's 'Lixir of Life? How many lives have not been preserved, how many souls pulled back from the very brink of eternity by twenny drops of that miraculous Water of Life?"

Eclipse stared in wonderment. "Mean t'say you done heard of it?"

"*Heard* of it, dear lady? Certain, have I. To you and your famed concoction do I owe the very breath in my body and this heart that beats, now faint, now strong in my manly breast."

He socked his chest; it made him cough.

"Don't get so carried away, my man," Sister said. "You're li'ble to pop a gasket."

"It's true, every word, I swear. And how often have I thought to myself, could I but one day be privileged to meet up with that same Sister Eclipse whose smilin' countenance is stamped on every label on every bottle of that fateful recipe, how dearly I would like to thank her for all I owe to her being. And I ask myself was not the very radio apparatus I hear broadcasting so dissonantly from yonder manse"—Banjo pointed toward the Cumberpatch house—"invented by Mr. Marconi for the simple purpose of bringing your wares to the 'tention of a blinded public? Was not the roadside billboard invented for a like purpose? Spread the word, good lady, spread the word. That has always been my motto: Spr-r-r-read-uh the-uh Wor-r-r-d. Pass along to the health-minded wayfarer the joys and blessings of your wonderful decoction. Though I fear no likeness on billboard or poster could do justice to the magnitude of your pulchritude."

Sister was enchanted. Granny Bid, too. "Why, that man's a poet," she called from her porch rocker.

"And he don't know it," Banjo added with a chuckle, whereupon he proved his mettle, in Opal's eyes at least, by showing that he knew just how and when to get himself off the stage. He took out his gold watch to check the time, dropped the watch back in his plaid vest pocket, then, flipping his hat back on his head, he bade farewell to one and all. Nodding genially to the Cumberpatches on the porch and acting the Lord of Creation, he stepped out smartly up the road to Peavine.

He was almost out of sight when Opal turned to follow Sister Eclipse toward the house to change out of her yellow dress. But before she could take two steps she was intercepted by the small, weaselly form of Henhouse Cumberpatch with his wall-eye and his mischievous look. He put out his tongue and jerked his thumb in the direction of Primrose Hill.

"Look like yer wanted," he said hoarsely.

"What?" asked Opal, who seldom understood anything Henhouse had to say.

"Wanted," he repeated just as hoarsely. "Up yonder."

"Up yonder" only meant one thing to Opal: up the hill to the big house. And if she was wanted it was Augusta Primrose who wanted her, and if it was Augusta who wanted her, it was for only one reason: Banjo B. Bailey, Esq.

Opal looked up the narrow dirt road that led from the Hollow up the back way to the Primrose mansion, but instead of Miss Augusta it was Miss Blossom she saw, coasting down the hill on her red bicycle. Henhouse fled in an instant, and Opal was glad to be left alone to greet her friend. Outside of Granny Bid and Sister Eclipse, Miss Blossom was probably the only other person in the world—except her daddy, too, of course—who really gave a hoot about what happened to her, and if there was trouble to come from Miss Augusta, she knew she could count on Miss Blossom to help her through it.

"Good afternoon, Opal," said Miss Blossom with her usual ounce of cheer as she skidded to a perilous halt at the side of the road. Leaving her cycle to lean on its stand, she took both of Opal's hands in hers, smiling and pressing them affectionately. "How nice you look. I'm sure you made a happy impression at church today." Miss Blossom stood tall and spare, and her hair formed little ringlets like grape clusters around her face. Her pink cheeks gave her the bloom of health and her voice sparkled with humor and friendliness.

She looked toward the porch, where Sister had resumed her visit with Granny. "Hello-o, Granny Bid! Hello Sister!" she called, waving energetically. When the two women returned her greeting, she smiled again at Opal. "Glad to see your granny's getting some air on such a fine day. A day with the gold in its teeth," she added, looking around with great enthusiasm, as if she was searching the sky for something.

Opal could tell Miss Blossom was beating around the bush, confirming her suspicions that something was up. As if reading Opal's thoughts, the woman explained in her gentlest manner possible—which was very gentle indeed—that, while Miss

36

Augusta had expressed concern that Opal had been seen talking earlier with a stranger of questionable character, Miss Blossom's errand was also of another nature. There was a visitor from Savannah whom Augusta wanted Opal to meet for reasons Miss Blossom didn't go into, and though it was Opal's day off, would she mind accompanying Miss Blossom up the hill for a formal introduction?

Despite her misgivings, Opal agreed to go—in truth, what choice had she?—but not until, she added, she had talked it over with Granny and made sure that Sister could stay on for a bit, it being the Sabbath and all.

"But, of course, my dear, I'll just wait right here. Run along, quick as you can, and be sure to give Granny Bid a hug for me."

While she waited, Miss Blossom turned her bicycle around, and before long Opal had returned to her side, still in her yellow dress and her only pair of good shoes, ready for the lecture and the "formal introduction" to come. As they started up the hill, she prepared herself for the worst, which she had learned was generally the best solution to matters involving the dreaded Augusta Primrose.

Chapter Four

On Primrose Hill

OPAL TRUDGED UP THE LONG RED ROAD WITH MISS Blossom, now walking her cycle, to the big house with the tall white columns and the cast-iron jockey on the lawn, the house where as an infant she used to play in her diaper on the kitchen floor. In fact, she'd been born in that house. The birth time had come upon her mother right in the middle of her dusting. The Primrose mansion was "historical," everybody knew that. The famous General Lee had slept there, in the very bed where Colonel Goodson Primrose first saw the light of day. Other famous folk, senators, even the governor of the state, had driven up this same hill, some in carriages, some in autocars. The president of the Confederacy, Jefferson Davis, had once dined on catfish pulled out of the river by Opal's great-granddaddy, old Johnny-Buck Thigpen.

And today, another visitor of consequence: Miss Augusta's

38

lady friend, come all the way from Savannah. Despite Miss Blossom's calm reassurances, the presence of this newcomer under the Primrose roof seemed not to bode well for Opal, and she had a presentiment that trouble lay ahead. They turned in at the front gates—thrown wide this day—with the gilt-lettered sign proclaiming *Primrose Hill* and *Goodson Pickett Primrose, Col. ret.* on it. This announcement was a matter of no small interest to Opal. For the life of her she never knew why Colonel Primrose was called colonel, since to the best of her knowledge he had never seen service in any conflict known to man.

Setting her bicycle against the porch, Blossom took Opal in through the back doorway and into the parlor. Standing behind Opal, her hands gently resting on the girl's shoulders, Miss Blossom announced, "Here's our dear Opal, Augusta."

Opal stood with her eyes modestly lowered, waiting for the axe to fall. It was always hard for her to look at Augusta Primrose, who had such a formidable manner that it made Opal's heart quail just to be in the same room with her. And not without reason: Augusta Primrose, the Colonel's spouse and helpmeet of many years, presented an imposing figure, an imposing manner, and an undeniably imposing bosom.

Augusta took an authoritative pose by the marble mantel. "Yes, here she is, indeed," she said, summoning Opal with an imperious gesture that had required her many years to perfect. "Take care you don't knock over anything," she added as Opal sidled like a crab across the oriental carpet.

"Now, young lady," Augusta began, "perhaps you can tell me just what you thought you were doing, dawdling along the Old Cotton Road on the way to church this morning?" Before Opal could get out a word Augusta went on. "*And,* if you'll be so kind, you may inform me how you came to be dawdling in the same manner along that same Cotton Peavine Road on the way *home* from church? And both times with the identical low and disreputable-looking character."

Opal did her best to explain the circumstances of her meeting with Banjo Bailey, both times, but her words had little or no effect on Augusta Primrose, who tossed her head so her many chins shook like the wattles on a turkey. And when Opal, ill-advisedly, happened to mention that Banjo was working in the show business, Miss Augusta was aghast.

"What!" she cried, bridling like a horse at the starting gate. "Do you mean to stand there on my best Bokhara carpet and tell me that good-for-nothing ne'er-do-well is connected with such a shocking enterprise as a traveling show? I am disgraced! May I remind you," Miss Augusta went on, "that it was the *show business*"—she filled the phrase with disgust—"that ruined your useless father and my dear Elizabeth. Yes, *show business* broke your mother's frail heart. When I think of that poor young woman, so graceful, a real lady of a lady's maid, falling for that slick character . . ." Overcome with emotion, Augusta's words trailed off. She sniffed and touched the corner of her handkerchief to the corner of each eye.

Opal felt bad that anything she had done could be so upsetting to Miss Augusta. Still, as she recalled, it had been the croup that had taken her mother, and what did that have to do with show business? "Mr. Bailey's the advance man for Beebee's Bantam Wonder Show," she offered, hoping to ease matters by commenting on Banjo's important status. "He tacks up the advertising posters on the telegraph poles."

"I do not care if he tacks up the five-pointed stars in the Almighty's glorious firmament, you are not to have truck with his likes," stated Augusta fearsomely. "I have no desire to be a hard-hatted Hannah, but I ask—no, I *demand*—I demand your promise never to have anything to do with this mountebank ever again."

Opal almost could have laughed at "hard-hearted Hannah's" new headgear, but she remained silent and Augusta waited.

"Well-ll . . . ?" said the woman finally in that terrible way grown-ups have of threatening young and unmeaning wrong-doers.

"I—I can't promise," Opal said softly. "It wouldn't be right."

"Wouldn't be *right*? And who, I ask myself, are you to tell *me* what may or may not be *right*?"

"I just can't, Miss 'Gusta. Banjo, he's my friend. He's a good person. He's happy and Granny Bid says he makes her smile. Sister Eclipse and he—"

"Ah-*ha!*" exclaimed the triumphant Augusta. "I might have known. Birds of a feather, I'll be bound. Would it not be exactly like that loud, bombastic creature to get involved with a repro-bate." She cast her eyes to the ceiling as though seeking the help of the Almighty. "I must speak to the Colonel when he comes in from his golf. Goodson will know what to do. He generally does. No doubt this friend of yours drinks. And if he plays the banjo, surely he is many miles beyond redemption. It is a fact of life that banjo players are the lowest creatures on the social scale. And he has now joined in league with that notorious Eclipse DeVere. Characters of her ilk should be run clean across the county line. We have no place for chicanery and knavery here in Peavine; it's bad enough having that terrible man, Franklin Delano Roosevelt, in the White House." Again she dabbed at her eyes and sniffed as though she'd lost a loved one. Turning, she called past the ruffles at the shoulder of her tea dress.

"Are you hearing all this, Amelia?"

"I am, alas," replied a voice from behind the bladelike fronds of some potted palms, where Opal could barely discern the fea-tures of a tall thin lady in a high-backed chair. "And I confess,

Augusta," the melancholy voice went on, "it saddens me to hear it."

"I shouldn't wonder," said Augusta in her best put-upon voice. Then, taking Opal by the scruff, she dragged her across the Bokhara rug past the palms. "And here, Opal Thigpen, if you can believe your eyes, is your benefactress, your angel from on high, ready to aid and assist you in your journey through life, and you have the nerve, the naughty nerve to thwart and balk me."

"Amelia," she went on, "*this* is the girl I have mentioned to you. Opal, this is Mrs. Vermilyea. Say hello, but pray keep your distance. There is no need to shake hands, it being so warm out."

"Pleasedtomakeyouracquaintance," Opal said, running her words together, bobbing a quick nod before this thin, parrot-faced, but most imposing lady.

"How old are you, Opal?" inquired Mrs. Vermilyea, looking the girl up and down through glasses on a silver stick.

"Thirteen last Valentine's Day, thank you kindly, ma'am."

"On Valentine's Day!" exclaimed Mrs. Vermilyea. She spoke rather like a schoolteacher in precise syllables and the tones of a ripe quince. "I think that's sweet. Did you hear, Blossom?" she said. "Saint Valentine's Day. That is the very day my poor Filsom gave up the ghost and went to his reward," she added with a sigh, fluttering her lashes.

"It's true," Miss Blossom put in, happy at last to be able to turn the conversation to more pleasant topics. "Opal was born on Saint Valentine's Day. In twenty-three—the year we voted out the last Republican in the Legislature." She smiled and ran her eyes over Opal.

"That will be quite enough, Blossie," said Miss Augusta in her most austere tone. "We may safely reserve these historical observances until some more appropriate moment. Just now we have

42

far more important affairs of business to consider." She trilled a little laugh that climbed up on the scale of C. "Affairs having to do with Opal and that may serve to alter her entire outlook on life. What have you to say to such a happy prospect, Opal?"

Since Opal didn't have any idea what Miss Augusta was talking about, she didn't know what to say, and therefore she said nothing. She waited politely, looking from one face to the other, searching for some clue that might tell her what important affairs were afoot.

"All of life is change," Augusta went on in a lofty tone, "and at thirteen one must always consider change. Therefore, Opal dear, we have decided, Goodson and I, that we must find ways, just as we did with your dear, departed mother, for a girl such as yourself to better her place in life, and through the kind auspices of our dear Amelia, we have come upon just such a niche." She pronounced the word "neesh." "As it happens—and please correct me if I am wrong, Amelia—it happens that Mrs. Vermilyea is without a second maid, and Goodson and I have prevailed upon her to consider you for that position. It will, I believe, consist for the most part in keeping a substantial collection of bric-a-brac dust-free. More importantly, Amelia will sponsor you to the Savannah School for Ladies in Waiting, where you will learn a most respectable trade and will learn it among a social set of a far better class than that Hollow riff-raff. Is that not so, Amelia?"

"Yes, indeed, you have put it perfectly, dear Augusta," said her friend. "There is no finer place to acquire the fine skills of dusting, mending, and servile manners than the Savannah School. And my rare and expensive porcelain collection will be an ample arena in which Opal can practice her craft." She smiled at Opal, showing her long yellow teeth. "*And* she shall have a new feather duster to start off with."

"There!" exclaimed Augusta. "Now what do you say to that, Opal? Is that not a handsome offer for a young girl poised on the threshold of life?"

Opal stared in confusion. She looked over to where Miss Blossom stood, helpless to say or do anything, then back to Miss Augusta. "Dusting? At Savannah?"

"That is correct. And a *firm* offer."

"But who would look after Granny?" Opal asked, feeling a tide of panic at Augusta's suggestion. Her? A parlor maid trainee? Living in Savannah? Without Lola and Lucerne and the Poland pig? It was too terrible to think about.

"It doesn't matter really. Your grandmother can just as well go to a home," she heard Augusta Primrose saying, and a cold knife cut through her heart. "There's a very nice place we have heard of. It's called the Bide-a-Wile—"

"Oh, Miss 'Gusta, we can't do that," Opal cried, filled with fear. "My momma'd turn over in her grave to know Granny Bid went to the old folks home. Not to mention what my daddy would do."

Augusta sniffed through her long nose. "Your father is hardly to be considered in any of this since his running off the way he did and leaving Goodson and I—and Cousin Blossom I might add—with the responsibility of his entire family." Opal attempted to defend her daddy's actions, but Miss Augusta went on like a train without brakes. "Now, your great-granny is old, very old, and a young girl like yourself can hardly be expected to take care of her till she simply passes on from old age. Ah, here is Goodson. Now let us hear what he has to say on the subject."

All heads turned as Colonel Primrose entered the hallway from the front door, setting his golf bag in a corner to lean against the draped marble statue of a goddess.

"Humph harrumph," he said, coming in. "And how is everybody faring? Eh? Ah, Opal, there you are. I didn't see you hiding behind the aspidistra. Step out where I can have a look at you. Dress looks familiar, yellow, is it?"

Opal mustered enough words to explain weakly that it was a hand-me-down from Miss Blossom, made over by Sister Eclipse.

"Yes? Good. Well, now." He glanced at his wife. "Has Opal been informed of our plans?"

"Yes, she has," replied Augusta.

"She has, indeed," said Amelia Vermilyea.

"And of course she concurs with our idea?"

All eyes fastened on Opal as the adults awaited her reply.

"Very nice of Mrs. Vernilla to ask," Opal began.

"Ver-mill-*ee*-uh," Augusta pronounced, "A fine old Huguenot name."

"Very nice of her to ask," Opal repeated, "but I can't go."

"*Can't?* And why not, may I ask?" said the Colonel.

"I can't leave Granny. She needs me. I'm all she has in the world."

The Colonel turned to his wife. "But, Augusta, did you not tell Opal about the Bide-a-Wile?"

"I did indeed. But Opal has seen fit to turn up her nose at the Bide-a-Wile. To think of it. A nice corner room and they play clumps on Friday nights."

"And Friday night is fish night at the Bide-a-Wile," the Colonel added. "We all know how old Biddy dotes on a bit of catfish."

"She only likes how *I* cook it," Opal said, her voice catching.

"Then she must learn, that's all," Augusta said. "Now let us hear no more about it. I say she shall go to the home, and to the home shall she go, while Opal packs her traps for Savannah." Augusta clapped her mouth shut, cutting off further discussion.

"Come, come, dear, you mustn't cry," said Miss Blossom. "Crying is only a waste of tears. Isn't that so, Goodson?"

45

"Indeed it is, Cousin," said the Colonel. "Besides, in no time you'll be all grown up, and you must give good thought to what you want to make of your life."

"Yes," put in Amelia Vermilyea, "and who knows, if you apply yourself, you might even be famous someday. Why, just look at Florence Nightingale!"

"Truer words were never spoken," said the Colonel, despite the fact that Amelia's reference to the famous nineteenth-century English nurse made no sense at all.

"But I don't want to be no Florence . . . whatever," Opal protested.

"Tt-tt-tt, Opal dear, such grammar," cautioned Miss Blossom. "You must remember what I've told you, or soon you'll be talking like those poor benighted Cumberpatches."

At the mention of the Cumberpatches, Augusta assumed her "persimmon" look. "A life under that depraved influence is not for the likes of this child! As anyone can see, Opal, you are meant for more gentile things. You're pretty enough, I'll say that. And you may take my word for it, you will do far better to make up your mind to accepting the position that is so generously being offered you, and to put all other foolishness out of your head."

"I think we can safely conclude this conversation right here," the Colonel said, consulting the mantel clock, for it was close on the dinner hour. "I hope, Opal, that you can see how generous Mrs. Vermilyea is being in offering you this superior position, and that when she returns from her holiday at Sea Island in the fall you will naturally wish to assume your place in her household, while, as I have already indicated, your grandmother will go to the Bide-a-Wile, where she will end her days comfortably and—gracious, what's wrong with the child?" He stared at Opal, whose eyes were wide with alarm. Clapping a hand to her mouth as if she were going to be sick, she dashed from the room, very nearly knocking over a Chinese vase in her haste to get away.

"What on earth's got into the poor thing?" asked a mystified Mrs. Vermilyea.

"I'm sure we've hurt her feelings," said Miss Blossom, and she hurried after the sobbing Opal.

"Some girls just don't know when they're well-off," commented Augusta with a sniff, and the Colonel said "Harumph!" which meant either yes or no, but who was ever to say which?

Miss Blossom caught up with Opal by the gazebo and gently drew her inside. "Opal, please, please don't be upset," she entreated. "Augusta and the Colonel are only trying to help you sort out your life. You really must start thinking of yourself. As for Granny Bid—"

Opal put her face in her hands and burst into tears again. "But how can I leave her to go to the home?"

Blossom couldn't bear to see the girl so upset, and she tried to explain that Granny Bid would have the best of care at the Bide-a-Wile, but her soothing words had no effect. Opal only sobbed as if her heart would break and wouldn't listen at all. She took off her shoes and ran down the red road to the Hollow.

She ran without let-up until she reached her rabbit hutch. Taking Lola from the straw, she carried her over to the pigpen, where Zephyr lay in the mud, enjoying its coolness. Lucerne was standing nearby, and when she'd brought them all together she began to talk to them, explaining about the visitor up the hill at the Primrose mansion.

Then, with a catch in her throat, she said, "I'm afraid I've got some bad news. I'll just pass it along so you'll know the true state of things, then we won't say any more about it. The truth is, it looks like I'll be going away from the Hollow. But that's not the worst. The worst is, Miss 'Gusta and the Colonel, they want Granny Bid to go away, too—to the Bide-a-Wile. I couldn't hardly believe my ears when they heard it, but it's true. Miss 'Gusta, she left it for me to tell Granny. Now how'm I supposed to do that?"

She stopped, thinking hard, and the animals just looked at one another, for the problem was such a knotty one that none of them had anything close to a solution. The only happy part of it was that Amelia Vermilyea wouldn't be back for Opal until the fall, and that gave Opal the rest of the summer to figure out how she was going to explain to Granny that the Primroses were planning to pack her off to the home.

One good thing happened, anyway: That evening, when Sister Eclipse drove her contraption up to the door, noisy as ever, she announced that Banjo Bailey had made good his promise. If Opal cared to take in the traveling show at Tilley, two tickets would be waiting in their names at the box office, compliments of Banjo B. Bailey, Esq.

Chapter Five

Opal Goes to the Traveling Show

THE FOLLOWING FRIDAY EVENING, OPAL AND SISTER
Eclipse drove over to Tilley in the Dented Dragon. Bid hadn't
wanted Opal going off at night, but the Tilley performance of
the Beebee show was just a one-night stand and the only chance
for Opal to catch the show on the free passes Banjo Bailey had
arranged. After the performance Eclipse was going to drive over
to Countytown to see about buying some radio time for her 'lixir,
and it was arranged that Banjo would see that his guest was safely
returned to Peavine at a reasonable hour.

Opal had never been to a traveling show before, and she looked
eagerly at all the interesting sights to be seen. The gray canvas
tents had been pitched in an empty field, formerly devoted ex-
clusively to the raising of the lowly rutabaga, now host to Beebee's
Bantam Wonder Show. On the way into the main tent she passed
the menagerie (featuring a sick chimpanzee and a loosely stuffed
alligator), as well as the famous baby in a bottle and the bearded

lady. Opal hoped to catch a glimpse of Cupid, the elephant she knew from the picture on Banjo's posters, but she was nowhere to be seen. She was probably putting on her makeup, as Opal had heard all circus folk did before the show. Still, she was in seventh heaven as she followed Sister into the show tent and took her seat, munching on popcorn from one paper sack and peanuts from another. (Sister Eclipse had allowed her a whole dime as spending money.)

The performance opened with a smattering of jolly painted clowns with red lips and pink hair, who did all sorts of amusing tricks. These were followed by a troupe of daring aerialists, who swung about on high trapezes. Opal got a crick in her neck, gazing up to the tent roof where small silvery figures, picked out in the spotlight, floated about as if they were among the clouds. Never had she seen such amazing stunts performed, and so high up in the air. At last it was time for the number one attraction: Nate Seeger's Wild African Elephant Bazaar, featuring Cupid, Queen of the Tanbark.

Opal thought she had some notion of what lay ahead for her, but she was wrong. When the red plush curtains parted and the elephants came parading ponderously and majestically into the ring, she felt a sense of wonder and excitement that she had never known. The huge beasts were done up in brass-studded harnesses and multicolored pompons, moving carefully in a circle with trunks and tails entwined. As Opal watched, captivated by their every move, one rolled over with an ease and agility that belied its size, another balanced on its hind legs as if it weighed no more than ten pounds, while another stood with all four feet set on a painted tub as it waved its snakelike trunk in the air. Then in the center of the ring another wound its trunk around the trainer—the one and only Nate Seeger, dressed in his Great White Hunter outfit, with shiny black boots and a cork sun helmet—and lifted him up into the air as if he were light as a feather. Seeger carried a whip, which flew through the air with a sizzling curl and, as he was set down, made a loud *snap!* to great applause.

When it seemed that the big gray lumbering beasts had used up all their tricks, Seeger gave his whip another smart crack and stepped aside until his elephants were all lined up in a row neat as could be; it seemed as if they had been turned to stone, so motionless were they. Then, suddenly, the trainer disappeared behind a canvas panel, to reappear in seconds leading onstage the star attraction of the act: *Cupid.*

"Laydeez 'n' gent-ull-min," began the ringmaster, resplendent in red coat and black top hat, "for your delectation and enlightenment, Colonel Claude Beebee takes great pleasure in in-tro-doos-ing that pulchritudinous pachyderm, that sweet and saucy minx, that cute cut-up—Queen of the Tanbark—the *gr-r-r-reat Cupid* and her bag of tricks!"

This announcement was greeted with another wave of enthusiastic applause and, not wasting a moment, Seeger cracked his whip over Cupid's head, cueing her to lumber around the ring by herself, while the other elephants sat watching without batting an eyelash. Opal thought it odd, the way Cupid acted, for though she moved at a good clip around the ring, every time she passed the spot where Opal sat with Sister Eclipse, the elephant would slow her pace and direct her look up into the stands.

Why, Opal thought, *it's almost as if she's looking at me, like she knows me. But I'm sure we've never met, or I'd remember.*

Then the ringmaster announced that Cupid would now stand on her two front legs while balancing a large rubber ball on the end of her trunk, but—and this was *very* strange—Cupid did no such thing. In fact she didn't do anything close to what the ringmaster said she'd do. What she did do was to turn her back on her trainer, and tossing her head and wafting her trunk in the air, she broke clean out of the ring and headed for the bleachers where Opal was sitting.

Then a strange and wonderful thing happened. When she got as close as she could to Opal, for there were lots of people around, all as astonished as Opal herself, she extended her trunk and touched its tip to the young girl's cheek. Opal sat motionless as the elephant began nosing around in her lap, and when she raised her trunk again it was clutching the bag of peanuts Opal had been eating.

Within seconds, the supple gray trunk curled under, shoving the peanuts, bag and all, inside the large open mouth. The audience was laughing and cheering to beat the band, but Opal just stared, speechless. She could feel the eyes of everyone in the tent glued to her, and it was embarrassing for her to be thrust into the spotlight—which she was, for the man working the big traveling spot had shifted its glaring beam from the ring over to where Opal sat. Meanwhile, Cupid continued to stand nearby, calmly munching the peanuts and ignoring the loud commands of her furious trainer, who cursed and scowled and stamped his shiny black boots, all the while circling the elephant's head with the tip of his whip and cracking it in her ears.

"Oh, dear," said Opal, touching Sister's arm, "I don't think he should do that, he'll scare her—besides, I can tell she doesn't like it."

This much seemed sure, for in a swift movement of her trunk, Cupid snatched the whip in midair from Seeger's hands and went lumbering across the ring with it. Swinging it triumphantly overhead, she dashed through the rear curtain and disappeared from view.

Infuriated, Seeger flung himself after her, shouting more curses and shaking his fists. Surely Opal had never seen anyone so angry, not even Old Man Cumberpatch that time a hornet stung him. One more thing seemed sure: the show was over. Still, Opal feared for the elephant, who could never hope to escape Seeger's wrath, for his red, angry face plainly told the sort of mean, vengeful character he was.

As everyone filed out of the big tent, Sister Eclipse waved Opal and Banjo good-bye and went off to the radio station in County-town. Banjo had to stop for a word with his boss, Colonel Beebee, so Opal wandered off by herself among the crowd, enjoying all the midway sights and hoping for a glimpse of the elephant who had proved so knowing and endearing. She found the other elephants outside their tent, huddled together in a placid group, their trunks hanging down limp as though the performance had exhausted them, paying no attention whatever to the people who stood by ogling them. As Opal leaned against the rope separating her from the large beasts, trying to discover which one was Cupid, she felt a nudge in the small of her back. But when she looked around she saw no one. A moment later she felt a second nudge, and this time, to her surprise, she saw the tip of an elephant's trunk protruding through a gap in the tent canvas and sniffing its way toward her.

"Looks like you've made a friend," said a nice man standing beside her, and he handed her a paper bag. "I think she wants some more of these," he added.

Thanking the man, Opal took a peanut from the bag and touched it to the elephant's trunk, which instantly curled around the treat and carried it out of sight. In mere seconds the trunk reappeared, but this time, instead of sniffing out another peanut, the trunk made a beeline for Opal herself. Gently it wrapped itself around her waist, and she felt herself being lifted slowly off the ground. To her astonishment, as well as to the delight of the onlookers, she was carried through the air and slipped through the opening in the canvas where she met the owner of the trunk, Cupid!

Being hefted by a one-ton pachyderm would have made most people nervous, but not Opal. The way Cupid set her down so gently and inched toward her with such dainty, careful steps convinced her of the creature's hospitable intent. Yet Cupid could carry her friendly overtures only so far because one hind leg was locked in an iron ring, and a length of chain fastened to a stout post held the animal prisoner.

Opal herself closed the gap, going up to the elephant and talking softly into her soft, floppy ear.

"Nice elephant, sweet elephant," she crooned. Stroking the rough skin of her trunk, she began to hum, and as she hummed she fed Cupid some more peanuts, reaching up (though the elephant wasn't awfully tall, Opal still had to reach on tiptoe) to place them in her mouth. Gazing at the large round eye that regarded her so solemnly, she thought she read a silent message in it. It was as if the elephant was trying to tell her something.

"Here, then," came a loud, stern voice. "What's going on in here!" Opal instantly recoiled as the elephant trainer, Seeger, stormed into the tent. "Feeding the elephants, are you?" he shouted, bearing down on her with a fierce scowl. "Can't you read them signs anyway?"

He pointed a dirty finger at the DON'T FEED THE ANIMULES sign. "Want to get yourself arrested?" he shouted. "Want to go to jail for life? Want to get *whupped?*"

At the word *whupped* he produced his long, thick bullwhip with its handle of braided leather tipped with silver, and before Opal could say or do anything, he'd swung his whip in a vicious circle around his head, then uncoiled it like a snake to produce an alarming crack close to Opal's ear.

With a cry, she ducked and turned to flee, hands over her ears, only to be stopped by Seeger's surprised shout. Looking back, she saw that the elephant had slung her trunk around her master's waist and had yanked him straight up off the ground, carrying him to a nearby post and hanging him by his big brown leather belt on a wooden peg.

Opal couldn't help laughing, so comical was the sight, but her laughter only made Seeger angrier.

"Blank the blankety-blank-blank, Cupid!" he cursed. "You had better put me down this blankety-blank minute, or it's the blankety-blank glue factory for you! I've warned you before, blankety-blank it!"

But the elephant ignored the threat, merely shuffling back toward the post to which she was chained. There she settled herself on the ground and observed her angry master from the corner of her eye.

Seeger's fury knew no bounds. "Hurry!" he shouted, flailing his arms at the innocent Opal whom, clearly, he blamed for his troubles. "Go find someone to get me off this blankety-blank-blank post!"

Opal looked over at Cupid. As Seeger continued to yell and struggle, suddenly the elephant's spirit seemed to ebb out of her, and the mischievous sparkle in her eye was gone. Concerned for her new friend and fearing what Seeger might do when he was freed, Opal rushed from the tent, calling for help. She ran right into Banjo Bailey, rounding the corner.

"Help! Hurry! This way!" she cried and pushed him into the elephant tent, while Pickles trotted on his heels.

"Get me down, you blankety-blank fool!" Seeger shouted, waving his arms and kicking his feet. "Did you hear me, you simpleminded bindle stiff! Will you do something or must I hang here all day?"

"Hanged if I know," said Banjo, slipping Opal a wink. "Maybe

I should cut your throat for you," he went on, producing a large pocket knife and unfolding it so the blade shone in the light.

"Great brass screws!" exclaimed the agonized man. "I'm going to be murdered as I hang here!"

With that, Banjo slipped behind the man and sawed away at his leather belt, and in another moment Seeger dropped from the peg and sprawled on the ground.

"By thunder, you'll pay for this!" he cried, shaking his fist, but Banjo chose to ignore him in the coolest way. He calmly folded his knife and returned it to his pocket, then crossed his arms over his chest.

"How'd you get hung up like that, anyhow?" he asked, plainly enjoying the sight of Seeger struggling to his feet, angrily dusting off the seat of his britches.

"This is the last time, by gum, this is the last blankety-blank time I'm going to put up with this sort of behavior!" he exclaimed, his face getting red as a tomato. "That blankety-blank elephant's nothing but a blankety prima donna. She got manners worse'n Paulina, her momma. I ain't gonna put up with no more tricks, y'hear me? Allus crabbin' the act, never helpin' set up the canvas like any right-minded elephant. By jingo, I've half a mind to—"

He sputtered and he fumed, and the angrier he became the more he cursed and swore; and the more he cursed, the longer the elephant lay there, looking weaker and more done in by the moment, her tongue hanging out, no longer pink, but a pale sickly shade, with bits of cottony foam in the corners of her mouth.

"She's looking a bit seedy, don't you think?" Opal ventured meekly.

Banjo hunkered down by the ailing beast and gently lifted her eyelids. "Not much action going on in there," he said.

"Won't somebody help her? Can't you call a doctor?" Opal begged.

"I'll help her, all right!" yelled the overly stimulated Seeger. "I'll help her to the boneyard is where I'll help her. I'll help her straight to the glue factory, where they'll boil her up into a big pot of glue, like they done with her ma, that's what I'll do! They'll use that elephant to paste up advertising bills!"

Opal was appalled by these nasty words, and horrified to think of the fate that Cupid's poor mother appeared to have met at the hands of this cruel man. No wonder Cupid hated him so much. "No, no!" she cried in alarm. "You can't do that! You mustn't!"

"Oh yeah? I'll show you what I can do," the angry Seeger shouted. "What else is she good for anyhow, I'd like to know? Am I supposed to pick the dad-blamed critter up in my arms and carry her around with me? Look at her, lolling there like the Queen of Sheba, like she owned the whole blankety-blank world and everything in it! Oh, if I could only get these two hands around that blasted throat, wouldn't I give her a good squeeze though! Nothin' I hates worse'n a low-down no-good dumb elephant!"

"Now, Nate," said Banjo, stroking Cupid's forehead, "you know she's a star, and stars is just temper-mental."

"Yeah, she's a star—star of goldbricking and discombobulating the whole blankety-blank act whenever she takes a mind to."

Opal was most sympathetic to the animal's plight. "But she's sick, poor thing. She doesn't know what she's doing!" she protested. "We must find some way of making her well again. Perhaps a veterinary might be called?"

"I'll vet'nary her!" shouted the irate fellow. "She'll find out what she's doing by the time I'm done with her! She ain't sick, she's jest funnin'! I seen her like this before, but this is a grandstand performance. And it's gonna be her grand finale, by dad!"

Seeger flung down his cork helmet and jumped on it, crushing it flat, like a child having a tantrum. Then he strode off, to return in a moment clutching a double-bore shotgun.

"Oh, no!" screamed Opal, rushing to where Cupid's inert form lay, as if to shield her from what was to come. "You can't shoot her!"

"You better believe I'm going to shoot her!" Seeger broke the gun barrel and socked in two 12-gauge shells, his face gone cherry red, his mustache bristling, and an ever darkening scowl creasing his brow. "By golly, I'll see her stuffed like a baked potato, I will!" He hefted his weapon and prepared to dispatch the poor beast.

Opal's heart was in her throat. "But she hasn't done anything but get sick on my peanuts," she protested.

Seeger wasn't interested in Opal's logic, and he had no compassion for the animal. "Think I'm goin' to let that dad-blasted critter make a fool of me, and eat me out of house and home to boot, when she don't do nothing but lie there, sick unto death? If she wants to go to elephant heaven, fine with me. One blast and I'll give her a good head start. Get out of my way, girlie!"

He cocked his gun and raised the barrel, placing the handle against his stubbly cheek. His finger tightened on the trigger, but Banjo sprang forward in the nick of time, knocking the gun barrel into the air, causing a shot to ring out and Opal to scream. Even Seeger looked palefaced and shaken from the explosion. Banjo tore the gun from Seeger's hands and addressed him angrily.

"You got no call to go shootin' up a helpless critter like that. Prob'ly wouldn't of been so ornery if you hadn't sent her momma to her Maker the way you done. Who told you you could do a thing like that, anyhow?"

Seeger stuck his face out at Banjo. "Nobody's got to tell me— Paulina was my elephant, and so's her young'un. I guess I can do what I like with my own property, can't I?" He squinted his red beady eyes at Banjo, and his adam's apple bobbed in his neck like an orange swallowed by an ostrich. "What else am I to do with her, anyways?" he went on, as if he was about to cry. "Why, she'll eat me out of house and home within a week." To Banjo's amazement, there were tears starting to roll down the man's cheeks.

But Banjo had no patience with such an obviously phony act. "Oh, can all that sob-story stuff," he said. "If you don't want the darned elephant, then get rid of her. But don't go shootin' her with that there shotgun. T'ain't nice."

From where she crouched, gently mopping the corner of Cupid's mouth with her handkerchief, Opal agreed. Shooting an elephant certainly wasn't nice at all. Especially an orphan elephant.

"Oh sure, easy for *you* to say," Seeger replied. "How's a man s'posed to get rid of a eight-hundred-pound elephant? I'm not no magician. I can't just make the critter disappear in no cloud of smoke, alla-kazam! And I can't go leaving her on no street corner waiting for the trash truck to cart her off, neither."

He looked from Banjo to Opal, but neither said a word.

"Of course," Seeger went on, studying his badly soiled nails, "if someone was to come along and take her off my hands . . ."

Banjo pushed his tall hat back and furrowed his brow thoughtfully. He slid a look from Seeger to Opal, who returned his wink and smiled. Then Banjo began a new tack with the elephant trainer.

"Now see here, Seeger," he said, "if you feel that way about it, why don't you just up and let this here li'l gal have her."

Seeger's eyes bugged. "What's that? What would *she* be wantin' with no elephant anyhow?"

"The fact is, Opal 'pears to have taken a fancy to this here beast. I know she'd give her a good home and care for her."

59

Opal felt a surge of excitement rush through her veins. "Oh, yes!" she pleaded. "Let me look after her."

"That's crazy," said Seeger. "What's a fool girl like you going to do with a sick elephant?"

"I'll take her home and nurse her."

"Are you crazy, gal? You think yore momma's gonna let you bring home a great big critter like this one and have it lyin' around the front parlor on the carpet? You ain't no Mary and this ain't no lamb, nosiree. Why, just look at that miserable beast. She can't hardly walk a single step." Seeger wagged his head dourly. "See her a-lyin' there pantin' out her life's breath. She's done for, I tell you. Ain't I ben around elephants all my life? Don't I know everything about the cussed breed? I mean it, this one's done for."

Opal was quick with a reply. "Well, sir, if she should expire, then we'll see she gets a decent burial." She stroked Cupid's side now. It felt hot and damp, as if she were running a fever—that is, if elephants ever got fevers; certainly it would call for a sizable thermometer to find out.

Seeger scratched his head thoughtfully, pondering the situation. "Well, all I got to say is, a person'd have to be pretty dumb to take on a sick critter like that."

"Say, lookee here, Nate," said Banjo suddenly, pulling out his gold turnip watch. "To cinch the deal I'll throw in this gen-you-wine fourteen karat gold watch, an old family heirloom. Worth two hundred dollars, cash on the drumhead." He let the watch spin in the light so it threw off bright flashes. Seeger's eyes glazed at the sight, and a second later the watch was swallowed up inside his pocket.

"Done and done!" he exclaimed. "I guess I'll know what time it is now."

Opal agreed that it was always a good idea to know what time it was, even for a man like Seeger. "Oughtn't we to have some kind of paper on it?" she suggested. "To make it all legal?"

"By golly, you're right, Opie," said Banjo.

Seeger was only too quick to write out a paper and sign it. "But you just listen here to me, you two," Seeger said, thrusting the paper at Opal. "Don't you never come runnin' back to me, sayin' I forced this here girl to take that cussed beast. I ain't lookin' to have you come leadin' her back to me to feed and nurse. I'm shed of that big-eared hayburner now, and that's that."

Turning on his boot heel, he tossed Cupid a contemptuous look, then marched away, nose in the air.

Opal was never so glad to see anyone go. She whispered words of comfort into Cupid's large, floppy ear, then glanced around, noting that all the while they had been bargaining over the elephant, the small tent they were in had been dismantled around them and packed up. All the circus trucks and trailers had driven away. With the departure of Seeger's outfit, she was all alone now in the deserted turnip field—all alone, that is, except for Banjo and the elephant. Yes—the elephant named Cupid, her very own Queen of the Tanbark, beside her in the dark amid the empty furrows, with the white moon riding high in the indigo sky.

"Well, I'll be jiggered," said Banjo, making a complete tour of Cupid with Pickles following on his heels, scrutinizing her carefully as she lay out on the ground, looking as sick as sick could be. "What do you think of that, Opie?" he wondered aloud. " 'Pears like you just became the owner of one sick elephant. Now watcha gonna do? She'll be a sight to hoist, I reckon."

Opal had her palm on Cupid's forehead. "Say, that's funny," she muttered in some mystification.

"What's that?" Banjo asked.

"Why, she seems to have cooled off some. She's not so clammy, either."

"You mean she ain't sick?" Banjo was both hopeful and astounded. "Well, if she ain't sick, why don't she get up?"

Then, even as they watched, an astonishing thing took place. No sooner had the words sprung from Banjo's mouth than Cupid gave a long, drawn-out sound through her trunk, like a deep sigh of relief. Tossing her head so her ears flopped, she got nimbly to her feet.

"Well, I'll be a monkey's uncle," the dumbfounded Banjo said.

Opal stared at the sight of the large beast solidly on all fours again. And what was that sly, knowing expression she had in her eyes? "You know, Banjo, I'm wondering . . ." she began.

"Whatcha wonderin'?" asked Banjo.

Opal smiled. "I'm just wondering if she was sick at all. I believe she was just funnin'." She went up close and looked Cupid straight in the eye. "Were you just funnin', Cupid? You can tell us. We're your friends."

Cupid's eyelid lowered momentarily, then raised itself again.

"By golly, did that elephant just wink?" asked an amazed Banjo. Cupid's lid dropped and rose again. "There, by gumbo!" Banjo exclaimed jubilantly. "If that wasn't a wink I'd like to know what it was." He gave Cupid's head a friendly pat. "You was just pullin' that rascal's leg, wasn't you, sweet thing? What a clever girl you are. I guess we put one over on ole Nate, didn't we?"

Cupid tossed her head again and waved her trunk victoriously in the air.

Banjo sucked in his cheek. "Well, here we are then. What say you, l'il bug?" he asked Opal. "What's your plan?"

Opal didn't know how to answer. She thought it must be quite late. Bid would be getting worried. She looked up at Cupid, whose large gray shape loomed in the darkness of the turnip field. "I wonder what we should do with her?"

"I reckon you better take her on home before the night air sets in and the dew starts to fall, or she'll catch a grippe for sure."

"Banjo's right, Cupid," Opal said, stretching to talk into the elephant's ear. "How'd you like to come along home with me?" Cupid jerked her head up and down, then wrapped her trunk around Opal's waist and gave her a big hug. "Oh, Cupid," she sighed rapturously, "I love you so."

She laid her cheek affectionately against the elephant's head and rubbed it up and down. The skin was just the least bit scratchy, but in no way unpleasant. Then she felt the trunk give a gentle squeeze, and before she knew it she was being lifted into the air and settled onto Cupid's broad neck just behind the ears. When she was safely balanced and holding on to the harness, with Banjo and Pickles the dog leading the way, they started off along the road to Peavine.

By now not a soul was stirring, no lamp showed anywhere. The moon was riding high in the sky, its bright beams turning the road pale and lighting their way. Though no one was there to see them, what a sight they made: the little dog prancing on its hind legs, followed by Banjo stepping out jauntily, his bundle on a stick resting on his shoulder, his tall hat tipped over one eye, while behind him, swaying in the moonlight, came the elephant, on whose back perched Opal Thigpen, gazing up at the bright twinkling stars, silently asking herself what Granny Bid would have to say when she saw what her great-granddaughter had brought home with her.

Chapter Six

By the Dark
of the Moon

BACK AT PEAVINE HOLLOW ALL WAS DARK AND QUIET.
The whole world seemed to be holding its breath in anticipation
of Opal's return from the traveling show. Along the roadside the
dewy sod muffled Cupid's footsteps as she walked tirelessly
through the darkness, and the great beast seemed to know that
she must move quietly, ever so quietly.

"Open the gate, please," Opal requested of Banjo as they arrived
home, but before he could get to it, Cupid reached over his head
and with the tip of her trunk deftly raised the latch and pushed
the gate open. When they had all passed through she carefully
closed it behind her and, as if knowing exactly where to go,
headed for Bid's little house.

At the front door Opal let Cupid's trunk assist her to the
ground, and, with the elephant following, she went around to
peek in at the window of her great-grandmother's room. In the

darkness she could make out the old bedstead, but so small was Bid's form that it was scarcely to be seen among the rumpled bedclothes. While Banjo and Cupid waited outside, Opal went around to the front and crept inside. Though she tried to be quiet, her foot struck something in the dark, and upon the instant came Bid's quavering voice.

"Opie, there's someone in the room!" Bid croaked. "Where you been, child? It's late and you promised me you'd be home at a decent hour."

Sitting down at the bedside, Opal lit the lamp and calmed her great-granny, explaining that she'd been delayed due to the illness of a friend.

"What friend?" demanded the old lady. "Sister's not sick, is she?"

Opal was hard pressed to reply, for she felt herself falling into a trap, one she'd have to fib her way out of, and she didn't want to do that. "No, Granny. It . . . it was a . . . a kind of . . . sort of a . . . *new* friend."

Bid sat straight up against the bolster and narrowed her eyes suspiciously. "What's that? *New* friend? What kinda new friend does a girl your age get to meet at this hour a'night?"

"Oh, we didn't meet *this* hour of night, Granny," replied Opal politely. "We met earlier this evening, as a matter of fact."

"And so, havin' met up," piped Bid, "you just decided to go out and have yourselves a high old time, is that it?" She fixed her eye on Banjo, whose shadowed shape looked in over the sill. "Some no-account buster like him takes you gallivantin' in the dead a'night—and you hardly out of rompers. I knew Sister shouldn't of left you with a man like that, who doesn't even know enough to remove his hat in front of a lady."

"Oh no, ma'am!" exclaimed Banjo, and he snatched the tall hat from his head. "We wasn't doin' no gallivantin', missus. We jest picked up this here friend of Opal's, and we come straight on home, like you done ast."

"Well, where is she, this friend?" demanded Bid.

"This is her, right here," Banjo went on. "Cupid, honey, poke your head in and say hello to Opal's great-granny." He stood a little aside so the elephant could stick her trunk into the room as if she were offering it for a friendly shake.

"Sweet Jesus in the clover!" cried Bid, shrinking back against the bolster. "It's a dragon! Gimme a stick an' I'll kill it!"

"No, Granny," cried Opal. "It's not a dragon. It's an elephant. And she's my friend. Her name's Cupid. She won't hurt you."

"Won't hurt me? Why, that critter could swallow me up at a gulp. Whoever heard of such a thing—bringin' home an elephant! Where's the rest of her?"

"It's outside, Granny," explained Banjo.

"That's as well. Seems to me an elephant her size'd be takin' up the whole place."

Cupid, who had been listening carefully to every word, wore an injured air. She never liked going anyplace where she wasn't wanted.

"What do you plan on doin' with her?" Bid wanted to know.

"Well, Granny, I was planning on keeping her," Opal answered.

"*Keepin'* her? You don't mean t'say you're plannin' to have that beast round here all the time? And your poor old granny havin' to look after her when you're back at school? Look there, what mischief is the nervy critter up to now?"

As Granny Bid had not accepted her offered trunk, the curious Cupid had begun to examine all the objects she could reach, the patchwork quilt covering Bid's toes, her worn-out shoes standing side by side under the bed, sniffing the flowers blooming in the mason jar, flipping through the few items on the bureau top.

66

"She's puttin' her long nose into ever'thing," said Granny disapprovingly. "Somebody's got to teach that critter manners." Cupid was running her trunk over the picture of Christ and the twelve Apostles. "Now she's snoopin' up on Jesus and His Brethren."

"Brethren?" exclaimed Banjo. "I thought Miss Mary just had the one boy."

If this was Banjo's idea of a joke, Opal had no time for it, for by now the elephant's examination of the picture had tilted it on its nail.

"That's enough, now, Cupid," Opal said severely. "You don't want people to think you're a nosy elephant."

Cupid dropped her head and withdrew her trunk. No, this elephant didn't want *anyone* saying *anything* bad about her. Opal stroked her ear flopping over the windowsill and blew in it to make her feel better.

"Opie, honey, how did you come by havin' this real live elephant, tell your granny," Bid said.

"Banjo got her for me. He traded off his twenty-four-carrots-gold turnip timepiece for her."

Granny was shocked. "Mean to say you got that whole big elephant for one bitty turnip?"

"Not a *turnip*, Granny, a turnip *watch*. It was twenty-four carrots of gold."

"Oh, carrots." By now Bid was confused as to which vegetable, turnips or carrots, had played a part in Cupid's purchase.

"And now she's ours, all ours," Opal said proudly. "We've brought her home to live with us."

"Good Lord in the morning!" exclaimed the old lady, shaking her head. "We're already mighty short on space round here, and that's a mighty big animal. Where you goin' to store her, anyways?"

"Don't worry, Granny, we'll find some shelter for her."

As she continued to lie in bed, Bid tugged thoughtfully at her lip. "I wonder what those lowdown trashy Cumberpatches are goin' to say when they see what you brought home with you? I reckon Old Man Cumberpatch'll be plenty mad. You best hope he doesn't take his gun to your elephant like he did to Brownie, makin' that poor rabbit into stew."

Opal refused to think of anyone else pointing a gun at Cupid. She was prepared for the Cumberpatches kicking up a fuss, but she was counting on Cupid's being able to charm them with her winning ways. Besides, Opal figured that God would find some way of working things out. He always did.

When Bid yawned, Opal suggested that Cupid say good night; it was time for Granny to get her beauty rest.

"Say good night to Cupid, Granny," and she handed Bid the end of Cupid's trunk to shake. "Granny, say 'See you in the morning, Cupid.' "

"See you in the mornin'," squeaked old Bid; the elephant's trunk twitched blissfully. Then Opal proceeded to sort of roll the trunk up like a firehose, and push it out the window. She drew the shade down, kissed her granny good night, put out the lamp, and stepped onto the porch, noiselessly closing the door behind her.

"This way, now, and be careful—don't stumble," she said as she guided her new pet along the side of the house. She went in through the door of her room, but when Cupid attempted to follow it became evident that the doorway was too narrow for the animal to negotiate.

"You ain't gonna get that critter in that little room nohow," Banjo pointed out.

"What should I do?" Opal wondered.

"You'll have to leave her outdoors, that's all."

68

"But I can't do that. What about the dew? What if she was to take sick for real?"

Banjo was looking around, scrutinizing the lay of the land. "That the Cumberpatch barn yonder? Look like there's room in there for such a beast." Softly whistling up Pickles, he started off, followed by the quietly plodding Cupid. With the lamp in one steady hand, Opal hurried after them.

Banjo was impressed with the barn, which seemed more or less to meet his mental specifications. "I think this'll serve the porpoise jest fine," he said with a wink. The flickering flame of the oil lamp made their shadows dance all about, and the scene had a spooky feel to it, as if somebody's skeleton might leap out at them at any moment. But Banjo was bold as brass as he tramped about the space, checking it for drafts and strange odors.

"We'll just stash you in one of them horse stalls fer tonight, my li'l popover," he said to Cupid. "I 'speck you is probably hungry, huh?" Cupid tossed her head twice. "Well, don't you worry none, Cupid honey," he went on, "Banjo'll scare up some grub."

As they moved further inside, Opal could hear the scurry of mice in the straw, questing for loose grain to eat. "Look here," she said, guiding Cupid to an empty stall, "this one's plenty roomy. I'll just put down a nice bed of straw for you to sleep on, and there's plenty of sweet clover for you to eat. And as an extra treat I'm going to fill that feedbag with fresh oats, so you just help yourself as you feel the need."

So saying, she patted Cupid's head and moments later she was guiding the elephant's trunk to the bulging feedbag. Then she went about bringing in straw and hay from the rick, some of which was extra for Cupid to eat, some to sleep on. The important thing now was for everyone to get some sleep before morning, when the Cumberpatch tribe would take to caterwauling upon finding an elephant in their barn; that was something Opal would have to deal with when the time came. Meanwhile it was more important to make sure that her new pet was as comfortable as possible, safe from drafts and wanting nothing.

When she said good night and took away the lamp, she followed Banjo outside. "You don't think she'll be scared of the dark, do you?" she asked him.

"Lan' sakes, li'l bug," Banjo replied, "that elephant done taken on the dread Nate Seeger. She could never be scairt of anything in the world. 'Sides, she knows she gotta home now."

The moon slid down the western sky, and Cupid was fast asleep in the stable; Granny was softly snoring in her bed; Banjo, his tall hat between his knees, was curled up on the porch glider; and Opal, in her little corncrib bed in the back room was too happy to sleep at all. She didn't know much about elephants, but one thing she did know—she had a friend; two, in fact: one with show-biz smarts like her daddy, and the other with a seven-foot trunk. And beyond the window, high overhead in the velvety summer sky the bright stars winked down, and even the moon's silvery face seemed to smile and nod that all was well. For as Banjo had said, Cupid had found a home with Opal Thigpen in Peavine Hollow.

Chapter Seven

Going Haywire

NEXT MORNING AFTER COCKCROW, OLD MAN CUM-
berpatch and all his sons came out of the house and went about
their morning chores, yawning so wide that their tonsils showed.
Number one on their list today was to see after the tractor's inner
workings, which had been acting up again. One thing Old Man
Cumberpatch couldn't stand was a persnickety engine, and today
he planned on fixing it or knowing the reason why.

So intent were the men on their mission that when they entered
the barn they didn't even bother looking in the horse stalls, just
went right to folding back the hood panels on the tractor and
sticking their heads in. Since Cupid never snored, no one realized
she was even there—and no one saw when she awoke. She came
to with a soft yawn, blinking her eyes as she looked around,
wondering where she was (even elephants forget *some* things).
Slowly she lumbered to her feet and began shuffling around the
stall, trying to get her bearings amid the unfamiliar surroundings.

Looking over the stall's half-door, she saw before her eyes a number of seemingly headless forms bent over some sort of noisy contraption that rattled and clanked and steamed and made terrible popping sounds. Ever curious, Cupid began feeling around with her trunk, grazing the rear end of one of the men leaning over the motor. Tulaine Cumberpatch jumped at the touch and said, "Hey, quit that!" to his brother Four Dice, standing next to him.

After a moment Cupid's trunk again brushed against Tulaine in the same way and in the exact same spot.

"Consarn it, Fordy!" exclaimed Tulaine, "Didn't I say quit that?"

"Quit what?" demanded Four Dice with a look as innocent as any angel's.

"What you just done—touchin' me intimate like that!"

"Listen here, Tulaine, I didn't touch you like nothin'. I had both m'hands on this here wrench," retorted Four Dice, shaking his oil-slicked socket wrench in his brother's face.

"Well, just you cut it out, anyways." Tulaine gave him a reproachful look and returned his attention to the troublesome tractor engine. When Cupid brushed him a third time, he jerked back, smacking his head on the hood panel. The blow made him see red and blue stars, and he got so angry that he hauled off and cut Four Dice a good one on the chin, knocking him to the floor.

"Gol-darn you durn-diggety pissants!" exclaimed their father—*pissants* was a word he enjoyed using when referring to his sons—"scrappin' agin! How many times do I got to tell you—"

He stopped midway in his sentence, for his eye had fallen on the elephant's trunk sticking out of the stall—and the elephant attached to it.

"Well, I'll be catechized," muttered the old man, dazedly. "If that don't beat all."

"What, Paw?" asked Buster.

"If that danged thing there don't look jes' like a elephunk yonder in Bourbon's stall."

"By dash, Grampaw, you're right," said Beaudine, looking around. "Ain't Grampaw right, Billy Rondo?"

"Hit shure looks like a elephunk to me," said Billy Rondo, whose eyes seemed to pop clear out of his head. "Hee-hah! Jes' lookit that there trunk, ain't that sumthin'! And lookit them big old floppy bat ears. An' them roly-poly eyes. If that ain't some kinda real elephunk, I'll get me some eye specks. How d'you s'pose hit got here?"

Opal, having finished tending to Bid, chose that moment to enter the barn, where she found herself face to face with the combined male line of the Cumberpatch tribe.

"Opal Thigpen—what you know 'bout this here funny-lookin' critter?" demanded Tulaine, planting his fists on his hips and giving her a menacing look.

"Hit some runaway from that travelin' show you gone to las' night?" Billy Rondo wanted to know.

"This is Cupid," Opal responded meekly. "Cupid's an elephant."

"See? I toldja," Beaudine asided to Four Dice. "Elephunk. I guess I knows a elephunk when I sees one."

"No, I told you, durn it," put in Billy Rondo. "Ah'm the one said it was a elephunk. I seen one in a box a'Animal Crackers one time."

"Opal Thigpen, just what in tarnation are you doin' with a elephunk?" demanded Renfrew Cumberpatch.

"I bet she done stole it," said Buster meanly.

"Buster Daltree Cumberpatch, don't be any bigger fool than you already are," snorted his father scornfully. "Folks of a right mind don't go around stealin' whole elephunks. They's far too big for thievin'. A body fer sure'd have a sight a'trouble hidin' one."

"I didn't steal her," Opal said. "She belongs to me."

"Oh say, I bet," said Buster sarcastically. "Didja buy it from the Sears and Roebuck catalog?" This remark provoked a lot of guffawing and thigh slapping among his brothers.

"A man at the traveling show gave her to me," Opal said, ignoring their hilarity.

"For what consideration?"

"For the consideration that I love her and look after her when she's sick and—"

Buster ran his finger across his forehead and flicked away the wet. "Naw, naw, I mean for what consideration of money? Legal tender. Hard cold bucks."

"No bucks was tendered, hot or cold," said a voice from outside. "It wasn't that kinda deal."

Banjo stepped around the corner of the stable. "Hidy, fellahs," he said, tipping his tall hat and smiling all around. "Fine mornin' and that's a fact." He smiled at Opal. "Mornin', li'l bug. I see you done got your night's rest all right. And our friendly pachyderm, she of the Circus Maximum, Queen of the Tanbark, I trust she too done passed a night of blissful slumber."

The Cumberpatch boys were casting looks of distrust among themselves; they didn't cotton to this big-talking fellow who'd suddenly popped up among them again.

"So whatcha gonna do with that there critter?" asked Tulaine.

"I hoped perhaps you'd let us put her up in your barn for a little."

Old Man Cumberpatch's mouth turned down at both ends. "You don't say? And who's to pay for her feed? Big job like that's bound to eat a body out of house and home."

"She's an elephant," Opal put in. "She doesn't eat either houses or homes. Just hay."

"That's right, gents," said Banjo with his friendliest smile. "Jest

74

hay. And not so much hay at that. Y'see, an elephant, he be like a camel. Now, a camel, he kin store up a whole load of water in his hump, 'nuff to cross the whole Sahary Desert, while a elephant, all *it* have to do is take a tiny li'l bit of hay and it'll store it up in its trunk and it'll go the whole day. Some folks keep old clothes in their trunk, but a elephant, he be keepin' *hay* in his."

Billy Rondo put his large red hand out at Cupid, who started and jumped back, her trunk rising in the air as a silent warning.

"Best not to touch her none, till she gets acquainted," Banjo advised him.

"Oh, that there elephunk, she like me jes' fine, don'tcha hon?" Billy Rondo said, giving Cupid a couple of strokes on the trunk. Then, like an angry python, the gray trunk whipped itself around Billy Rondo's middle, yanked him clear off his feet, then turned him upside down and dropped him headfirst into the horse trough. Sputtering and fuming, Billy Rondo pulled himself out dripping and turned to his father.

"She dropped me on my haid, Paw," he whined as he rubbed his scalp. "Lookit the danged ol' bump she raised on me."

"Serves you right, pissant," said Old Man Cumberpatch. "You was told not to touch that critter. Next thing you'll lose a whole arm."

The old man spat through the fork of two fingers and spoke to Opal. "Well, girl, you just cart her along outta there now, and you boys, hop on into that stall and do a clean-up job."

Ever obedient, Opal led Cupid out of the barn and along the path to Bid's house, while the Cumberpatch men stood in the doorway scratching their heads and drawing down on their elastic suspenders with their thumbs, marveling at the strangeness of a full-grown elephant turning up overnight in Bourbon's stall thataway.

"I've got to dope this whole thing out," Opal said to Banjo. "An elephant needs a roof over her head the same as folks do. And as her new owner it's up to me to provide it. Any thoughts?"

"She do take up a sight of room, don't she?" Banjo agreed. He scrunched up his face in deepest thought. Suddenly the little light in his brain went on. "Say, whyn't we just toss all that junk outta the back shed and stick her in there?" he suggested.

Opal had her doubts; that shed was filled with all sorts of castoffs. "I don't expect Cupid'll fit in there. She's awful big— shed's awful small."

"You won't never know till you try, li'l bug," was Banjo's sensible reply.

He was right there. You never knew *anything* till you tried. Opal decided to try. She went to where the elephant stood patiently waiting, with her trunk curled under. "Come along, Cupid," she said, "and let's see how we can get you in the shed. But first we got to empty it out or there won't be any room at all."

She peered inside the small building, which was pretty dark, there being only the one window along the side. The inside was jam-packed with everything under creation: rusted motor parts, a pile of barrel staves, gardening tools, parts of vacuum cleaners, pieces of a broken chair, a misshapen wire dress dummy, some worn mule tackle, a horse collar, a strap of jingle bells, all kinds of things that nobody wanted but kept around in case they came in handy someday.

"I never seen sucha messa stuff," Banjo grumbled, ejecting a treadless tire that rolled away among the nasturtiums. Cupid tossed her trunk and nodded in agreement.

"See here, Cupid," Opal said to the elephant, "if we're goin' to stall you here, you've got to help out a little. Some folks aren't as able-bodied as they might be."

Cupid tossed her head again, then inserted her trunk into the shed. When she withdrew it, it had half a dozen tires skewered on it, like doughnuts on a stick. She held them to one side, patiently waiting to be told what to do with them.

"Oh, that's all right, just go ahead and drop them anywhere," Opal said, and with a flick of her trunk Cupid flung the tires away among the tall weeds.

"Good work! Now see what else can you yank outta there," Banjo told her.

Cupid advanced farther into the dim interior, and in no time a whole explosion of objects came flying out so fast that Opal had to jump lively to avoid being hit.

"Now that' ain't no way t'do," Banjo admonished Cupid. "Don't go throwin' 'em ever' which-a-way like that. Make a nice pile, keep things neat, all nice 'n tidy. Sure, that's the way. You catch on fast. Now go on and hand me out that there old icebox."

"Oh, I don't think she can move that all by herself," said Opal. "An icebox is bound to be heavy, don't you think?"

"Pshaw," said Banjo, "she'll handle that icebox like it was a box of matches. See, a elephant's built for heavy-duty movin'. Once I seen a elephant pick up a big ole Lincoln Zephyr in his trunk. Why, in Africa, they move whole buildin's. Let's go, Cupid, send 'er out."

Sure enough, in a moment, out flew the old broken icebox, and quickly after it a broken extension ladder, a broken bicycle, and yet another tire, which landed atop the pile.

"Now do us some real good with that there iron anvil," Banjo instructed Cupid.

"Goodness, that's bound to give her a strain," Opal said fearfully.

"Naw, twon't neither. Ever hear of a elephant with a hernia? Heave 'er out, Cupid. There's a good girl."

And indeed, out came the anvil, which when Cupid uncurled her trunk, struck the ground with a heavy thud.

"We best leave that where Jesus flang it or *I'm* the one'll get hisself a hernia," Banjo said.

When the shed had yielded up its final discard, the two of them looked the place over, trying to decide if it would make suitable living quarters for an elephant. Banjo paced off the length, which seemed fine, but the width caused him some problem, and he decided there was no ideal way to estimate.

"C'mere, honey," said Banjo, reaching for Cupid's trunk and coaxing her farther into the shed. Opal peeked in, observing with interest as the elephant filled up the small space, while the figure of Banjo disappeared altogether from view, for Cupid's swelling sides had blocked out the window, leaving the place dark as pitch.

"Here, now, back 'er up," commanded Banjo's disembodied voice as he tried to maneuver the elephant back out of the shed. Cupid gamely attempted to locomote in reverse, which proved an impossible task since she now took up every inch of width between the two side walls and was stuck tight.

"Dagnabit, she jest won't go," Banjo said, puffing as he crawled out of the shed from between Cupid's hind legs. He set his tall hat on the trampled grass and instructed Opal to give Cupid's tail a pull.

"I don't like to do that," Opal said anxiously. "It might hurt her."

"Naw, naw," said Banjo, "you can't hurt no elephants by pulling at their tails. Their tails is all discombobulated, like. Just give her a good yank, that'll do her."

Opal did as she was told, reaching up and giving the tail a gentle tug, but nothing happened; Cupid didn't budge. Opal wondered if they hadn't made a mistake putting her in the shed in the first place.

Just then, Tulaine Cumberpatch passed the shed on the old rattletrap tractor, which his tinkering had finally got working again. On his lap sat his baby girl, Precious One, who loved nothing more than going for a ride on her daddy's tractor. The motor chugged and smoked and clanked as the wheels bumped their way across the field, heading for the spot where Tulaine would hook it up to the cultivator. Suddenly the tractor jumped and sputtered, and there was a loud *pop!* as the engine exploded, then died.

Cussing a purple streak, Tulaine jumped down, setting Precious One on the tractor seat while he yanked up the hood panel and stuck his head inside to see what had gone wrong this time. He fiddled and he fussed and he cussed and he kicked, then he stood by the driver's seat, where he yanked the choke out, fiddled with the magneto, and depressed the accelerator, then he went back and fussed some more under the hood. At last the motor started up again, and the machine began to quiver and shake to a fare-thee-well. Tulaine pulled down the panel and as he leaned to latch it, the tractor leaped forward with a violent jerk, knocking him to the ground and taking off—driverless but for a highly alarmed toddler.

Precious One let out a cry and clung with her little hands to the seat. While the tractor careened wildly across the field, she let go of the seat and clutched desperately at the steering wheel, turning the speeding tractor, first this way, then that.

"Hang on, Precious! Your daddy's a-comin!" shouted Tulaine, hightailing it after the runaway vehicle. Hearing the commotion, the rest of the Cumberpatch tribe came dashing one after the other out of the house or the barn to see what was happening.

"Hang on, Precious!" they shouted. "Hang on! Life is dear!"

Precious One was hanging on for all she was worth, clutching the wheel so that her baby knuckles turned white and the tractor ran in circles. Her daddy was still hotfooting his way behind it, whooping like an Indian in a Tom Mix movie and calling on the Lord to avert a tragedy. Melissande Cumberpatch was watering her rhubarb when she saw what was happening and, catching up her Mother Hubbard skirts, went running like a turkey after Tulaine. Four Dice set down the piece of harness he was repairing and ran after his ma, and Billy Rondo gave off hitching up the team and ran after Four Dice, to be followed by Buster, and Buster by Henhouse, and he by Yclept, then Miss'sipp, who sprang out the front door of the house to run after Billy Rondo, and Desiree, still putting curlers in her hair, ran after Miss'sipp, and Etoile, who was redding up the kitchen, ran after Desiree, screeching like a stuck pig, and Fayette took out after Etoile, and after Fayette came Sally Dawn, and after Sally the hound dog, Sad Man, until there was a long line of Cumberpatches stretched out across the turnip field, all chasing after Precious One aboard the tractor and trying to keep her from getting killed.

Then, just at that moment, for reasons best known only to itself, the tractor reversed, and, making a quick spin, started back in the direction it had come. Tulaine had to jump plenty quick to get out of the way, Maw dove for the sidelines, and Four Dice was next, moving his clodhoppers faster than they'd ever swung. Then Billy Rondo, wheezing like a steamer, nearly got run over, and when he pulled up short Buster and Henhouse and Yclept came near to running straight up his spine, then the wild-eyed Etoile flew screeching from the path of the oncoming monster, dragging Miss'sipp along with her, while Desiree and Fayette yowled in fright and leaped to save their mortal souls.

Opal gazed on the scene horrified. The mindless, driverless

tractor was now heading straight for the mudhole, and with Banjo right after her, she took off after it in a desperate effort to save Precious One. Meanwhile, in her newly emptied out shed, Cupid sensed that something was wrong. Since she was facing inward and unable to see, she attempted to turn herself, a feat that proved even more impossible than backing up, wedged as tight as she was against the boards. In her excitement she began to strain and heave, waving her trunk in the dark space and trumpeting her loudest call. As she attempted to free herself, she became more and more violent, pulling and yanking every which-a-way. Suddenly there was the horrid screeching sound of rusty nails prying themselves loose from the bone-dry timbers, and in moments the shed tore itself away from the adjoining house.

Freed at last, Cupid went dashing after Opal, wearing the shed across her back as if it were some sort of medieval armor. Still waving her trunk and trumpeting loudly, as if to let everyone know that help was on the way, she lumbered across the field, quickly overtaking all the Cumberpatches galumphing toward the mudhole. With every step she took, whole sections of the shed came loose around her and dropped away; the shingles flew up one by one, and the board siding fell off, until only the bare framework clung to her back, and as she thundered on, even these scant pieces were shaken off, freeing her of all encumbrance.

By now the tractor was on a collision course with the mudhole, whose brown, turgid waters seemed to beckon the machine in sinister fashion.

"Precious One!" screeched Etoile, fearing the worst. "Oh, someone save my Precious One!"

Hearing those words, Cupid redoubled her efforts to reach the child before the tractor could hit the mudhole, straining every fiber and muscle in her elephant's body to avert a terrible tragedy. Taking in deep gulps of air through her open mouth, her trunk held stiffly out in front like the barrel of a cannon, she pelted on, her heavy flanks heaving as she gained ground.

The driverless tractor bounced helter-skelter along. Hitting a hillock, it leaped high into the air, shaking up Precious One, who somehow still managed to hang on. Then, just as the machine jolted toward the edge of the mudhole, Cupid gave a final bound and, seizing the child in her trunk, snatched it from the jaws of certain death, while the tractor landed with a wet *splat!* in the water where, within seconds, amid rings of increasing size, it sank from sight.

"God in Heaven and all His Saints be praised!" shouted Tulaine, who hadn't been inside a church since the day he was baptized.

"Cupid, bring that poor child here," Opal ordered, and the brave beast turned and obediently deposited the frightened infant in Opal's arms. Etoile, her face all red and tearstained and her mouth wide open and in danger of catching flies, came screeching up to reclaim her offspring. Then she dashed off across the field with Precious One, followed by her mate and all the other Cumberpatches, the whole tribe departing without one single word of thanks for either of the child's saviors. But Opal didn't care; neither did Cupid. The baby was rescued and that was the main thing. Saving babies was always a good thing to do. It was always good to do good in the world when the chance was offered.

Chapter Eight

The Song of Summer

IT DIDN'T MATTER THAT THE CUMBERPATCHES HAD neglected to thank Cupid for her bravery in saving Precious One, because while they may have ignored the elephant's heroism, others did not.

Ever since the tractor had sunk from sight in the pond and Cupid had saved the day, passersby pointed out the Cumberpatch place as being something noteworthy. Photographs of Cupid pulling the tractor out of the mudhole had been in all the rotogravure sections, as well as bold newspaper headlines that read something like this:

HEROIC ELEPHANT SAVES INFANT FROM DROWNING!!!
PRODIGY'S CRIES FOR HELP ANSWERED BY VALIANT PACHYDERM WITH BRAIN OF EINSTEIN

A banner headline like that was surely bound to turn a person's head; yes, but not Cupid's. Having such prominent notice taken of her exploits was nice, but she didn't go overboard about it, just took it all in her stride like she did that sort of thing every day—saving drowning children and then hauling out tractors from some old sump.

As things turned out, the incident had proved a pretty lucky thing. Putting a roof over an elephant's head and walls about its body, with a rain barrel close enough at hand for drinking purposes, was a tall order, one Opal wasn't sure how to deal with, especially now that the shed had been reduced to kindling wood. But Melissande Cumberpatch came to her rescue. Reminding her husband of Cupid's quick thinking, Melissande talked Old Man Cumberpatch into allowing the baby's savior to go on staying in Bourbon's barn stall, sort of as a belated thanks. And so Cupid became an official resident of Peavine Hollow, and no one was happier than Opal.

No one could imagine her happiness over having Cupid, because it was simply not to be imagined. Cupid wasn't like other children's pets, a hamster or a rabbit or a pig or a cow or even a dog; she was a great big elephant, big enough to receive all the love Opal had to give. And big enough to be loved and admired by all kinds of folk, too. For it was true: after the newspapers got hold of the story, people began flocking from all over the place to see this wonder of nature. Now a day seldom went by when there wasn't a line of autos parked along the roadside with all kinds of rubberneckers trying to get a gander at the remarkable beast. And when they drove away they called out that they'd be back; they wanted to show Cupid to Grandmaw Fester or Aunt Hattie or Uncle Rhubarb.

The way things were heading, even the Cumberpatches stood to profit from Cupid's presence on the property. Miss'sipp and

Henhouse set up a roadside soft-drink stand and sold lemonade at five and ten cents a glass, while Melissande hung out some of the quilts and pucker-patch bedspreads from the cedar chest and let them go at ten or fifteen dollars a whack. Four Dice got to ogle the girls in their high heels and marcelle hairdos, while the unwed Fayette Cumberpatch got to make calf eyes at the boys in long pants. All in all, the Cumberpatches found their lives considerably changed in a relatively short time. Fact was, Cupid was changing a lot of people's lives.

The elephant's presence in the Hollow seemed a tonic for young and old alike—but especially for the young. All the children from around the neighborhood couldn't think of anything more fun than having that big beast to come and look at any time they liked. The whole idea seemed impossible, like a dream. But it was no dream, for there she was, right before your very eyes, a pet who was so sweet-natured and such fun to play with, whose broad, strong back could carry so many riders on it, who acted almost human sometimes. It seemed to Opal as if Cupid understood what children were all about and was willing to let them behave just as they were meant to do, to laugh and joke and have the kind of fun children liked to have.

Of course, Old Man Cumberpatch stayed grouchy as ever. He made no secret of how much he hated having a passel of kids running all over his place, heedless of tramping down his cotton and his butterbeans. But he didn't give a rap how much they played in the mudhole. A deep spring fed the hole, so the water was always cool, and when Cupid waded in to revel in its oozy, muddy chilliness, in went every child in the neighborhood, too, slopping around and having big old mud fights.

Afterward, they'd all troop down to the riverbank where Cupid would wade out and take the water in her trunk, a full two gallons of it, and spray it over all the children, head to toe, while they pranced around and squealed with delight. And when they were all clean, Cupid would carefully wash herself off, and the faithful Opal would stand by with a long-handled janitor's brush to scrub her pet's back where she had trouble reaching herself. That done, Opal would take a large rag, and standing on a stepladder, she'd wash inside the big floppy ears, taking care to wash behind them as well and trying not to get soap in Cupid's eyes.

Of course, the best place to sit back, take the sun, and dry off was on Cupid's own back, and it was one day when Cupid was performing just such a service for Miss'sipp and Henhouse and Precious One, that Opal had a thought. Old Doc Beezer had come to visit Granny Bid that morning, and he'd left saying that she needed some nitroglycerin tablets for her heart. This was bad news, for Opal knew there was no money to buy the medicine with. But the sight of the Cumberpatch kids up on Cupid's back was a moment of sudden inspiration, and in that moment lay the seed of Opal's entire future. That same afternoon she walked Cupid out by the vegetable stand, and they tacked up a sign, Opal holding the tacks as Cupid hammered. The sign read:

ELEPHANT RIDES
5¢—10¢
(OVER FORTY POUNDS—2 BITS)

This was bad news for Henhouse Cumberpatch. He was considerably over forty pounds and had to pay twenty-five cents, and this made him good and mad.

Someone else whose ire was aroused proved to be Augusta Primrose, who had been watching the busy activity down in the Hollow from the big house porch ever since she'd read of Cupid's feat in the *Clarion*. Augusta did not approve of this sort of commercial carryings-on in the neighborhood.

86

"What's the place coming to, anyhow?" she wondered aloud. And, indeed, what *was* the place coming to?

Cousin Blossom, however, thought it a capital idea. "My!" she exclaimed, shading her eyes and peering down at the Hollow. "Opal seems to be doing a land-office business with that elephant of hers. Before we know it, she'll be a regular entrepreneur, won't she?"

"Hmph!" said Augusta, annoyed when Blossom used that sort of highfalutin vocabulary. Nor did Augusta take kindly to Blossom's sympathetic support of such a common undertaking as offering elephant rides for cold hard cash practically on her doorstep!

"We are not moneygrubbers," she declared through that long nose of hers. "The Primroses have never been in trade. I think it's a disgrace. *And*, to be perfectly frank, I wouldn't be the least bit surprised if that ugly beast keeled over in all this heat." She drew out her hanky from her belt and sniffed the floral-scented *eau de toilette* she had sprinkled on it. "And I shudder to think how many of those urchins who ride her may be squashed to death."

"Gracious, Cousin!" exclaimed Miss Blossom. "We mustn't say such things. We musn't even *think* them. I'm sure the elephant's perfectly well looked after. Opal sets such a store by her. And after all, elephants do come from a hot country, don't they? And they're terribly strong, aren't they? Just look how Cupid dragged that heavy tractor out of the mudhole. To say nothing of saving the baby."

"Nevertheless," said Augusta, "something must be done. At summer's end Mrs. Vermilyea returns from her vacation at Sea Island, and then these antics must stop. The proper place for an elephant is in the zoo, and *that*, I can assure you, is where your large-eared African friend will end up."

Blossom was horrified at the thought of Cupid being placed

behind bars, to stand about being ogled by a bunch of rubberneckers who didn't know an elephant from a zebra. However it
was to be done, Augusta must be forestalled in her plan.

Meanwhile, there were the rides. But ten-cent excursions atop
an elephant's back were only the beginning; more, much more
lay in store for Augusta, and had she known what it was, she
would have thrown herself into the backseat of her Rolls-Royce
and ordered Jekyll to drive her off a very tall cliff.

While Augusta continued to fret and stew about the goings-on
down in the Hollow, Cupid continued to prove herself a great
help in a variety of ways. Though she'd hardly been taught anything at all, she seemed to know a lot just on principle. And what
she didn't know she certainly picked up in a hurry. She would
get herself fitted into a horse harness and pull the plow, she would
water Bid's kitchen garden with her trunk and pull up weeds, and
when Opal was busy at the Primroses or at church, she would
sit with Granny Bid and look after her, using her trunk to rock
Bid's chair or to waft a fan and keep her cool. And when it came
to household chores, who in the world was more useful and
practical, or neat and clean and quick? To all her tasks Cupid
brought a quiet strength and intelligence, and a genuine affection;
she seemed to possess all those highly prized traits that most
humans were lacking in, and when Opal knelt to say her prayers
at night, she blessed the good fortune and thanked the good
Lord for bringing her such a friend.

Unfortunately, Opal's nights were sometimes sleepless. She
would toss and turn in bed remembering her visit with Miss
Augusta, weighed down by the abiding fear that when this perfect
season was over Granny Bid would be sent to the Home, and
herself to Savannah to dust Amelia Vermilyea's bric-a-brac. But
come the wee small hours of the morning, she would realize that

in the end it would all be up to her: Opal Thigpen would be the one to figure a way out of the predicament. She was only thirteen, and she didn't have the experience to handle such problems cleverly, but still, ever optimistic, she would remind herself that where there was a will there was a way, and if there was a way she would find it.

Meanwhile, her perfect summer unfolded. Most afternoons, with her chores attended to and a bit of free time on her hands, Opal could be found down by the river with her fishing pole and line, sitting under the cottonwoods and discovering what catfish there were to be caught. Naturally, when she went fishing she was accompanied by Cupid, who, like Mary's lamb, went nearly everywhere that Opal went. There they would sit side by side along the shady bank, Opal with her bamboo pole, Cupid with a line tied to her trunk, casting her hook in and out of the water, hopeful of a fat bite.

For an elephant, Cupid was a darn good fisherman. She'd sit there on the bank until she felt a tug on her line; the cork would bob, and she'd have a nibble. Quick as a flash she'd toss her trunk back, and out of the water would flash a catfish or a perch, and Opal would drop her pole and run to unhook the catch. Then Cupid would throw the line back in the water again and settle herself to wait for another fish to swim by. Opal didn't think there was anything odd about an elephant who sat by the river and fished, and it was a cause for wonder, the dither some folks made of such a sight. Augusta Primrose wasn't the only one having trouble with the idea of an elephant roaming up and down the Old Cotton Road, drinking from the river and fishing for catfish along its banks.

But as the days wore on people got used to the notion, and they began to pay more attention to the splash of the catfish and the babble of the brook than to the elephant on the bank. For it was deepest July from one end of the Cotton River to the other, and in the Hollow the folks who lived along the waterside were content just to sit under the cottonwoods and listen to the lovely song of summer, to the sighing of the breezes among the green leaves, the creak of the rope hammock slung between two bottle trees; to hear the lazy bumble of the bumblebee as it buzzed from clover to buttercup in search of honey and the happy chirping of the birds.

How wonderful, Opal thought, to feel the still, summery hush that lay over everything, in a time when everything moved so slowly, and July and August promised faithfully that December would never show its face again. So it was that the happy summer days melted like honey and butter on warm pancakes, one into the other, and Opal, happy with Cupid, sang the song.

And the day would end, the dusk would creep across the land, and the last rays of sunlight would wink in the river. As the velvety darkness closed in around her and the moon rose in the sky, Opal would reach beside her and take the tip of Cupid's trunk and wind it around her narrow waist, stroking and caressing the rough, leathery skin as if it were the softest, most fragrant skin in the world, the kind they talked about in bath soap advertisements. Then, feeling Cupid's trunk respond with a gentle squeeze, before she knew it she would be lifted into the air and onto Cupid's neck, where she would sit perched as they went for a walk in the cool night air.

What a thrill! What excitement! What happiness! *Why,* Opal would think, *I could be a king or a queen, riding up here on my elephant.* How regal she felt, how elegant, and as Cupid lumbered slowly along, gently rocking Opal under the tree boughs, under the starry sky and the light of the silvery moon, she told herself she was the luckiest girl in all the world. No matter how long or hard she was obliged to labor at her chores up on the Primrose Hill, earning enough money to keep her and Granny alive, it was all worth it—since the coming of Cupid. And she resolved to take care of Cupid the best way she knew how; to love her and never let her be lonely. These were good things to do when you cared about someone, especially if that someone was an elephant.

Late one night a big fat watermelon moon came riding up over the hill, shedding its light across the tops of the rippling cornfields. In the river the catfish jumped and splashed, and on its banks the crickets chirped. Opal listened from her bed. Then, when no other lights shone but the stars and she was sure everybody was asleep, she stole out to the barn to chat with Cupid as she often did late at night, and to see that she was nice and settled in her stall. As Opal shared her thoughts, something told her that tonight especially she wasn't speaking in vain, but that every word she uttered was perfectly comprehended, and that Cupid was absorbing the words into her brain and storing them there and would never forget them—for that's what elephants did best, wasn't it, never forget?

"Oh, Cupid," Opal said finally, "I love you so. I hope you know that." Cupid nodded. "And I also want you to know that no matter what happens to us—not that anything will, of course," Opal added quickly, "I'll always take care of you." Again Cupid moved her large head up and down, and they were quiet for a moment. Then, as Opal lay her head affectionately against Cupid's trunk and nuzzled in close, she had an idea. And no sooner did she whisper it into Cupid's ear than off they went, out the barn and across the yard, hand-in-trunk.

Because Cupid's feet were thickly padded on the bottom, she was able to step quiet as a mouse, making hardly a sound as she moved toward the edge of the cornfields. By the same token, because Opal was in her bare feet, she made hardly any noise either, and silence was all important now. Granny Bid always said that in the still of the night, if you didn't make the slightest sound, you could hear the corn grow, but you had to be quiet as a stick or you'd never hear a kernel. Opal loved the notion, and so, obviously, did Cupid when Opal suggested the excursion.

"This is a pretty good place, don't you think, Cupid?"

They had stopped at the end of a dark row of corn with slender leaves fluttering gently in the night breeze. Cupid tossed her trunk to show agreement, and there they stood, outlined by the light of the moon, listening as hard as they could.

"Listen!" whispered Opal, straining every fiber of her being and putting her ear up close to an ear of corn sticking out from a tall stalk. In the soft, slight rustling of the leaves she thought she could hear it enlarging itself. Yes! There! A little puffing sound— *pffffffff*—then a bit of a *snap!* and always that faint rustling that seemed to go on and on in the darkness all around them.

"Grow, corn," Opal heard herself say, "grow big and tall. Ears, grow fat and sweet and juicy for nice corn pudding." She felt the tip of Cupid's trunk lightly touch her shoulder, which meant she was in complete accord, and Opal was pleased that Cupid could also hear the corn growing. But then, with those big floppy ears, why not?

The moon climbed higher, the hour grew later, and the dark sky was ablaze with stars. They could see the Milky Way, like a road of jewels so bright and white that you could almost walk on it. Why, she thought, it was like the Great White Way that Daddy wrote about, the place where all the shows were put on in the theaters, the main street of New York: *Broadway!* She put her head back against Cupid's shoulder and talked about her daddy, for she knew Cupid liked to hear stories of how Jimmy-Jack Thigpen was making it big in the Big Apple. As she spoke she felt the tip of Cupid's trunk gently stroking her cheek; it was like her mother's fingers when she used to rock her to sleep.

She continued to gaze up at the wide, all-covering, blue-black sky, so alive with gleaming light, those millions of stars tossed like so many planting seeds across the firmament, adding their silvery beams to the light of the moon. Suddenly, a bright light streaked across the heavens, with a long, silvery tail blazing gloriously behind it, only to disappear in moments, back into the great darkness.

"Did you see it, Cupid?" Opal asked excitedly. "Did you see the shooting star up there in the sky?"

Cupid nodded and waved her trunk up at the stars.

"Then you must shut your eyes and make a wish," Opal instructed, as she closed her own eyes and wished with all her might. But Opal's wish was so big, so impossible, that she was sure it had no chance of coming true. Still, it was her wish, and she would keep it safe in her heart just in case.

She turned to look at Cupid. Her eyes were still obediently closed, and Opal gently kissed her cheek. "Did you make a wish?" she asked in a whisper.

Cupid opened her eyes slowly, but didn't nod; nor did she shake her head. She just looked into Opal's eyes with a steady, unflinching gaze. It was as if she was trying to tell her friend something, as if she wanted Opal to know that she loved her, too, and that even though she'd seen the shooting star and had closed her eyes like Opal had instructed, there had been no need for her to make a wish. For Cupid, her wish had already come true.

Chapter Nine

A Grand Idea!

DURING THE TIME THAT OPAL'S SUMMER IDYLL WITH Cupid was taking place, Banjo Bailey never wavered in his heartfelt admiration of Sister Eclipse, and, true to his word, he kept very close company with her. Though not a generally known fact, Sister was well past forty (which seemed quite old to Opal), and squarely set in her ways. Nevertheless, Banjo had made up his mind to woo Sister however he could and have her for his wife—all two hundred pounds of her. To this end he had left Colonel Beebee's show and taken a small room in town. Of course, he was still in the show business, though now the posters he tacked up were for Elbowtown's one movie house, the Dreamland Theatre. While his days were still spent on the road, when the sun set he could be found at Sister's gate, where he'd invite himself to sit on the stern of her houseboat, twang his banjo along with the frogs lining the riverbank, and watch the fireflies turn their little orange-and-blue lights on and off.

Being of a forthright and candid character, Sister Eclipse had made it known to Banjo that she wasn't interested in finding herself another husband, but Banjo never let that daunt him. "A woman who says she don't want to get married is a woman just kiddin' herself," he declared. "That selfsame woman, she'll come 'round, just like Christmas, just like the bill collector."

"That man's just after my money," said Sister, but Opal confided to Granny Bid that Sister seemed pleased all the same by Banjo's attentions.

The harder Banjo courted, the more forcefully Sister repelled his advances, but she never once told Banjo *not* to come 'round, and she never turned down any of the little presents he brought, either.

One early evening before the sun had set behind the cotton-wood grove, Sister Eclipse came by to visit with Granny. Soon after she got herself settled on the porch Banjo showed up. "What say we takes in a show together, you'n' me?"

Sister snorted. "Where'd *you* get the price of a show, you old flimflam man?"

"I got me a whole quarter right here," Banjo replied, producing a shiny twenty-five-cent piece from the pocket of his red plaid vest.

Sister hooted and threw up her hands. "Lord, if you're not the richest man in the country," she chortled. "A whole two bits, I'll be jiggered." Just then she caught sight of Opal, coming up from the riverbank with Cupid. She heaved herself up, making the porch planks groan, and called, "Opie, honey, you look like you could use a little adversion. Whyn't you come along with this old hobo 'n' me and take in a pitcher show?"

As much as Opal enjoyed the thought of going to the movies, she had to think of her granny. But Bid assured her that Cupid had already proven herself quite capable of keeping her company, and for her part, Cupid was only too happy to stay with the old woman while Opal enjoyed herself at the picture show.

"I won't be gone long," Opal assured her pet before leaving, "and when I come back I'll tell you all about the movie, every word, will that be all right?"

Cupid nodded agreeably, though Opal secretly wished she could take her along, despite the fact that she knew the theater seats would be too small for an elephant to sit in.

As they drove to Elbowtown in Sister's contraption, Opal was secure in the feeling that Cupid had understood the situation completely. Arriving in town they found that on so fine an evening people were out in numbers, lallygagging along the wooden sidewalks or sitting on soda pop boxes, just watching the passing show. Outside the Dreamland Theatre the moviegoers were already lining up, waiting for the box office to open. Banjo escorted Sister Eclipse and Opal into line, where he tipped his hat to several passersby and had a friendly word of greeting for all.

"Howdy, Miss Elthea, you're looking mighty peart. Nice evenin', Jojo, you are certainly in fine fettle. Fancy seein' you round here, Daniel; I thought you was still in jail for circulatin' that numbers bag." Banjo flashed his smile and looked over at the box office, where Sister Eclipse had wandered and now stood reading the prices with an indignant expression.

"Look here, Banjo Bailey, how do you expect you're going to get the whole three of us into that there movie house?" she demanded. "It's ten cents apiece and you only got you a quarter."

Banjo wasn't the least bit cowed. "Never you mind, delicious lady, you just leave everything to old Banjo." He gave Opal his broadest smile and slipped her a wink as if to say nobody had anything to worry about. Pretty soon the ticket lady arrived and squashed herself into the little rainbow-painted box office. Opal watched her drop the *Closed* sign and touch her pink hair in a couple of places (as if to make certain it was there), before she began handing out the tickets off the roll.

"Now you two just wait yourselves right here," Banjo said conspiratorially, and Sister Eclipse and Opal watched him step up to the window and bend low to talk through the little round hole in the glass. Once he glanced over his shoulder and nodded energetically, then the box-office lady looked over and she nodded back, and they talked together some more. Pretty soon Banjo slid his quarter across, and she rolled him off three tickets.

"Okay, ladies, come along," Banjo said, taking Opal by the arm and escorting her into the lobby. "Careful, don't stumble now," he told her, and Sister Eclipse followed them through the doors to where the ticket-taking man stood.

"Three, sir," Banjo announced grandly, handing the tickets over and getting back three torn stubs. Still clutching Opal's arm he led her toward the stairs leading up to the balcony.

"Make like you stumbles a time or two," Banjo whispered in Opal's ear, giving her a little push so she missed her step and nearly fell over. "Thatta girl," he said encouragingly, "couldn't of done it better myself."

"What kinda nonsense you up to, Banjo?" demanded Sister Eclipse suspiciously.

"Ain't I told you I'd get us in for a quarter?"

"Yes, you did."

"And ain't I done it?"

"Yes, you has."

"Well, then. Be 'preciative some. Banjo Bailey is a man of intrepidness and distinction, and he never lies! 'Course, a stretch or two of the truth can come in handy." He beamed at Sister and gave Opal a little nudge.

"But what's all this stumblin' around foolishness? You like to of kilt poor Opal, knockin' her about that way."

Banjo put up a conciliatory hand. "Easy, Sister, easy. I just told that li'l old box-office bug that you an' me was takin' this li'l gal to the pitcher show, only, since she done been blind since birth and 'cause she couldn't see the pitchers maybe they'd let her in fer nothin'. Only that li'l old box-office bug, *she* says, 'Maybe she can't *see* but she can *hear*, can't she?' So we done compromised on half-price, five cents. And here we are."

Opal thought that was very clever of Banjo except for the fact that he'd had to tell an untruth to pull off his stunt. She decided that some day he'd tell one untruth too many, then he'd really be in the soup.

They sat down in the very front row of the balcony, where the seats were already nearly filled. Pretty soon the newsreel started up and Opal sat fascinated as the pictures danced and flickered on the screen. After the newsreel there were *Prevues of Coming Attractions*, and finally the feature picture.

The movie was called *Down on the Farm*, the story of a bunch of kids who lived on an old rundown country place called Penny-whistle Farm, and two of the kids, Eddie and Geraldine, got the idea of putting on a show in the barn. They wanted to make believe it was a real live theater and charge admission and sell popcorn and taffy apples. They wanted to wear costumes—top hats and spats and long dresses and fur tippets. They wanted to sing songs to please the audience and do dances for them, and they had a trick horse with a swayback, and its name was Dough-boy. He wore an American Legion cap—and Doughboy could count to ten with his hoof and shake his head yes and no, and he let Geraldine ride around on his back in a bareback rider's outfit.

Of course, the grown-ups all made fun of the kids' idea—the way grown-ups are often inclined to do, since they forget they were young once themselves—and they said no, there wasn't any use, and who would come, and it was a lot of trouble to little worth, and so on and so on. But the children would not be dissuaded, and in the end they prevailed. Their show, Barnyard Follies, was a big hit. Everyone enjoyed it, especially old Gramps, and the money they earned was given to the Home for Children. Both Eddie and Geraldine were pleased with the show's success; they had improved their dancing skills, and it was hinted that they might just put on another show, or, more, might even get married one day. To each other.

All the way home Opal thought about the movie, and all that thinking gave her an idea. It came to her in the middle of the night, waking her up and causing her to sit bolt upright in bed. She didn't holler "Eureka!" or "Excelsior!" or anything like that, but as she lay back in her bed in the dark, she knew she was on to something exciting. If only she could put her plan into effect, all might yet be well.

In the morning when she went out to feed Cupid, she sat right up close and talked into the elephant's ear, the way she always did, but instead of telling her the story of the movie she said, "Listen to me, Cupid, this is serious, so lend an ear."

Cupid flapped her ear so it fell across Opal's cheek and she had to push it aside. She confessed her fears over losing Bid and being sent to Savannah. "And I don't know *what* would become of you, Cupid. I hear Miss 'Gusta is talking about sticking you in some zoo somewhere."

With these words Cupid's whole body began to tremble, and Opal's heart went out to her. "It's going to be all right," she said firmly. "I'll never let you be put behind bars. I promise. Last night I had a swell idea. I got it at the movies. I want to put on a show. A real live show in the Cumberpatches' barn. We'll charge admission and have costumes and sell popcorn, and m'lasses taffy. And we'll make some money, and if we do maybe we can keep Bid out of the home."

Cupid swung her trunk into the air. She thought this idea of Opal's was a good one, but there was a question in her eye that Opal had difficulty answering.

"I don't *know* how much money we'll make," she responded, "we'll just have to see. If we do one show, we might make two or three or even five dollars—if we get a really good house. And if we did two shows, we might take in ten dollars. So, if we did four shows, that would be twenty dollars, and six shows thirty dollars."

Opal stopped; Cupid got the idea. She had a fine appreciation for the multiplication tables.

"And now for the big surprise," Opal said, and Cupid stiffened in suspense.

"Every show must have a star. Banjo says a good show always depends on its star to pull in the customers and do a big box office. And if a show is *really* good, then it can have *two* stars. And *that's* how it's going to be. Our show's going to have two stars, and the stars are going to be you and me!"

It was Cupid's turn to sit bolt upright. She looked at Opal as if to determine for herself if her words were really meant.

"I'm glad to see you like my idea," Opal said. "Oh, I forgot, we'll even get Banjo's dog Pickles into the act. She's so talented and light on her feet." Cupid liked this idea, too, and Opal made herself a bit more comfortable. "Now, this is how I plan to do it. First, I'm going to have to teach you some really neat tricks, the kind of tricks most folks wouldn't think an elephant could do. And most elephants couldn't—but *you* can." When Cupid looked doubtful, Opal hastened to reassure her. "I *know* you can. I believe in you, you know I do, and I know that if we work very hard and are diligent in our rehearsals we're bound to be a smash with a capital S. And then, when we've put on enough shows so we have maybe fifty or sixty dollars, we'll take Granny Bid and we'll leave Peavine before Miss 'Gusta ships her off to the home and me to Savannah to dust for Mrs. Vermilyea. That way we'll be able to live our own lives and not have other people telling us how to live them. What do you think? Be frank."

Cupid nodded her head in her frankest fashion. The whole thing sounded like one terrific idea to her, and she'd give it her all.

"Now here's another idea," Opal went on, grateful that Cupid was so much in accord with her plans. "I'm going to get Banjo Bailey in charge of the whole goods. He's been in the show business since Hector was a pup. He knows all the angles, and he'll steer us right. He talks a blue streak, but he can run the business e of things, and we'll cut him in for a percentage of the profits. How does that sound to you?"

Cupid made it clear that she thought Opal's plan an excellent one—especially for a thirteen-year-old girl—and should be placed in operation right away. So, as soon as breakfast was over and Opal's chores for the Primroses were done, she led Cupid, followed by Pickles, into the meadow and taught Cupid her first new trick. It was a somersault, something she'd never done in Seeger's act. There was nothing to it; Opal just tucked her skirts in her bloomers and did a somersault herself. When she was on her feet again she said, "Come on, cutie, let's see you do it."

And Cupid ducked her head between her two front feet and did a perfect somersault. That was pretty good work, but then Opal made her do it again, this time with Pickles curled in her trunk. Anyone could do a somersault, but doing it with a dog in your nose was a different story.

They passed on to more difficult business. Cupid had to learn to stand stock-still while Opal danced and performed all manner of feats and tricks that she'd learned from her daddy and, more recently, from Banjo—over, under, in front, in back, and all around Cupid. And this wasn't very hard, for Cupid had great stores of patience and always seemed to know instinctively what it was she was supposed to do.

Nothing gave Opal greater confidence than the knowledge that she was putting her entire life and well-being into the hands of Cupid—or into her feet, since elephants didn't have hands. If one little thing went awry, one wrong move, all those pounds of good gray elephant could come tumbling down on Opal, crushing the life out of her. Yet such was Opal's faith in Cupid's ability to perform these feats with care and exactitude that she never for an instant felt a twinge of fear. And with each newly learned trick, the program was that much closer to opening night.

When Opal went to bed that evening, she didn't dream of Savannah and bric-a-brac and no more Cupid or Granny. She and Cupid were together on a stage before a huge audience, there was a hundred-piece orchestra playing "On the Good Ship Lollipop," and the audience was clapping like crazy, Granny Bid, too, as Opal tap-danced on a small platform strapped onto Cupid's back! All the tricky steps that she'd picked up from her daddy on the back porch were now put to good use, and as far as Cupid went, you'd never know she was aware that there was a girl on her back doing the Shuffle-Off-to-Buffalo.

Up on the hill, Miss Blossom, who'd been rocking on the portico, looked down upon the Hollow, where she could see Opal and her pet out in the meadow, rehearsing a series of maneuvers over and over.

"Such patience," she sighed admiringly. "I do believe Opal is teaching that elephant some tricks."

"Tricks!" snorted Augusta, almost knocking over the geraniums she was watering. "The only trick that creature needs to learn is how to get to the zoo pronto. As for Opal, if she's not careful she won't have any prospects at all, for, assuredly, Amelia Vermilyea is not going to turn over her lovely home in Savannah to some nitwit with elephants on her brain."

Cousin Blossom didn't like to hear Augusta talk that way about Opal and was at pains to say so. Something in her observations of the girl and the elephant left her with the idea that something rare and different and exciting was afoot, and that same afternoon she got out her English bicycle and rode down the hill to check on the goings-on.

She found Opal still out in the meadow with Cupid, sporting an open umbrella that she employed to balance herself gracefully atop Cupid's shoulders.

"My stars, Opal, if you're not the cleverest thing!" said Miss Blossom, clapping her hands appreciatively. "I can't balance the least bit. At the rate you're going, you could be in the Barnum & Bailey Circus some day."

Opal, to whose ears these words were music, signaled to Cupid, who used her trunk to carry the girl to the ground. Both were tired from their labors, so Opal sent her pet for a refreshing wallow in the river, while she and Miss Blossom sat under the tree in the shade. There, because Blossom had always shown only the friendliest feelings toward her, she confided her plan for putting on a show in the Cumberpatch barn. Miss Blossom, though an adult, was not the kind to throw cold water on an idea, and she confessed to being enchanted herself. In fact, she became so excited she could hardly speak, but she sputtered out that she'd be happy to do what she could to help things along.

"I'm very good with a needle," she admitted shyly. "I wonder if I couldn't cut and sew a few costumes?"

An offer of this nature was exactly what Opal had been hoping to hear. Miss Blossom would make a wonderful designer for the costumes, and because she did paintings and made sketches, she could use those artistic talents toward the creation of a poster, like the ones for Beebee's Bantam Wonder Show, and Banjo could tack them up.

But then there was the all-important matter of the barn, a thorny problem, since the building belonged to the Cumber-patches. Providing a horse stall for a homeless elephant was one thing, but letting that elephant take over the whole barn was another matter, one Opal didn't feel up to dealing with.

"You just leave it to me," said Miss Blossom firmly. "I'll get that barn for our show, you'll see."

And Blossom did get the barn. Opal never understood how that prickly business had been arranged, but the next morning Tulaine told Opal the barn was hers. Miss Blossom, who was all smiles, gave no clue as to how the matter had been arranged, but Opal told Cupid there was more there than met the eye, even an elephant's, which was higher than most people's.

The rehearsals continued. The work went well. And whenever Banjo could get some time off from his employment with the movie theater, he would stop by and put in his two cents, which usually amounted to a lot more than two cents. Sister Eclipse would come around, too, and she and Granny Bid would sit on the porch watching Opal and Cupid perform more and more complicated tricks: Cupid would hold sticks and play the trap drums while Opal made music on a harmonica, Banjo on his banjo; she would make a hoop of her trunk for Pickles to leap through; she would do a handstand while Opal balanced with an umbrella on Cupid's rump; she would prance around and play the tambourine with her trunk, and when Opal dressed up as an infant, Cupid would play Moma, nursing her with a baby's bottle, then rocking her to sleep.

With each passing day their repertoire of tricks grew more extensive, and Opal couldn't have been more pleased and proud. Talk was already going around about what was happening, and folks in the area were eager for the big opening night.

This turned out to be a splashy event, with a full house and all; only the Primroses were noted for their absence. But everyone who did attend was crazy about the show, especially the showstopping finale, when Opal did her imitation of Stan Laurel (who never looked skinnier), while Cupid impersonated Oliver Hardy (who never looked fatter). All told there were four performances, the audiences ate it all up, and they netted a grand total of thirty-seven dollars and ninety-nine cents. With the show's success, Banjo promised Opal that he'd get their act booked at the County Fair come September. Sister Eclipse said Banjo was just bragging, but he kept on talking about the Big Time so much that after a while Opal got to believing it too.

Then, suddenly, they saw all their plans and dreams kicked into a cocked hat by a startling series of events that, while painful at the time, were eventually to set Opal's and Cupid's feet on the road to fame and fortune.

And they had Augusta Primrose to thank for it all.

Chapter Ten

Augusta's Great Disaster

WHILE OPAL AND CUPID PERFORMED THEIR ENTER-
tainments for the neighboring Hollow folk, Miss Augusta was
planning a do of her own, the famous annual Primrose garden
party. Held to honor the anniversary of General Lee's visit to the
Primrose mansion, it was *the* important event on Peavine's social
calendar. Jekyll would don his best livery, with a waistcoat of
striped satin and silk stockings, while Melba, who had done for
the Primroses ever since Granny Bid retired, would get into her
good alapaca and wear a freshly starched cap. Cucumber sandwiches thin as poker chips would be served from sterling silver
salvers, and for dessert, three flavors of ice cream: spumoni,
tortoni, and tutti-frutti (all favorites of the Colonel). Coffee, tea,
and punch would also be served, but without spiritous content,
for Augusta never permitted the ingesting of alcoholic beverages
under, or even near, her roof.

"I have a thought you might be interested in, Cousin 'Gusta," said Miss Blossom, who was washing out her hair under the set-tub taps. "What would you say to inviting little Opal to bring her elephant to the garden party to entertain all your guests?"

"Surely you are joking!" exclaimed Augusta. "An elephant at a garden party? What if it were to step on someone's foot? Or put its trunk in the punch bowl?"

"Oh, no," replied Cousin Blossom, "Cupid is very well-behaved and she would never do that. I don't even think she drinks punch. I'm sure your guests would treasure the memory of Cupid's somersaults. And Opal's dancing has improved by leaps and bounds. Thanks to Mr. Banjo Bailey she can now do a buck-and-wing and even a triple time-step. You might be surprised at what he has taught her." Miss Blossom had become so excited at the thought that she was getting copious amounts of water all over the linoleum.

Augusta was not so sold on the idea. "Are you suggesting we allow that misguided girl to tap-dance all over Primrose Hill? What will our guests think?"

"Why, they'll love Opal's dancing just as I do, and you will too. If only you had come to their little show. It's quite a novel act."

"Novel act? Really!" Augusta ran the silver-backed brush from her vanity set through her hair. "I won't have it. I simply will not consider it."

"All right, dear," said Miss Blossom. "It was just a suggestion. I'm sure Cupid would much rather go for a nice cool swim in the river anyway."

The minute she said that, Augusta started thinking things out a bit more clearly. If there were any chance of improving the shining hour with a dancing elephant or indeed a young girl dancing on an elephant, she didn't want to miss her chance to make a sensation. Besides, Fulvia Pinckney was coming; Fulvia was the social columnist at the *Peavine Daily Clarion* and would be writing up the garden party. Think if people read that there was a live African elephant amusing her guests with a tango—or even a rumba!

"On second thought, Blossie dear," she said to her cousin, "you might mention to Opal that if she's free, she and her elephant might just drop by. She's not to expect a fee, however."

"But she's an entertainer. Entertainers are usually paid," Miss Blossom objected.

"Oh, Blossom, don't be silly," said Augusta. "In the first place, the child is quite well compensated by Goodson and I for the small amount of work she does around this house, not to mention the additional sum that we contribute monthly to her great-grandmother's existence. In the second, she isn't really an entertainer. Believe me, if I'd seen anything down in the Hollow that smacked of the entertainment business, I'd have put a stop to it in an instant. No, Opal is a child putting on childish little shows in barns and things."

"That may be where she started, yes, but everyone has to start somewhere. Just think where she may end up."

"*I* know where she'll end up, my dear. Getting a proper schooling and learning a proper trade, so that she can return to service here on Primrose Hill in the tradition of her antecedents. So let there be an end to this talk." She walked quickly out and then walked quickly in again, saying that Blossom might suggest her idea to Opal, but if they planned upon appearing (without fee, she stated again) Opal and Cupid must wear costumes and the costumes must be gay and pleasing to the eye.

And that was the end of it, for this was how Augusta wanted it, and what Augusta wanted she usually got.

After drying her hair, which stuck out every which way as if she'd been electrified, Miss Blossom rode down the hill to advise

Opal of the coming event. Banjo had stopped by, with Pickles at his heels, and he quickly agreed to the playdate on Primrose Hill, relishing the idea of a free write-up in the paper. There was much to be seen to by way of preparation, he told Opal when Miss Blossom had gone in to visit with Granny Bid, a new specialty to be rehearsed, new skits of an appropriately entertaining nature for a garden party, a different dance for Opal incorporating all the new steps she'd learned, new songs as well, and naturally a new Grand Finale fitting to the occasion, for, as Banjo always said, it was by their finales that the Big Time show business acts were most often judged.

It rained by the bucketful the night before the party, but the great day faired off nicely, and by midmorning the last-minute preparations were all well under way. The handsome marquee of blue and white Venetian stripes spread its scalloped canopy where the lawn was greenest, Miss Blossom's French harp had been moved—ever so carefully—to the gazebo, with a little gold-painted chair for her to sit on while she played.

The Colonel chose to ignore the pre-party hubbub and spent the morning out on his green with his shiny new club, putting away as was his habit, and missing the hole every time. In the meantime, Augusta sat fanning herself on the porch, for though it was not yet eleven, the day was already warm, and she asked herself crossly what idiotic notion had possessed her to plan a party in such dreadful weather. Surely this was the hottest August she could recall. But these thoughts were not unusual for her; Augusta Primrose often found herself not enjoying her own parties, regardless of the temperature, wondering why she'd bothered giving them in the first place.

Upon the stroke of one, the first autocar rolled up the drive and deposited the first partygoers. And since the event was marked as such a special one, the guests were decked out in their best finery, rather too warm for the weather, but making a gala effect just the same. When all of her guests had partaken of the refreshment and dipped into the cut-glass punch bowl, Augusta felt the need for a bit of music, and so she ordered Miss Blossom into the gazebo, where "Cousin Blossie" offered one or two musical selections. No sooner had this presentation ended than the most important part of the program was offered.

All craned their necks at the sight that now presented itself before their astonished eyes. Decked out in a costume of rosebud pink, with a ballet dancer's skirt, and flowers in her hair, carrying a tattered umbrella to keep the sun off her face, picking her way carefully across the lawn, Opal Thigpen approached, followed by Cupid, whose head was crowned with a generous garland of white daisies. Behind them came Banjo and Pickles the dog, and these in turn were followed by a strange array of folk, the sight of which caused Augusta Primrose to draw herself up and say, "Hmph! And who invited those ne'er-do-wells?".

She was of course referring to the Cumberpatches, who had all turned out, but for a few of the boys, to watch the fun. They stood along the roadside, peering over the rambling roses trailing across the fence, waiting for the show to begin. Henhouse Cumberpatch swung on the gate, holding in his grubby hands a shoebox, whose contents remained—for the present—undisclosed.

The Primroses' guests hardly knew what to make of this dismaying appearance, and felt it was naughty of Opal to have invited them. (Opal had not, they had simply invited themselves.) As for Opal herself, the sight of the girl under that ridiculous-looking umbrella, leading that grotesque beast, was too much, and Augusta's guests tittered behind their hands.

They changed their tune quickly enough when Opal began to put the elephant and the dog through a few of their paces. Cupid balanced her rubber ball while standing on her two front feet, then swung Opal onto her back to perform her tap dancing routine. The gathering clapped their white-gloved hands enthusiastically, and everyone agreed it was all too sweet for words. What would Augusta think of next? Augusta herself was obliged to admit she found it amusing. And when Banjo strummed "I Wish I Was in Dixie" and sang "Love Among the Bluebells" for the folks, and Pickles did her little somersaults and other clever tricks, the applause was like a heavy rainfall.

Then came the super-socko finish Banjo had designed just for the garden party, in order to impress Augusta and her guests. The number had a patriotic theme, presented to the tune of "Stars and Stripes Forever." Up the hill came Tulaine Cumberpatch (he and his brothers were willing to help out Opal in a pinch) as Uncle Sam, with stripey pants, a tall hat, and a spade beard. Then came the "Spirit of '76." (This was Billy Rondo, with Beaudine as the wounded fife-and-drummer, and brother Renfrew carrying Old Glory.) The sight of the Stars and Stripes got more applause (Banjo was no dummy, he knew how to milk an audience). Then, on came Opal dressed as Miss Liberty herself, looking just like the postcard of the statue Daddy had sent, carrying a torch and a big book (a borrowed world atlas Miss Blossom had found), and a spiky crown in her hair. She was followed onstage by Cupid, clad in the American flag, and after Opal lit up boxes of sparklers and handed them around, Cupid picked her up in her trunk and swung her high into the air. The show ended to a rolling thunder of applause with people shouting "Encore!" which meant they wanted to see more; but that's all there was, there wasn't any more.

And so the curtain came down—except there wasn't any curtain—and no one could say that the show wasn't a big success. Augusta was showered with the sincerest kind of compliments while the cast of overheated performers was given warm lemonade and wilted sandwiches behind the kitchen trellis. As soon as their glasses were empty, however, they were dismissed by a haughty Jekyll, thank you very much. Then, as Opal was leading Cupid away, crossing the lawn by the lilac bushes, an unfortunate thing happened: the soiled, nasty little face of Henhouse Cumberpatch popped out from behind one of the shrubs. Suddenly, he sprang into Opal's path, and Opal's eyes widened as he slowly lifted the cover of the shoebox he was clutching. The box contained a live mouse, which Henhouse seized by the tail and dangled in Opal's face. Only it wasn't Opal he wanted to scare—but Opal's elephant!

"Here, big ole' thang!" the wicked boy exclaimed, "take a ride on this!"

With that he swung the squirming mouse right under Cupid's eyes, then dropped it on the ground. The terrified mouse, not knowing which way to run, beelined it straight up Cupid's leg, possibly mistaking it for a tree trunk. When Cupid realized she had a mouse somewhere on her person, she let out a bellow that caused the party guests to freeze in their chairs. Trumpeting loudly, the panicked elephant wheeled, then went stampeding across the lawn in the opposite direction while the mouse dropped safely to the ground and scurried toward a group of ladies sitting on their little chairs, with teacups and saucers delicately balanced on their laps.

"*Eek!*" screeched Fulvia Pinckney, the social columnist, tossing up her cup and splashing tea all over her garden outfit as she sprang onto her chair seat and clutched her skirts around her legs. "*Eek! Eek!*" she screeched hysterically. "*Eek!*" and she showed more of her calves than could be deemed discreet.

And "*eek!*" screeched the other ladies, upsetting their teacups as well and losing their balance and falling into the gladiola bed as the confused mouse darted frantically about between their feet seeking escape.

"Look out! Look out!" shouted the Colonel, unavoidably repeating himself as he pointed at the lumbering elephant who, utterly unnerved by the sight of the scurrying little mouse, was running in crazed circles around the lawn, heedless of where her feet trod, madly tossing her trunk and bellowing in fright.

"My petunias!" cried the outraged Augusta. "My marigolds! Do something, somebody! Don't make me institute a lawsuit for damages!"

As Cupid dashed about, Opal and Banjo rushed pell-mell after her, trying to calm her. Pickles, too, sprang high in the air, attempting to reassure Cupid with her excited bark, but to no avail. Cupid would heed nothing but the frantically darting mouse.

Shying away from Fulvia Pinckney, whom she desired at all costs to avoid, Cupid wheeled and bolted in the direction of the tent, a reminder of her circus home and safety. But that way lay disaster. As she charged toward it all four legs became entangled in the ropes supporting the canvas top, and as the pegs were yanked out of the ground the whole tent came tumbling down around her. Inside the tent the surprised guests found their plates of tutti-frutti ice cream upset in their laps, while servants carrying trays collided head-on and stacks of china and glassware went crashing to the ground.

Still, the berserk elephant plunged ahead, dragging the canvas along with her, a piece of which had fallen across her eyes, impairing her vision. It wasn't until Cupid blundered up the front steps of the house and onto the porch that she was able to free herself of the tent—too late, however, to avoid overturning a wicker chair and several large flowerpots and making hash of Miss Augusta's good raffia runner.

This destruction accomplished, Cupid went careening off the far end of the portico, to land smack in the Colonel's prize rhododendron bushes. Momentarily recovering her balance, she turned once again in frenzy, only to strike a starchily dressed waiter carrying the last of the unbroken dishes. The stack of plates and cups shattered on the slate flagstone, knives and forks and spoons flew among the hollyhock bushes, and the luckless waiter spun off into what remained of the prize rhododendrons.

But it was not over yet, not by a long shot. That same little mouse belonging to Henhouse Cumberpatch, having been hiding under the porch out of harm's way, decided at this moment to make a break for it. He scurried across the lawn as fast as his little legs would carry him, just as Cupid was showing signs of calming down. Spying the mouse again, she reared up on her hind legs, and this time went thundering off toward the gazebo. As she crashed into its support posts, the entire structure came apart, Cupid tripped and tumbled backward, and—horror of horrors!—crushed Miss Blossom's French harp to smithereens, narrowly missing its owner, who fortunately had some idea of when to stay put and when to make herself scarce.

Just then, the dazed mouse came scurrying back across the lawn, heading straight for Cupid and provoking yet another fit of terror in the beast. Cupid tossed her trunk and bellowed as loudly as she knew how, then went rampaging across the lawn, clearing a wide path through the tables and chairs, sending their shrieking occupants flying helter-skelter. With Opal now just a tail's breadth behind Cupid, the elephant suddenly turned, heading on a collision course with Augusta's fountain. But rather than colliding, Cupid opted for a high arcing leap into the pool, landing with a giant splash that soaked everyone within a forty-foot radius. Making matters worse, her backside struck the waterspout, smashing it, so that water began to squirt in all directions like a runaway firehose, soaking all those who'd missed the first deluge. Out on the road, the Cumberpatches began cheering and clapping in unison, for to their minds this was definitely the best part of the program.

"That's a good 'un!" cried Old Man Cumberpatch, slapping his thigh and spitting into Augusta's cabbage roses, while Melissande positively huffed with pleasure.

"I never seen no funnier sight than that big old elephunk settin' in that there pool a'water," screeched Etoile, while Miss'sipp nodded agreement. The cause of all the chaos, Mr. Henhouse Cumberpatch, was laughing fit to beat the band and calling out names at Cupid—mean, nasty names that ordinarily would have had the elephant snorting with rage. But not now. Now her expression was one of the greatest confusion: she was asking herself how such a thing could have happened to *her*, a great big elephant, and why she had been so frightened by a tiny little mouse.

Yet the elephant's seeming calm did not put an end to the pandemonium in Augusta Primrose's garden. For the Colonel, who had witnessed the entire rampage from atop one of the little gilt chairs, waving his arms and calling for cool heads to prevail, had now come to the conclusion that words were useless and some real action was called for. As his wife continued to proclaim herself in every danger of fainting, the Colonel leaped down from his perch (actually he didn't leap; he fell off the chair) and shouted for Jekyll to bring him his elephant gun.

"By Jove!" he shouted. "I'll put an end to this mayhem!"

When Jekyll reappeared with the weapon, his master wasted no time in popping two shells into the chambers and cocking the large shotgun. He threw up the muzzle and fired, two loud blasts in quick succession. Fortunately, his shot was wide of the mark, and instead of hitting the elephant in the fountain, he hit what was left of the gazebo and Miss Blossom's harp, an explosion that sent a thousand fragments high into the air to drift to earth in bits the size of matchsticks. The guests were forced to laugh:

They all knew that despite his bragging, the Colonel was really a bum shot, and Fulvia Pinckney, despite her dismay, jotted a quick note to this effect. Guests sighed with relief that the worst was now over, and they set about putting their clothes to rights, grateful that no one had been seriously injured.

Meanwhile, the pathetic Cupid remained knee-deep in the fountain, looking like some mammoth-sized statuary figure in a park—a very wet park, indeed. Bent on helping, Banjo rushed up and tugged her by the trunk until she reluctantly abandoned the fountain and stood dripping on the grass, where by degrees she regained a measure of calm and assumed a shamefaced expression at the wide array of destruction she'd caused. Opal hurried to her and whispered in her ear.

"It wasn't your fault, Cupid, honey, you were goaded into it." Her look fell on Henhouse, who at that moment had ventured through the gate and stood on the flagstones ogling both Opal and Cupid. The moment she saw Henhouse, Cupid's whole body began to tremble. With lowered head she charged, and in four giant steps she had reached the mischievous little boy, whom she caught up in her trunk and swept off his feet, raising him high into the air.

"Looky what that elephunk is doin'!" screeched Etoile, clambering over the fence and catching her skirt on the rose thorns. She stared helplessly at the sight of the enraged elephant wafting her hapless son above the heads of the alarmed crowd. "You put Henhouse down this very instant!" she screeched, waving her arms as she tried to unhook herself from the rose bushes.

"You heard the lady!" shouted her husband, Tulaine, who came crashing through a nearby hedge, followed by the rest of the Cumberpatch tribe, all pushing their way onto the Primroses' property, waving their arms and hollering at the elephant to set

Henhouse down. But Cupid was having none of it. Like a halfback with the ball tucked under his elbow, she ran with her prize, heading straight down the hill, kicking up a cloud of red dust as she went. Not to be outdone, the Cumberpatches gave chase, like a bunch of crazy Keystone Kops, shouting, "Don't you hurt our Henhouse none, you danged elephunk!" and praying aloud to their Maker that the boy should not be harmed.

Augusta's damp and sodden guests stared in horror, wondering how it would all turn out, for clearly the elephant was on a rampage, and who would calm her distraught nerves? Only Opal and Banjo maintained their equanimity, watching with half-hidden smiles as Cupid reached the river and plunged right into the water with Henhouse still in her jaws. There she proceeded to dunk the boy, once, twice, thrice, until, sputtering and hollering, he slipped from her mouth and flailed about until Fayette Cumberpatch, catching up her skirts, jumped into the river and pulled him out by his collar.

Up on the hill, Augusta noticed none of this. She simply stood staring at her fractured fountain as it continued to gush forth with might and main, shooting a thirty-foot-high geyser into the sky.

"And did Opal teach her elephant to do all *this?*" Augusta Primrose demanded of Miss Blossom. Having recovered from her near faint, she was taking stock of the damage: the trampled flowerbeds, the flooding lawn, the gazebo in smithereens, the ruined tent, the scattered tables and broken chairs, the sodden guests, and, everywhere, mud—a sea of ever-increasing mud.

Blossom was at a loss for words. She'd had the highest hopes that if the entertainment was a success Augusta would relent and not send Granny Bid to the Bide-a-Wile or Cupid to the zoo, and further, would allow Opal to stay and get her education right there in Peavine. But with this catastrophe, evidence of which lay all about, Blossom feared that the end had come and Augusta would prevail. There was no one to turn to for help, and without help the situation was hopeless.

But this was without reckoning on fate, which was about to take a hand. It had been waiting in the wings, and was preparing to make an entrance; and when it did, it would alter the entire course of Opal's life in one brief night.

Chapter Eleven

The White Doves

FULVIA PINCKNEY DID HAVE HER SAY IN THE NEWS- paper, and the disaster of Augusta Primrose's garden party became the talk of the town. Naturally, everyone blamed Opal, saying she ought to have known better than to take an elephant to a fancy-dress garden party, completely forgetting, of course, that Opal and Cupid had been *invited* to appear, *and* without any fee. Still, most admitted that, despite the loss of property and poise by many of the guests, the incident had brought the folks in the Hollow a good deal of amusement.

Alone among all concerned, Augusta Primrose could not put the tragedy behind her. "There is nothing further to be said," she declared to Blossom and the Colonel over a cold supper on the porch, where she stared angrily down at the Hollow. "This sort of nonsense must cease! It is time the girl took her head out of the clouds and got her feet firmly planted on terra cotta. I have said and I'll say it again: Young girls, soon to be young women, do not play with oversized toys like elephants. They simply learn what a young woman must know and keep the station such young women must keep. And so it shall be with your Opal, Cousin Blossom."

Miss Blossom was close to tears. "Oh no, 'Gusta, I beg you, don't send the child away. And for pity's sake, do not part her from Cupid. They love each other so!"

Augusta was deaf to all entreaty. "Blossom, think what happened the last time I listened to you about those two. No, I said Opal shall go to Savannah and to Savannah she shall go! Old Biddy shall be sent to the Bide-a-Wile, that beast will be placed behind bars, and there we shall see an end to the matter."

Augusta stormed off and Blossom finally let the tears fall as they would have chance to fall again, for more sadness was to come before day's end.

Returning home from a visit to Sister Eclipse's, Opal stepped through the hedge to see the Primroses' Rolls-Royce drawn up at the front door. Jekyll had his feather duster out, and was giving the grille a good going-over, but of his mistress there was no sign.

As Opal came in at the back of the house she heard the inimitable voice of Augusta Primrose coming from Granny Bid's room.

"Biddy Thigpen," she was going on, "you're far too old to be acting so hard-nosed about this business. You really mustn't make me angry, you know. My constitution won't stand for it."

"I don't care," came Bid's reply. "I can't stand to go, and if I say I can't stand to, I can't stand to!" Opal knew that her great-granny, despite her weak state, could be as firm as Augusta Primrose.

"And I say you *shall* go, so there you are!"

"No, ma'am, *here* I am and *here* is where I'll stay. Where's my Opie. I want to see Opie."

"Here I am, Granny," said Opal, stepping into the room. Bid was propped up in bed, her red taffeta cap on her head, making a border of ruffles around her thin, gray face. The imperious Augusta, sitting stiff-backed in the one chair, eyed the girl with ill-disguised suspicion.

"Have you fallen to eavesdropping?" she demanded. "Have you sunk that low?"

"No, ma'am, I wasn't eavesdropping," Opal replied politely, although she didn't like being accused of doing naughty things when she hadn't been naughty.

"Come give old Granny a kiss," Bid said. Opal went and kissed her, trying to avoid Augusta, not an easy thing to manage in the tiny room.

"I've just been explaining to your grandmother about the home . . ."

"I already said I'm stayin' here."

"Hush, Granny," Opal put in, "let Miss 'Gusta finish."

". . . where she shall have the best of care," Augusta went on. "At the Bide-a-Wile she'll have three meals a day, a bed of her own, and a roof over her head. That should be enough for anybody. In any case, there is no question of Granny's *not* going, since whether she agrees or not, you will no longer be able to avail yourselves of *this* roof."

Opal felt a sharp pang of apprehension.

"What're you talkin' about, 'Gusta?" asked Bid from her pillow.

"I am merely telling you that this—this *house* of yours is going to be torn down. There! It's out! *Now* you know the truth."

"Torn down? But how could that be?" Opal asked.

"It's very simple. Goodson and I have decided to sell off all of this bottom land. And when that is done, this little house of yours will be removed, along with those dreadful Cumberpatches. The new road is going through here, right where we're sitting."

This was news indeed! Opal said she hadn't heard talk of any road going through there. Augusta sniffed again.

"Grown-ups are not obliged to go about informing young girls of their plans for laying down new traffic arteries," she stated loftily.

"But we don't need a new road. We have the Old Cotton Road."

"*Old* is right! That washboard road has shaken the bolts off the transmission of my automobile. It's rather like driving one of those midget bumpo-cars at Fun Land."

"But our house. What will become of it?"

"It will become rubble, that is what will become of it. A very big tractor is going to come rolling in here and push down the walls and pull it apart, and then a truck will come and carry away the debris until there is nothing left of the place. *Then* Biddy will be happy enough to go to the Bide-a-Wile, even though she at present declines to do so. And *you*, young lady, will take the cars to Savannah, where you will receive an education of the highest quality possible with Amelia Vermilyea. As for your elephant, well, it will just have to go to the zoo, where I'm sure the children will relish all the tricks you've taught it. And *that* is all I have to say about *that*." She rose and shook out her coat. "Please to understand, I have given all concerned fair warning, so if you are wise you will prepare yourselves accordingly. Now I have an appointment to have my hair done, which will make it a very full day for me."

After Augusta had driven away in the Rolls, a badly daunted Opal plumped up Granny Bid's bolsters and made her comfortable. She fixed her a cup of chicory, put in the twenty drops of 'Lixir of Life, then sat down on the chair Miss Augusta had vacated. Bid gazed at her great-granddaughter with tears in her eyes, then spoke meekly.

"Perhaps we had better do as Miss 'Gusta says, child."

"Oh, Granny, don't," Opal protested, trying to keep from weeping, too, but the look on Bid's face made the sobs rise in her breast.

"It's true, honey." Bid reached out and took Opal's hand in hers before going on. "When you get to be old as Granny is, you get grateful to think of walkin' through those Pearly Gates, where you get to hear that Heavenly Choir and all those golden harps twangin'—just like Miss Blossom's."

"Yes, Granny, I suppose." Opal hadn't had the heart to tell Bid about the fate of Miss Blossom's harp at the garden party.

Bid subsided a bit, falling back against the bolster, her eyes closed, then presently she began to mutter again.

"If only I could see my Jimmy-Jack one more time. If only he'd come back and I could see him before they take me away."

"Yes, Granny, you know Daddy'll come if he can," Opal said.

"My, my," Bid went on, "if I had him here I'd sling him over my knee and give him a good tarrin'. What a mischief-maker he was, that Jimmy-Jack. Still 'n' all, he was a mighty slick fellah, your daddy. Lordy, how he'd get all duded up of a Sunday in his pretty polka dots and stripes and one a'those bright ties he fancied."

"Yes, Granny, I remember. But you must rest now. Miss 'Gusta has tired you out with all her talk."

She waited until Bid's eyes drooped again, and when it seemed certain she was asleep Opal went out and had a talk with Cupid in the shed, repeating everything Augusta had said about their losing their home, but not daring to mention what had been said relative to Cupid herself. Cupid's expression grew serious as she gravely considered the matter, and though she didn't come up with any quick answers, Opal could tell that she was thinking hard. And who knew, the elephant might just have a good idea. It wouldn't be the first time.

▲

Old Biddy slept the peaceful sleep she deserved, the sweet blessed rest that comes to all those who have reached the end of their lives; as Bid had now come to hers. It was soft evening time and the air had turned all violet and green, shot through with golden motes from the rays of the setting sun. The pigeons with their white feathery wings were fluttering around the open windowsill, and then a sweet musical voice called, "Biddy—Biddy, dear, it's time, come now, come," and Biddy in her white nightdress and red ruffled cap rose up out of her bed and floated across the floor to the window, and over the sill she went, out into the warm evening air, floating off across the rustling corn tops and the cotton patch, along by the Cotton River where the green ducks paddled, up and up into the golden air of summertime. And, as if a little reluctant to leave, part of Bid remained below, with the aroma of chicken fricassee in the skillet and collards on the hob, the leftover scent of the flowers that were just closing their heads against the coming of night. But the better part of her rose up to heaven where the gates were all pearly and gold, and white-winged angels played on golden harps their song of welcome to the newcoming soul who had waited so long and patiently to get there.

And that was how, at three months short of one hundred and three years upon the planet Earth, in the land of Dixie in County Cotton, in Peavine Hollow, Biddy Chippingdale Thigpen went to her reward. It was both rich and bountiful.

When Opal brought in the supper plate—steamed collards sprinkled with nutmeg and vinegar, and a nice chicken piece—Bid's eyes were still shut. She lay in exactly the same position Opal had left her in, hadn't stirred a wink. Opal set down the plate and waited, thinking her grandmother would wake up. She waited quite a while, but Granny never stirred. Never moved at all. Opal glanced over at the plate, then covered it with a napkin. Bid wouldn't be eating the chicken, wouldn't be eating the collards, wouldn't . . .

Opal couldn't help it: She began to cry. Two large tears slid down her cheeks and she wiped them away, thinking: *I mustn't cry for Granny Bid. She's gone to her reward. She's with the angels now.* And Opal dried her tears and said she must get on with things, for that was the way of life. People were born, they lived, and then they died, and those who came after had to see to their own living, before their own time came.

Outside, the purple dusk came on, birds were cheeping their evensong high in the catalpa tree. It was very still. Opal left the room and went to find Cupid.

"Granny's dead, Cupid," she said to the elephant. "She's passed through the Pearly Gates and now she's in the arms of the great Lord God Almighty. We mustn't cry. She's happier there. We must be glad she died the way she did, peacefully, in her sleep. You think that, too, don't you?"

Cupid nodded her head slowly, then softly curled her trunk around Opal and drew her close and held her, while Opal stroked the elephant's soft ear. Then, when they had both taken their comfort, they went about the tasks they knew must be done. First, Cupid was dispatched to Sister Eclipse's houseboat with a note from Opal, just a few well-chosen words saying that Granny Bid had passed over and for Sister to let the preacher know what had happened, so he could start making up the funeral talk.

When Cupid was on her way, Opal sat and thought about what she must do. She knew the animals would have to be fed, but she had no time right now; she slipped through the hedge and asked Henhouse if he'd be good enough to slop Zephyr, feed Lola and the rest of the rabbits, and put down some hay for

Lucerne. For once in his life, Henhouse agreed to help out without making a fuss.

Old Melissande, who was setting in her chair, giving the rocker a good go, looked up as Opal came onto the porch. She peered over at Bid's house. "How's yore grammaw, girl? You better stoke up with some firewood, with fall comin', she'll want to stay warm."

"I'm sure she'll be warm this winter," returned Opal, smiling to herself, for she knew heaven was always pleasantly warm, especially for old ladies of a hundred years or more.

Opal went inside to find Etoile and Tulaine and told them the news, saying very simply, "Granny's passed over. I have to make the arrangements." Etoile's eyes popped out of her head.

"*Dead?* Granny Bid done *died?* That ole lady done kicked the bucket?" Etoile went running in circles, breaking the news to her family, crying, "Granny's dead! Granny done cashed in her chips at last!"

"Gosh almighty," said a stunned Tulaine, "who'd of believed that old lady'd ever die?" Even Beaudine looked sobered by the news.

"I have to go get things ready, Tulaine," Opal said quietly. "Cupid has gone to bring Sister Eclipse. She'll bathe Granny and then we'll dress her."

"Why? She ain't goin' dancin', is she?" Beaudine slapped his thigh and Etoile gave him the heavy knock he deserved. Then she and Miss'sipp went off looking for something black to wear to Granny Bid's funeral party.

The service next day took a full hour, for Biddy Thigpen had lived a long life and in consequence the preacher had a good deal to say about her. There were flowers and singing, and when the burial was over those in attendance filed past Opal to express their sympathy. The last of these were Miss Blossom, then Miss

Augusta, who leaned to Opal's ear and spoke in doleful tones.

"We are all *very* sorry, Opal," Augusta Primrose began, "of course we are. We'll miss her in the years to come. She served the Primroses long and well, and now she has earned her just deserts." Even at a time like this, Opal thought, there went Miss 'Gusta mixing up her words again.

Nonetheless, she thanked Miss Augusta for her words of comfort, adding her suspicion that Bid didn't want to go on living with the thought of losing her house. "It was all she had," she explained.

"Not a house, my dear." Augusta corrected. "A shack, and no one will miss it when it's knocked down."

Opal didn't like having the place where she grew up referred to in such a way. "A shack to you, maybe, but not to Granny," she returned staunchly, right there in the cemetery. "Folks like you have everything, but you never stop to think about people who have nothing. Granny fetched and toted for your family till she couldn't tote anymore. And what thanks did she get? A bag of turnips."

Augusta colored at these candid words and looked around in embarrassment. "Goodness me, to make such a fuss over an insignificant piece of real estate. She'll be better off, anyway, and so shall you. You will enjoy living in Savannah, Opal. Of course, it does get rather hot in the attic, where you'll be quartered, but you'll soon get used to it." She smiled sweetly as if that would make everything right. "Now, if we can just decide how to get rid of that pesky elephant . . ." Augusta was not allowed to finish her sentence, for Opal burst into tears and ran to meet up with Cupid, who was waiting with Banjo and Sister Eclipse out by the road.

Despite Miss Blossom's wave from the Rolls, where she sat in the front seat with Jekyll, and her insistence that Opal spend the night on Primrose Hill ("in the room off the kitchen, of course," Miss Augusta added as she came up), Opal declined, adding pointedly that her granny wouldn't want her to be anywhere that she and her "pesky" elephant weren't really wanted.

Later that afternoon, as she sat with Sister Eclipse, rod and reel in hand, fishing from the bow of the *Bouncing Bett*, Opal tried to puzzle things out.

"What am I going to do, Sister? Miss 'Gusta's going to send Cupid to the zoo! Or worse, to the glue factory! They'll make stickum of her!"

" 'Gusta wouldn't sell that animal up for stickum, nohow. She's too valuable." Sister considered the situation. "She *might* sell her to a menagerie, though. We'd better consult with Banjo when he comes this evenin'. He'll know what to do."

As things fell out, Banjo was unusually punctual in arriving. They heard Pickles barking out on the road, then the little dog came dashing across the gangway to leap happily into Opal's lap and start licking her face with her warm moist tongue.

"Oh, don't, Pickles, please, not tonight," Opal said, setting her on the deck.

Having heard earlier of Augusta Primrose's plan, Banjo had had time to think, and he now put in his judgment. "We gots to scotch her, tha's all. We gots to put some crimps in her ruffles and stop her dead in her tracks."

"But how?" the anxious Opal wanted to know.

"Simple. Miss 'Gusta can't send you away if you ain't on hand, now can she?"

"No . . ."

"Well, then, just don't you *be* on hand. Don't you nor Cupid either be anywheres 'round here."

Sister spoke up. "Listen, bigmouth, is you advising Opal to run off on Miss 'Gusta?"

128

"Run off? *Abscond!* Yes, abscond! That's the word! Her and Cupid, abscondin' all over the place. And I believe *I'll* just abscond right along with them."

"Whatchou mean, Banjo Bailey? You is tellin' this chile to run off and take her elephant, and you is fixin' to run off with the pair of 'em?"

"That's how *I* see the situation, you big old bug, you." He gave Eclipse's rosy round cheek a tender pinch.

"But how can we leave?" Opal wailed. "Our home—our things? Our friends and all?"

Banjo shook his head gravely. "Be prack-tical, li'l bug. Your home is about to be kindlin' wood, you don't have much in the way of stuff, and you got your best friends right here with you."

"I have Miss Blossom," Opal said loyally.

" 'Deed you does. Miss Blossie, she be a fine friend. *And* you has Cupid. And it's Cupid that's goin' to get you outta the hole. That elephant's worth her weight in gold. All you got to do is go profesh'nal."

"Go professional?"

"That was my word. In the show business. And I'm just the man to do it. The County Fair's on over at Tilley. The Solo Brothers' Lively Arts Fun Show is playin' there. And I'm going to have me a li'l talk with that pair, see if I don't."

"Now what pair would that be?" asked Sister.

"Why, Sam 'n' Tam, the Solo Brothers. Twins, you know, as like as two bugs in a rug." (Opal thought probably he meant peas in a pod, but let it pass.) "Even their own mother couldn't tell them apart," Banjo declared. "Not till she painted the toes of one of 'em blue."

"Which one?" Opal asked.

"Dunno, we'd have to ask Sam 'n' Tam 'bout that. But I'm just goin' over yonder and git them two dudes to write you up a contract that'll put you on Easy Street."

Sister Eclipse scowled and shook her chins at him. "Oh, you is just one big talker, Banjo Bailey! How is you gonna put this here chile on Easy Street when you ain't got a telephone slug between the two of you?"

"You is gonna eat your words, honey lamb," replied Banjo sweetly. "Because pretty soon now this li'l bug here is goin' to be appearin' in the circus. She is goin' to be in the show business. Her and Cupid."

"Izzat so?"

"Yup. Zat is so."

Sister gave him a shove that almost knocked him over the rail into the river. "Well," she said, "if anyone can do it, I b'lieve *you* can."

Opal was unable to believe her ears. Her and Cupid—in the *show business?* Were such things possible in this world?

"But when do we leave?" she wanted to know.

"When? Why, right now."

"Right now?" cried Sister. "We ain't had no supper yet. I done fixed you's fav'rite beans 'n' ham hocks."

"Skip the feedbag, honeypot, we can eat later. Right now we gotta git the jump on them Primroses. So, lambie-pie, you just put on you's hat and let's git you's contraption cranked up while Opal fetches Cupid, and we'll be off to the fair! And purty soon we won't be eatin' beans fo' supper neither, we'll be feastin' on Oysters Rockerfeller! Let's us get goin' 'fore someone rings the knell on us."

As Banjo went to help Sister get the truck out, Opal was left wondering if Oysters Rockefeller had anything to do with the Rockefeller Center that she'd seen in one of her daddy's postal cards. If they did, maybe everything was still going to be all right. According to Banjo's plan, Cupid was going to be saved from the zoo or the glue factory, and they were headed for the show business. Maybe soon they would be eating Oysters Rockefeller in Rockefeller Center with Daddy in New York. Imagine that! She couldn't wait to see the look on Cupid's face when she told her all about it.

Chapter Twelve

Along the Sawdust Trail

LATER THAT SAME EVENING, AS THE MOON ROSE OVER the dark treetops, when the Peaviners were sitting out in the evening cool under the cottonwood trees, the Dented Dragon was seen chugging along the Old Cotton Road, with Cupid stored in the back and Opal seated beside her in the straw for company.

Opal had left a note for Miss Blossom, attached to her bicycle, explaining everything and asking her to write her daddy for her (she was still so much better than Opal at penmanship) to tell him that Granny Bid had died peacefully. She promised to let Miss Blossom know how their plan turned out and where Opal could be reached if there was any news of Daddy.

She knew Miss Blossom would keep Banjo's plan secret, and even with her heart sorely laden over Bid's death, she couldn't help smiling at the thought of Augusta's reaction to their escape. Banjo was smiling too over his bold stroke, but frankly by this time he couldn't see his future without either the girl or the elephant.

The moon was high by the time Sister Eclipse's contraption reached Tilley, and the fair was just closing down for the night. When Banjo asked to speak with the twins he was informed rather rudely by the show boss that the Brothers Solo were at present elsewhere engaged and wouldn't be back until Sunday. Opal suspected that the man was just being mean and trying to make trouble for them, and Banjo must have been thinking along the same lines because he talked extra nice to the boss.

Smoothly he said, "Look here, m'man, I've got the best act in the whole show business right here, and I'm prepared to let you have it in your show. This little lady here is Opal, Opal Thigpen, and this big ole here critter is Cupid, Queen of the Tanbark, and they do tricks. Amazing tricks." He and Sister Eclipse stood aside so the man could get the benefit of the view, which consisted of a tired thirteen-year-old and a sleepy elephant. "Now what do you think of that?"

"Not much," said the man, whose name was Sweeney and who had a very red face from drinking too much of the hard stuff. He scowled fiercely, first at Opal, then at Cupid. "We don't need no elephant act round here. We don't need no little girls, and we don't need no animules, neither."

Banjo was charm itself. "Now hold on just a minute here, m'good fellow," he said, stepping up closer. "I b'lieve you're looking at this thing hind end to."

"Yeah," said Sister, putting in her two cents' worth. "Don'tcha think you ought to give this little girl's act a chance?"

"I don't think I orter do nuthin'," said Sweeney. (The Cumberpatches were one thing, but Opal was certainly reaping her share of bad grammar so far in the show business.) "What *I* think is, you and this here fat lady and that kid and her lousy elephant orter be on your way, *that's* what *I* think."

"Say, Buster, who y'all callin' fat lady?" demanded Sister Eclipse, who knew she was fat and didn't need the likes of Sweeney to point it out.

"If the shoe fits," said Sweeney and started to go, only to be restrained by Banjo.

"Say, m'man, no need to get tough about it. Maybe we'll just wait around until your bosses get back from wherever they are."

Sweeney scrunched up his brow. "Lissen, hustler, ain't I just tole you, they's gone—to Elbowtown—and won't be back till Sunday? *I'm* the one in charge here, and I say get goin'. Less'n you want me to call the sheriff and book you a cell in the pokey."

"Don't you go givin' us no talk 'bout no pokey!" cried Sister Eclipse. "This here's my man, *my man,* you hear me, and nobody ain't puttin' him away in no jail, got me?"

"Aw, shut up your face, fat stuff!" shouted Sweeney, who had a temper and had never liked fat people at all.

"Say, listen, bigmouth, that's the absolute las' time you talk to her that way," said Banjo. "This lady is going to be my wife and bear my children!"

"What?" cried Sister stoutly. "Banjo Bailey, is this a proposal?"

"It most assuredly is!" cried Banjo just as stoutly. "My helpmeet and my big bug, that's what you is goin' to be!"

Opal felt a nudge from Cupid, and they exchanged a sly glance that said they found this a funny way for two people to get engaged, in the middle of a quarrel with another person.

"Come on," snarled Sweeney, "I want the whole of you no-a'counts offa this place right now. Otherwise—"

He got no further in his threats, for at that moment an automobile swung through the gates and blinded the group with its headlights. "Why, whaddya know, I think I see Mr. Sam 'n' Mr. Tam just driving up," said Banjo.

Spotting his employers, Sweeney came pushing past Banjo and ran up to the Solo boys, saying, "Mister Sam 'n' Mister Tam, these here folks is bein' an annoyance, and I want to call the sheriff to throw them off our place."

"No need for that sort of behavior, Pete," said one of the brothers. (Opal didn't know which, because she couldn't see his toenails.)

"And who would you be, sir?" inquired the other brother.

Banjo politely removed his tall hat and said, "You 'member me, Mr. Sam 'n' Mr. Tam, I used ter work for old Colonel Beebee's outfit. I was the advance man."

"Oh, yes, to be sure, certainly," said Mr. Sam 'n' Mr. Tam together, though Opal suspected they really didn't remember Banjo at all but were simply trying to be agreeable because they knew their employee had been giving them trouble. Banjo quickly took advantage of their considerateness to explain what had brought them here to Tilley, namely to have Opal and Cupid audition for them with the idea of spotting them in their circus.

The twins looked over at the elephant, who waited patiently a short distance away, her eyelids drooping with sleepiness, and the girl who stood yawning by the elephant's trunk.

"Good golly, she's only a child," said Sam with concern.

"She certainly is," agreed his brother Tam. (Sam 'n' Tam usually agreed on most matters.) "And it's nearly midnight, well past her bedtime, I should think."

Sam thought so, too. Their doubtful expressions indicated that they thought a girl of thirteen couldn't have much to offer for their purposes, but Banjo soon had them convinced otherwise. "We'd be willing to audition right here and now, if you both were of a mind."

"Aw, cut it out, you big bozo," said Sweeney, sensing that something was up, "it's late and the lights are all shut off."

"Turn them back on, Pete," said Sam with a curt nod.

"Yes, Pete, turn them back on," said Tam with as curt a nod.

Grumbling, Sweeney went and did as he was told. On came the bright lights, and in their white beams both Opal and Cupid sprang to life again. They were pros. They'd done the shows in the Cumberpatches' barn, they knew exactly what was expected of them, and they performed with a will. Golly, how they performed! Without costumes or makeup, without music or a ringmaster, and the stands bare of an audience, the pair gave it their all.

"Gracious, that little girl is talented," declared Sam enthusiastically.

"And the elephant, what about him?" asked brother Tam.

"*Her*," Banjo corrected politely. "Cupid, she's a girl."

"And so she is!" cried Sam, looking at Tam. "What d'you say, brother-mine? Are they hired?"

"Hired they are!" cried Tam in return, putting out his hand to Banjo. "Hired on the spot, as they say!"

And so they were. Sam marched over and gave Banjo's hand another shake, which meant, pure and simple, that Opal and Cupid were now in the show business and would get to strut their stuff eight times a week at a salary of five dollars a show—not a lot, when Opal thought about how much money somebody like Shirley Temple must be making out there in Hollywood, but as Banjo had already pointed out, you had to start somewhere.

As soon as the deal was set, Sister Eclipse turned over the motor of her truck for the drive back to Peavine. She kissed Opal and gave her a hug and said to be a good girl, and then reminded Banjo of his promise to marry her.

"I ain't fergettin', honey lamb," he said.

"I'll be countin' on it," said Eclipse, tipping her hat over her eye and driving off. When she was gone Banjo took Opal's hand and led her and Cupid around to the tent where they were to sleep. Opal's bed was to be the lid of a wardrobe trunk covered with stickers and labels bearing the names of famous cities like Fort Wayne and Duluth and Ausable Chasm, all the big metropolises the Solos' show had played in. Before she fell asleep Opal made out the name of one city stamped right into the side of the trunk: OSHKOSH.

Opal liked the sound of it.

And so it was that a new and exciting life began for Opal and her friend Cupid, with the Solo Brothers' Lively Arts Fun Show. Now they were really in the show business. And heading for the Big Time. Opal couldn't imagine any happier way to spend her itme than performing in a circus with her elephant—out there in the big ring, filled with sawdust, six shows a week and matinees on Wednesdays and Saturdays.

Just to feel those warm, bright, colored lights on her cheeks, just to hear the audience applauding as it watched the show, to know that as a stage partner Cupid was incomparable and would never make a mistake of any kind, gave Opal a wonderful feeling of confidence and assurance. This was what she'd been born for, everything in her life had led only to this, and she could imagine doing nothing else for the rest of her days.

And there was Banjo. Being a kind of silent partner and manager, Banjo was quickly proving an invaluable adviser, just as he had proved an invaluable friend and companion. At sunup he made sure Opal was keeping up with the schoolwork provided by the County Social Services. A far better cry, Opal thought, than the school in Atlanta that Miss Augusta and Miss Vermilyea had had in mind. Then, every morning he was out there in the ring with his shirtsleeves rolled up, putting Opal and Cupid through their paces, devising new bits of business and improving on the old ones, smoothing out the kinks and making the performance as professional as he knew how. And at the end of every day he would faithfully remind them that they were getting closer to the Big Time, and how they would strut their stuff then!

Meanwhile, Opal took to circus life like a baby duck to water. At "half hour," which was the time when the performers would start getting ready for the show, she would go into the tent and join the others in putting on their makeup, and she would chat with all the new friends she'd made, who only a short time ago were strangers on the circus midway: Zelda, the snake charmer, and her pet python, Oscar; Leilah the Fat Lady, who weighed over four hundred pounds yet could still manage to sit on a single chair; Zoltan, the Hungarian sword swallower, who could also eat fire; Mercy, the sweet little lady who had a beard down to her waist; and there were the Flying Marchesis, the troupe of death-defying Italian acrobats, and the Wild West Cowboys, the gang of rootin' tootin' daredevil Western riders in white hats and red shirts, riding white horses; and Sid Kolodony, with his funny toupee and his trained seal, Cliquot; and the clowns, for the Solo Brothers were of the old school, firm believers in giving the customers lots of clown work.

Together they would all sit in the makeup tent at their long oilcloth-covered tables, painting their faces before the brightly lighted mirrors, putting on putty noses and dyed wigs, while the acrobats in white tights gilded each others' torsos with gold paint. As Opal listened to the talk and gossip among these show business folk, she had the feeling that she was being let in on a way of life that was reserved for very few people in the world. And though a short while ago she'd had only Cupid and Banjo and Sister Eclipse as friends, now she had a host of them, including

138

a pair of "Balloonists Extraordinaire" named Buddy Pepper and Betty Buckeye.

Buddy and Betty had joined the traveling show for a limited engagement a few stops before Tilley, and it was especially exciting for Opal to work with real live hot-air balloonists, courageous adventurers who earned their living in so dangerous and glamorous a way. And Cupid enjoyed them, too. Buddy presented such a dashing picture of daredevilness, dressed up in snazzy jodhpur riding pants, a turtleneck sweater with his initials sewn across the chest, pigskin gloves, a tan leather helmet with goggles, and a long white scarf fringed at both ends. And with his trim dark mustache, prominent ears, and pearly smile, he could easily be mistaken for Clark Gable's cousin, Opal thought.

As for his partner, Betty Buckeye, she was every bit as daredevil as Buddy, which for a girl was quite a lot, and she was pretty enough to be in the movies, too. She had masses of golden curls, big blue china-doll eyes, long curvy lashes, and a curvy figure to go with it, and Opal and Cupid and Banjo thought she was not only fetching (and don't tell Sister, Banjo chided), but nice as pie, too. And they all got on famously. Betty liked nothing more than having Cupid hoist her onto her back, where Betty would turn nimble handstands and spin a silver baton. Actually, there was one thing she liked more, for the fact was that she was madly in love with Buddy Pepper, and fortunately, he was in love with her, too.

Buddy and Betty had also given Opal and Cupid a hint of just how big time the Big Time could be. Betty had been keeping a large scrapbook in which she posted all the newspaper accounts of their exciting adventures, with pictures and autographs of the many famous people they'd met, and she would hold the book open across her lap so that Opal, seated beside her, could look her fill, while Cupid stood behind them turning the pages with the tip of her trunk. Here were all the greatest animal acts in circus history, like Frank Buck of "Bring 'Em Back Alive" fame, and Clyde Beatty, the hotshot circus animal trainer. Then there was Mrs. Eleanor Roosevelt, with whom they had shaken hands, and Fiorello La Guardia, the mayor of New York. They'd even been to Hollywood, where they'd met Shirley Temple (Opal's idol) at the Brown Derby restaurant, and talked to Shirley's studio about appearing in a movie called *Balloons A-Weigh* with the famous child star.

Opal was fascinated. Why, the Big Time was even bigger than she imagined, and she resolved to work twice as hard so that one day she and Cupid would get to see some of the exciting places that Buddy and Betty had seen, and maybe even meet some of the famous people they'd met. Imagine, Shirley Temple, all the way out there in Hollywood! It was too exciting to think about.

In the meantime, Opal was grateful for how far they *had* come in such a short space of time. And look at all the fun they were having. Why, with the Solo Brothers' Lively Arts Fun Show they were always on the move, seeing places Opal had never been to (since she'd never left Peavine Hollow, except for Tilley and the movies in Elbowtown, in her whole life), never playing any place longer than a week, and sometimes laying out for what they called a "split week," which meant playing two towns within seven days. After the fair closed at Tilley, they'd bused and trucked over to a place called Titus, then on to Shelby, over to Frisky Hollow, up to Decatur Rim, and down along to Chivaree, with stops at Putney Ford, Little Church, and a place called Benign and another called Terwilliger Corners, where there was a hot-dog stand in the shape of a hot dog on a bun with real-looking mustard and relish painted on! Even Nabisco Falls and Potts Dam had seen the Solo Brothers' dust. Not much in the way of places, of course, just dots on the map or maybe even no dot at all (what Banjo referred to as "whistle-stops"), but that was the kind of show the Solo Brothers' Lively Arts Fun Show was.

And moving about from town to town on the bus, along the "sawdust trail," as the traveling show circuit was called, Opal and Cupid had found out just how important it was to work hard if you wanted to make it big. So, every morning as soon as breakfast and her school lessons were over, there they were, out on the side lot, practicing, practicing, practicing—making sure that when their time came out there on the tanbark, under the warm pink lights, the paying customers would be dazzled by what they could do and amazed at how effortlessly they did it. And just like those first customers back in Peavine Hollow, they would go home and tell their friends about the little girl and her amazing elephant.

Meanwhile, something else was happening along the sawdust trail (something Opal and Cupid were scarcely aware of), that Banjo had promised would happen. With every passing day, with every whistle-stop and tank town they performed in, the two ex-Peaviners were climbing from one rung to the next on the ladder to stardom. There was no denying it. While Betty and Buddy were the prime attractions that helped bring in the customers to the open-air show and "rake in the dough," as Banjo put it, Opal and Cupid were now attracting a major share of paying customers to the Big Top. Happily, there was never any question of professional jealousy between the two acts; how could there be when one featured balloonists, the other a girl tap-dancing on an elephant's back?

And so (for this was how most things went when you were finally in the show business), first their names appeared way down at the very bottom of the bill in very small print, like this:

. . . ALSO WITH OPAL AND HER ELEPHANT, CUPID

Then, one day, with winter around the corner, a newspaper reporter with a turned-up hat brim and a press pass stuck in the band came around. He said he was after the "big story," and asked a lot of questions of Opal and Banjo—which showed up as an interview in the *County Gazetteer*, along with a photograph of Opal and her elephant taken especially for the article, letting people know just how the two performers looked in the spotlight. And it wasn't long after that the size of their letters in the playbill went up to something like this:

FEATURING THE ONE-AND-ONLY OPAL
AND HER SENSATIONAL SIDEKICK
THE MIRACLE WORKER
CUPID, QUEEN OF THE TANBARK!!!

which in printer's language is known as 12 point type. Now, for a little girl and her pet elephant to get their names printed up in 12 point type so quickly was something of a wonder, and the upshot was: the more the customers the larger the print, and the larger the print the more the customers. It was what Banjo called a "vicious circle"—except it wasn't vicious at all; it was nice and good and fun, and with each passing day Opal had a better idea of who she was and what she wanted out of life, which is a good thing for any young girl or boy to know.

And so, day by day, the two performers became more well-known, more sought after by the press, more loved by audiences. Cheers and applause were theirs everywhere they appeared, and, best of all, the children loved them! Yes, it was to all the children that they played their act, for Opal and Cupid knew that if the children really liked them they'd get their mothers and fathers to bring them back, time after time, and that one day when these children were grown and had children of their own, they'd bring them to see their favorite attractions, too.

The other important thing that happened, affecting not only Opal and Cupid but the whole show and everyone in it, was that the Solo Brothers, Sam 'n' Tam (Opal never heard them called Sam *and* Tam, only Sam *'n'* Tam), were now able to book the show into larger towns, even cities. Taking their cue from the inflated box-office receipts, they ordered up a larger tent and larger stands, had new costumes sewn, and added more musicians to the band. Then the most wonderful thing that could possibly have happened did. The Solo Brothers, Sam 'n' Tam, promoted Opal and Cupid to full stars!

It was true. Now the posters read:

THE SOLO BROTHERS' LIVELY ARTS FUN SHOW
TAKES PRIDE IN PRESENTING
IN PERSON

OPAL AND CUPID

A glorious circus Queen and
her 1,100-pound Pachyderm

READY AND WILLING TO TITILLATE
EVEN THE MOST BORED AND BLAH-ZAYED
APPETITE FOR ENTERTAINMENT AND
ASTONISH ALL COMERS

The Tiny Tapping Tot and the Garbo of the Sawdust!!!

Three-color flyers were printed, and handbills, too, to be pasted up and handed out by the advance man in every town that the show was scheduled to play. Mammoth six-sheets were slapped up on board fences and vacant walls, advertising the Solo Brothers' glorious attractions, leaving no doubt who the headliners were. Small outfit though they might be, Sam 'n' Tam had given their little girl and her pet elephant the Star Treatment. Opal now had her own dressing room, with a gold star on the door, while Cupid had her own gold star pasted on the side of her stall.

And, best of all, Miss Augusta still didn't know where they had gone! Opal and Cupid were amused, picturing her scouring the countryside trying to discover their whereabouts. Still, it was possible for Augusta to have strayed across their pictures, for almost every place they went they could see the publicity posters tacked up for all to see.

As for Sister Eclipse, though she had gone back to Peavine Hollow and putting up her 'lixir, she hadn't forgotten Opal and Cupid, or "that ole fool," Banjo B. Bailey, *or* his promise of matrimony. And speaking of matrimony, Opal thought that Buddy and Betty seemed to enjoy each other's company so much, too, it was only natural that they should be hitched. But according to Banjo, a wedding was often the surest way to end a good working relationship. Look at him and Sister, he said. Why, she'd changed him from a no-account without a penny to his name to a man salting away money in the bank. Why would he want to spoil that? Still, Opal knew that, in truth, Banjo was really waiting for the day he had a nest egg worthy of his Big Bug, which was how he always referred to Sister now, and until that day came, he'd be happy with opening nights in places like Sizes and Sorghum, when his Big Bug would come and sit right there in the front row, clapping to beat the band and having the best time in the world.

And it continued to be the best of times for Opal and Cupid as well. At every performance, there they would be, the star attraction under the Big Top, Opal in her spangled tights and pink tutu, with her silver wand and gold crown fastened into her soft brown curls, tucked safely in Cupid's trunk, smiling to applauding audiences. How proud Daddy would be to see his little girl now, about to turn fourteen and starring with the circus at the same County Fair he used to take her to as a child. How proud he would be to see her fancy footwork, and what a performance she and Cupid would put on when that day came.

"You'd really love my daddy, and he'd love you too, I know," she said to Cupid one night before bedtime. "He always loved animals. I remember he had this big old hound dog named Trace, and when Trace died, Daddy sobbed to beat the band! I just hope he got Miss Blossom's letter about Granny, and we'll see him soon. Do you suppose we'll ever get to strut our stuff for him, Cupie? Do you?"

Cupid didn't have to think long before she nodded, and Opal detected the slightest trace of a smile in the corner of her mouth, as if Cupid was trying to remind Opal about something she had forgotten, but Cupid, being an elephant, had not. It was something they had discussed often, about how people, no matter how young or old, could accomplish anything in the world if they just put their minds to it.

As Opal hugged her elephant, she remembered something else she'd forgotten. It was the wish she'd made in the cornfield that night when she and Cupid had listened to the corn grow and had seen the shooting star. Opal's wish was still locked inside her heart, and now, more than ever, she knew she must keep it there, for one day it would finally come true. Thanks to Cupid, she was sure of it.

In the meantime there was a reunion in the offing that would bring plenty of tears. But they would be tears of sorrow, not of joy, for it was a reunion of a different kind than the one Opal was longing for. An old enemy had been using certain show business connections to keep close tabs on the Solo Brothers' new stars, and at this very moment he was driving over to Beauchamp, unbeknownst to them, to take in their next show and, no doubt, stir things up a bit.

Chapter Thirteen

A Face from the Past

BY NOW, WITH BANJO'S CONSTANT ATTENTION TO detail and interesting new ideas, and his daily routine of rehearsals, Opal and Cupid's act had come to shine like a sparkling gem. So polished was it that their performance under the Big Top in Beauchamp that night, in front of a multitude of cheering fans, was one of their best shows ever. Unfortunately, it was on this night when they were at their peak that a terrible thing happened. Right there in front of the whole world, practically, Cupid began acting oddly. Her skin began to twitch, she tossed her head nervously and began to swing her trunk in wide, agitated arcs. Then a low, keening sound issued from deep inside her throat, and her eyes took on a wild and frantic look.

Obviously something was upsetting her, but Opal was unable to fathom what it could possibly be. As one trick after the other fell flat, Opal could see the agitated and disappointed expressions on the faces of the crowd. Suddenly, the cold creep of stage fright set in as Opal's eyes traveled among the rows and one face in particular leaped out at her. It was a face she knew all too well, a face that fully explained Cupid's odd behavior, and she was at once panic-stricken. The dark features were wreathed in pleasure at Opal's obvious discomfort, not to mention the humiliation she was feeling, for by this time the band had stopped playing and the audience had begun to murmur and hiss its displeasure.

In the center of the ring, Cupid stood paralyzed with fright, for of course she too had spotted the face in the crowd. But although Opal was badly shaken, she knew she must remain calm at all costs in order to prevent Cupid's primitive animal urges from popping out. At any moment she could go berserk and maybe even trample someone. Opal approached her carefully and whispered in her ear.

"It's all right, Cupie," she said gently, stroking her elephant's trunk and trying to keep her tranquil. "I know what you're going through—I feel the same way, too."

But she could always tell when Cupid was paying attention, and at that moment the animal was ignoring everything she was saying. In a sudden rush Cupid yanked free of her owner's restraining hand, wheeled, and, furiously tossing her trunk, went stampeding across the ring, launching herself into the stands. The audience fled in alarm, women and children screaming, men shouting, everyone trying to get out of the path of the enraged beast, whose angry trumpetings pierced the air.

"Cupid! Cupid, come back!" Opal cried, but the elephant paid her no mind, just went on pounding up the steps, heading for the middle section where some people were trapped in a row. Making her way toward a man who seemed stuck in his seat, cringing in fright, she opened her mouth wide, flared her large ears, and emitted the most bloodcurdling sounds any beast could make. Then, wafting her trunk, she threw several loops around the man's waist, wheeled, and carried him swiftly back to the ring, creating an even greater furor among the crowd. Opal stared at the amazing sight, for, wrapped in the elephant's trunk, like someone in the coils of Zelda's python, Oscar, his head all but in Cupid's mouth, was none other than her former master, Nate Seeger!

"Cupid, put him down!" Opal ordered sharply. She was not about to have a man's blood on her hands, even Nate Seeger's. For it seemed that the evil trainer who had treated Cupid so cruelly was now about to pay for his sins; either to be devoured wholesale or to be flung to the sawdust and trampled upon!

"Do as I say this instant, Cupid, or I'm going to send you to bed without your supper, do you hear me?" Opal spoke to her elephant just as any mother would to her naughty offspring, but like so many naughty offspring Cupid paid her mother no attention. Strengthening her grip on the detestable man, the higher she raised him into the air, the louder he hollered and shouted.

"Put me down, you blankety-blank pachyderm! Set me on the ground or I'll sue! I'll sue you and your owners blind! I knowed I shoulda shot you when I had the chance!"

Such heated words served only to incense Cupid further. She had not forgotten the treatment she'd received at the hands of this enemy of all jungle beasts, nor had she forgotten being chained up and whipped and cursed at, not to mention the cruel treatment her mother Paulina had received at those same hands.

Meanwhile, the louder Opal ordered Cupid to drop the man, the more worried Sam 'n' Tam seemed by the threat of a lawsuit, and finally Opal got close enough to grasp Cupid's harness with one hand and lift herself onto the elephant's shoulders, where she leaned forward and began speaking softly and gently into her big, floppy ear.

149

"It's all right, Cupie, honey, you've given the nasty man a good enough shake. Now put him down before we all end up in jail. Elephants can get sued, too, not just Sam 'n' Tam. And think how kind they've been to us. We don't want to make trouble for them, now do we?"

Sam 'n' Tam watched with bated breaths, but Cupid surrendered her victim only with the greatest reluctance. Drawing back on her hind legs and rising up to her full height, she swung her trunk aloft and flung Seeger out into space. The eyes of the audience remained riveted. There he went, right through the air, describing an arc like that of a shooting star through the tent heavens, to land safely in the net that had been readied for the next act, which was to be Ironhead the Human Cannonball.

That so thrilling and dangerous an episode, which might have ended in disaster, had concluded in such a lucky manner was in no small degree due to Opal's clever mastery of her enraged elephant, and she was congratulated by one and all. As the Human Cannonball began his act and the audience resettled itself for the continuation of the show, Banjo and Buddy helped Opal coax Cupid back toward the dressing room tents, where she was calmed and given a large ration of sugared rhubarb and an extra bale of hay to munch on.

Meanwhile, Nate Seeger, free of the net that had caught him, ranted and raved loudly, threatening the Solo twins with the total extinction of their show, declaring that they were harboring a crazed beast that should be put out of its misery before she really injured someone. Limping, and holding his neck, which he claimed was paining him, he finally withdrew from the fray, but not before shooting a look at Opal and her elephant, as well as Banjo and the Solo Brothers, a look that clearly said they hadn't seen the last of Nate Seeger.

▲

The bad pennies of the world always had a way of turning up, didn't they? And despite his nearly being killed by a crazed jungle beast, Nate Seeger wasn't going to have plans he'd hatched upset in any way. Would-be killer or not, Nate Seeger was going to have that elephant back for his very own.

As he drove away he cursed himself for ten kinds of fool for ever having let himself be tricked into getting rid of the blankety-blank animal in the first place. He'd been so sure that the blasted critter would be dead within a week that he hadn't given it another thought, and now here she was a star attraction. It made his blood boil to have traded away such a valuable property, and he stepped harder on the gas pedal of his rusty old truck as he continued to fume and scheme.

Cupid's whole trouble was that business with her mother. Old Paulina had put some bad ideas into her child's head. If Seeger hadn't sent Paulina to the glue factory, Cupid wouldn't have gone rogue on him, and Nate would probably be rolling in money. But, he reminded himself, Cupid wasn't going anywhere, and there'd be time enough to bring her around again with the old tools of whip, stick, and pistol. Beasts were dumb all right, but if you learned them good and gave them a healthy knock now and then, they'd play ball. It was never too late for an enterprising and ambitious party like himself to rake in money, especially when he could outsmart a little girl and that numbskull of a manager any day.

His first step, he figured, was to ankle on over to the circus the next day, where a friendly little visit backstage might be in order, just to check on how the land lay and maybe have a little talk with his old friend, Banjo B. Bailey.

"Howdy, there, Bailey," he said, encountering Banjo behind

the red velvet curtain, where the performers made their entrances and exits. "How ya ben?"

"Ben okay," said Banjo, as Pickles growled at the man's heels. Banjo was also distrustful of Seeger's oily manner. "How's things been with you?"

"Not bad. Not bad," said Seeger. This was obviously a lie because from his shabby appearance it looked like Seeger had fallen on hard times.

"What can I do for you?" Banjo asked.

"Well, I just stopped on by to say hello. Sorry 'bout that misunderstanding yesterday. Hope there's no hard feelin's."

"None," Banjo replied politely, though all he wanted to do was throw the bum out.

"Looks like you're headed for the Big Time," Seeger went on.

"We surely are." Banjo was most emphatic. "We surely are."

"You and that little toe-tapping tot and that big old elephant over there." As he pointed over to where Cupid stood, the elephant turned away. " 'Garbo of the Sawdust,' huh? Reg'lar, buddin' movin' pitchah star, I guess. Heh-heh." He chuckled and scratched his head. "When I think the merry chase that critter used to lead me. My my."

From the corner of his eye Seeger saw Opal appear around the side of the watering trough, where Cupid was now taking a drink. She was with Buddy and Betty, and Betty was speaking gaily.

"Opal, since it's your birthday tomorrow, Buddy has a surprise for you. He's going to give you and Banjo a ride in his balloon. Won't that be fun?"

Opal grew excited at the prospect of such an excursion. She'd been secretly hoping Buddy would take them up one day. Seeger, who had been listening, brightened, too, and nudged Banjo.

"Why, durned if that ain't the little gal comin' right there!" he exclaimed. "Turned out right pretty, didn't she?"

152

"She did some, at that," Banjo agreed.

Seeger tipped his weathered fedora at Opal. "Hidy, little lady. I'm dashed if I could reckanize you, all got up so spangly and pretty in your tights. You're a reg'lar little sawdust star these days, aren'tcha?"

Opal didn't want to be rude, but the sound of Nate Seeger being so slippery made her apprehensive, so she said nothing. It didn't matter, really, because as Buddy and Betty went off to their trailer, Seeger went right on talking.

"I see that big old elephant of yours recovered from whatever was ailin' it."

"Oh, sure," said Banjo, answering for Opal. "That girl, Cupid, she was up and around in no time 'tall."

"How'd you get her over that bout of colic she had? It *was* a colic, wasn't it?"

"Colic?" Banjo shifted his shoulders around under his coat and chuckled. "Why, shucks, man, that elephant was just puttin' on, was all. That Cupid, she took a fancy to the li'l bug here. You was beatin' on that critter and all, and Opie, she was feeding the old girl peanuts—and you know how a elephant relishes peanuts— so she gets it into her head to just lay out flat and play dead."

"She did, huh?"

"That she did," Banjo replied, realizing for the first time that maybe he was giving Seeger more information than was necessary. "Sure fooled you, I guess," he went on, watching Seeger carefully, then adding quickly, "You sold that elephant to Opal, don't forget. You was paid in gold."

"Oh, I ain't fergettin'," said Seeger smoothly. "Don't worry none about that. But how I figure things, I figure that by rights that animal's still my property."

"How you figure that, m'man?"

" 'Cause it was extracted under fraudulent circumstances."

"Mean t'say you's accusing us of acting fraudulent? I traded you my papa-daddy's gold turnip watch."

Nate ran his tongue around his lips and stretched his eyes a bit. "That watch wasn't no gold! I tried t'hock it. They told me quick enough, that watch case was brass-plated tin. And you was pure brass to pass it off as fourteen karats."

"Well, sir, if that watch was brass-plated tin, it's news to me. My daddy give me that there watch and he says to me, 'Son, this here watch is solid gold and is worth two hundred bucks, so as long as you keep her you'll always have money on you.' Now if you don't want to keep it, I'll buy that watch back from you. Where is it?"

"Happen I ain't got it no more. A man stole it right outta my pocket in a saloon one night."

Banjo gave him a shrug. "Well, there you are. Tough luck, pal, tough luck. Now if you'll 'scuse us, it's time for Cupid to put on the feed bag. Come along, Opie."

He moved to go but Seeger detained him.

"Hold on there, Bailey, just a minute. As things stand now, I don't have no watch and I don't have no elephant neither. And seein' as you cheated me, you just hand me over that there animule and we'll call it square, okay?"

"Not okay, pal. Then was then, now is now. Things change, that's how it goes."

"Well, look at it this way, then. Since you ben usin' my property to earn money with—quite a bit of money, as I learn—I figure I got a percentage of those profits comin' my way."

"Uh-huh? Do tell. That's how you figure it, hm?"

"Sure do. But since I'm a nice fellow and I like you. I'm going to let you keep all them shiny profits you ben rakin' in. Every dollar, every simoleon, right down to the last spondulick."

"Well, say, that's mighty generous of you, m'man. I am impressed. And we thanks you kindly for your generosity, don't we, Opal?"

"Y-yes," said Opal, wishing Seeger would go away and all the talk about Cupid and money would cease.

"Fine," Seeger went on. "I figure I'll allow for you to keep the money you took in so far, *if* you return my property to me. *Then* we'll call it fair and square."

"Again we thanks you, but, you see, we don't have no property of yours."

"The heck you say! You got that elephant, ain'tcha?"

"Sure I do, but that elephant's not *your* property; she's Opal's property. You signed her over. Ain't I got a legal document to prove it? Didn't you, party of the first part, sign a paper deeding that elephant over to the party of the second part? Sure you did. You didn't want that elephant, anyways," Banjo went on, still cool as a cucumber. "Ain't that so, Opal?"

"It's true," Opal said. "I was there. You were going to shoot her!"

"I was not!" returned Seeger. "I was just makin' like I was, that's all. Say, girlie, I wouldn't hurt a hair on that elephant's head. Just look how she looks at me." He grinned a stupid grin at Cupid, still over by the water trough. "Lookee there—why, I b'leeve she's smilin' back at me."

Seeger had no sooner got his words out than Cupid turned and, in one swift movement, pointed her trunk directly at him and let loose with a blast of water as strong as a busted fire hydrant. Then she wrapped her trunk around the man's soggy waist, hoisted him into the air, and dumped him with a loud *splish!* into a large pile of manure.

Opal tried to hide her amusement as Seeger extracted his sodden, dripping form from the mound of animal droppings. He glared angrily at Cupid.

155

"Lookit what this blankety-blank beast done to my suit," he shouted, "and my brand-new three-dollar shoes! Why she's a menace to s'ciety!"

His suit and his yellow shoes were so covered with manure that he looked more like a farmer after a hard day's work than a desperate animal trainer. He shook a furious fist in Banjo's face. "You ain't heard the last of this, Banjo Bailey. You and that little knee-britches girl there. I've got the law on my side! I got important people knows me. You'll find out what the law can do."

"Never go to law, Nate," said Banjo philosophically, "never go to law. That's what my pappy used ter say, and it's good advice. Whyn't you just hustle yourself along now, 'cause you know what, m'man—you stink to high heaven!" Banjo held his nose and turned away and, finally, Opal couldn't help but laugh, enraging Seeger all the more.

"Maybe come around tomorrow," Banjo added. "We'll ask Cupid to turn her hose on you one mo' time so's you smell better. Our stars'll even take you up for a nice balloon ride. Won't that be nice. That is less'n you wants Cupid to hose you down right now."

Seeger snarled like a wounded bear. "You're a dirty lowdown skunk, Bailey," he spat out. "You already took me fer a ride, thank you ver' much!"

As he turned to leave, Pickles, who had been showing her sharp little teeth at Seeger all this time, took her cue. She sprang at his rear end and sank her teeth into the seat of his mucky pants. And what a comical sight it was to see, Seeger prancing about in a circle while Pickles spun around with him, hanging on for dear life, her tail all uncurled, growling as heartily as any jungle beast.

That night Nate Seeger went to bed in his truck with a sore rear end and sorely distressed, vowing to get even with everyone

156

who'd poked fun at him and put one over on him. He would get that blankety-blank elephant back if it was the last thing he did. But how? He lay awake into the night thinking hard, trying to cook up a plot that would show Banjo B. Bailey who was the smarter of the two.

As he looked out through the window of his truck, he saw the full moon up in the sky, like a big white bouncing ball. Not bouncing, just floating there like a big balloon. Like the balloon that was the Solo Brothers' other star attraction—that same balloon that would be taking that ninny Opal and the dratted Banjo Bailey up for a ride tomorrow.

Wait a minute—that was it! If they were up in the sky tomorrow, that meant they wouldn't be on the ground. And if they weren't on the ground—why then they were powerless to stop Nate Seeger from doing what he had a mind to do, which was bad business all the way around. Now he had it, at last—a way to get back at his enemies and to make himself rich into the bargain. He leapt out of the truck and went at it tooth and nail, hammer and tongs, until by daybreak, he had set in motion the perfect plan.

Chapter Fourteen

The Grand and Glorious Balloon Chase

THAT MORNING, OPAL'S BIRTHDAY, WHEN THE SUN was well into the sky, Buddy Pepper set up his balloon as planned, secured the restraining ropes, and turned up the gas ring to heat the air in the bag. When it was nice and full he called for Opal and Banjo, as well as Pickles, to climb aboard the basket. Sister Eclipse was coming to visit that day and had been included in the balloon ascension as well, but something must have delayed her—Banjo was laying short odds on the Dented Dragon's fickle engine. Meanwhile, Betty Buckeye arrived carrying a straw hamper: She'd thought to bring along sandwiches and coffee in case anyone got hungry, as well as a small birthday cake in celebration of Opal's big day.

Finally, after waiting as long as they could and still catching no sign of Sister Eclipse's truck, they were obliged to leave without her. All the circus folk were on hand to wave them off, and at

Buddy's signal two roustabouts cast off the ropes, and the balloon began its slow ascent.

Almost as soon as it left the ground, Nate Seeger, who had been watching from the road, went into action. With an accomplice driving his truck, they rolled onto the circus grounds and pulled up at the tent where the animals were quartered. As luck would have it, Cupid happened to be outdoors having her morning wash. A roustabout, who sometimes looked after Cupid for Opal, was hosing her down after a good sudsing. Seeger and his accomplice, a man named Bendix, got out of the truck and ankled on over to the roustabout.

"Whatcha say, son," Seeger began. "And what would your name be?"

"My name's Henry, but folks jes call me Harve," he responded in a friendly way.

"Well, well, Harve or Henry, I'm happy to know you. I'm glad to see you've got Cupid all nice and clean for her little trip this ay em."

"Huh?" Harve's jaw dropped in surprise. "Opal didn't say nothin' 'bout no trip. You a friend of hers?"

"You bet." Seeger held up two crossed fingers to demonstrate how close he and Opal were. "Friend enough to take the day off to drive her elephant to the dentist."

"The *dentist*?"

"Sure. Didn't Opal tell you?"

Harve shook his head. "No, sir, Opal sure didn't say nothin' about the dentist."

"Must've slipped her mind. Cupid's got a cavity."

"She does?"

"Uh-huh. Got to have it filled."

Harve shook his head again. "Cupid don't have no cavity. I

159

clean her teeth two times a week. I'd sure know if there was somethin' wrong."

"Well, just goes to show you how we can often miss the important things in life. You take a look, you'll see it. You don't want her comin' down with no toothache, do you?"

Nosiree, Harve didn't want his charge coming down with no toothache. He went over to have a look. He stood on a Nehi soda pop box and told Cupid to open up. Cupid, whose entire body had begun to shake at the sound of Seeger's voice, tossed her head and stubbornly refused to show her teeth. She bucked and reared and did everything to resist being party to this fraud, for she knew that where Nate Seeger was concerned no good could come.

Finally, after wrassling around with the elephant, Harve managed to get her mouth open, and he stretched his full length to peer inside.

"Shucks, man, I don't see no cavity."

"It's there, Harve, you look harder, you're bound to see it," said Seeger, urging him on.

"No, sir, I don't see it." Harve's voice created a robust echo inside the elephant's mouth. "Nary a cavity in this cavity." He pulled his head out, for it rang from the echo, and Cupid shut her mouth instantly as Harve got down from the Nehi box.

"Well, it's there all the same," Seeger assured him. "And you know how partic'lar Miss Opal is 'bout her elephant here. 'Sides, the appointment's made. If we don't keep it, that dentist'll charge us anyhow. You know how *they* are. So whyn't you just go on and load 'er up?"

Harve pointed to the balloon up in the sky.

"If Miss Opie, she come down from upstairs and she see that elephant ain't here, she gonna be mighty upset."

Nate flashed his palms. "Naw, naw, you don't know Opie. You leave it all to me."

"What's your name, anyways?"

"My name? Why, it's Thomas Jefferson."

Harve scratched his head, then nodded. "Seem like I heard that name somewheres before. I guess you must be a frien' of Opie's all right."

Duly convinced, Harve unchained Cupid and started to lead her to the truck. But Cupid would have none of it. She began to buck, rearing back and tossing her trunk with wild syncopation, trumpeting her distress so loudly that the circus folk stopped their chores and came to see what was happening. When Harve explained that Cupid had an appointment with the dentist, but like all kids she was unhappy about going, the others offered help. Together they pushed and prodded and coaxed, until, finally, they were able to march her up the planks into the truck bed. The wily Seeger and his pal Bendix lost no time in sliding in the tailgate so that Cupid was securely trapped, and her loud, trumpeting protests were in vain.

"Thanks a whole lot," Seeger shouted over Cupid's mournful cries. He saluted the group and hopped into the truck cab, while Bendix slid behind the wheel and started the engine.

"When'll you be bringin' her back, Mr. Jefferson?" Harve called as the truck made a half-circle and started for the road.

Seeger stuck his head out the window and hollered. "When'll I be bringin' her back, you ask? I'll tell you when, you big dumb ape! *Never!* That's when I'll be bringin' her back, and you tell that to your friend Opie-dopey! And Thomas Jefferson, he's the one wrote the blankety-blank Gettysburg Address! Step on 'er, Earle!" he ordered Bendix, who floored the gas pedal, leaving Harve staring openmouthed at the truck's receding tailgate.

Just as Seeger and Bendix reached the entrance to the circus grounds, they met up with another truck coming straight at them. Bendix threw his wheel to the right, and the truck veered over, narrowly missing the oncoming vehicle.

"Why, that dumb female come *that* close to messin' us up!" shouted Seeger, looking back as the driver and her truck bounced around in the road.

"She's a menace behind the wheel of anything that moves," Bendix declared, watching in the rearview mirror.

"It's that nutty dame with the 'lixir! Goldarn it, I wisht we'd of hit her," Seeger said emphatically, and they drove on.

It was indeed Sister Eclipse in the Dented Dragon, but though she was busy trying to keep her wheels on the road, Sister had got a good look at both Seeger and Bendix and had seen the elephant in the back of their vehicle.

"Why, I believe that's Cupid in that truck! Those varmints are making off with her!"

And sure enough, there went the faithful Harve, now the mad-as-a-hornet Harve, waving his hat and hollering Cupid's name as he chased after Seeger's truck. Meanwhile, Sam 'n' Tam Solo, who'd come rushing out of the box office when they heard the commotion, alerted other circus folk, and off they went in one of the show trucks, giving speedy pursuit. Sister Eclipse didn't wait to see more, but turned on a dime and started out after the thieves herself.

Behind her came the troupe of clowns in the big red fire truck they used in their act, and behind them the roustabouts, who stopped long enough to pick up Harve, who had already reached the road. Then Colonel Eddy's Wild West Cowboys took off in a thunderous herd, hollering like a pack of wild Indians (or cowboys, in this case) as they followed the others.

Up hill and down dale the quickly improvised posse raced along the red ribbon of country road, engines clanking, horses whinny-ing, clowns hollering, roustabouts shouting and waving their arms, everyone following the long plume of dry dust that rose in the distance behind the tailgate of the getaway truck. Seeger and Bendix had got a good head start, and besides, their truck was a big Mack with a powerful engine, and that engine was steadily pulling them and the kidnapped Cupid ahead of the posse.

Up in Buddy Pepper's balloon all was serene and quiet. *What a thrilling thing to do on my birthday,* Opal thought, as they rose like a soft cloud, hearing nothing but the sigh of the wind and the creaking of the waxed lines, watching everything grow smaller and smaller beneath them. Her single regret was that she couldn't share the glorious experience with Cupid. But when she came down again she'd certainly tell her all about it.

Scanning the landscape below, Opal saw the familiar sites take on a whole new appearance. The farmers' fields in the neighboring countryside, so limitless from the ground, now looked like a broad patchwork quilt. What could be more peaceful looking, Opal thought, than this toy world, the pretty little villages dotting the landscape, with their white church steeples, red barns, and silos, which looked so minuscule. The herds of cows gathered around the ponds, the people hurrying about, why they were less than ants, practically invisible.

Gazing back at the circus grounds, where by now the tents and vehicles were so small she had to squint to make them out, something caught Opal's eye. She asked to borrow Buddy's brass telescope, and as she put the lens to her eye it all came into focus—Harve Poplin wasn't sudsing Cupid anymore; he was shoving her into the back of a truck!

"Why . . . why . . ." Opal was nearly speechless with shock and outrage.

"What is it, honey?" asked Banjo. The now wordless Opal handed over the telescope and pointed down to the ground. Banjo took a look and let out a yowl.

"Why, that's that hound dog, Seeger, down there, and he's makin' off with Cupid!" Banjo was mad as a wet hen. He gave Buddy a look through the lens and went on fuming. "That dad-blasted Seeger, I'll bet he was just waitin' for us to take off so's he could drive up and make right off with Opal's elephant."

Opal agreed. "He said he'd get her. He just was waiting for his moment."

Betty anxiously clutched a rope and jumped up and down, pleading with Buddy to do something.

But how to do something when you were high up in a balloon and somebody was kidnapping an elephant down on the ground was a tricky proposition. There were only so many things you could do in a balloon, and preventing the theft of an elephant was not one of them. But they could give pursuit, Buddy added, just as Sister and the circus folk were now doing.

"Move along, Big Bug!" Banjo hollered, as if Sister could hear him from the Dented Dragon. "Go git that varmint!"

"Never fear! We'll catch them!" Buddy shouted. "We'll chase them all the way to Timbuktu if we have to!"

The wind was with them and on they sailed, following the route of Seeger's truck, the Dented Dragon, and the parade of other vehicles and horseback riders continuing their mad chase, not catching up with the kidnappers, but not losing sight of them, either. By his clever manipulation of the pressure valves, Buddy was able to lower the balloon, and he used his telescope again for a closer look at the getaway Mack truck ahead of them. As he watched, the door on the passenger side of the truck swung open and a man got out and stood on the running board.

"It's Seeger," Buddy shouted, "and he's got a shotgun, by golly!"

With his feet planted wide on the running board, Seeger had shoved his hat brim back, and was squinting along the sights of a double-barreled shotgun. It was the same gun that had once been pointed at Cupid's head, only now it was pointed straight at the balloon!

"He's fixing to shoot us down!" Opal cried out in alarm.

"He surely is!" thundered Banjo. "He's fixin' to shoot us outta the sky like a flock of pigeons."

"Pigeons, hah!" crowed Buddy defiantly. He tossed a stout line around a pin, then yanked the cap on a valve, and the balloon sprang upward as if it were on a rubber band. But even as it climbed, the occupants of the basket made out two puffs of white smoke blossoming like cotton balls at the end of Seeger's gun barrel. Two reports echoed and there was a loud pop overhead, followed by a hissing sound as a sinister hole appeared in the skin of Buddy's balloon.

"Jumpin' Jehosophat, we's been hit!" shouted Banjo, while Betty clung to a line and, trying to remain calm, sized up the situation.

"Banjo's right, Buddy," she reported, looking up at the balloon. "It's quite a large hole. What do you think we ought to do?"

"Let's have a look." Buddy quickly leapt into the rigging, and, climbing as high as he could, investigated the damage more closely. Betty was right, the tear was a serious one, and with every second the balloon was growing saggier and baggier as more and more hot air escaped. And without any hot air to keep it aloft, there could be only one result: The balloon would crash to the ground, carrying its load of passengers with it.

Opal and the others clung to the ropes breathlessly as the basket started plummeting toward the earth, drifting in the wind closer to Seeger's truck as if they might even crash right into it. And Cupid still inside! It was a terrifying feeling, and what to do? Suddenly it didn't seem so much fun to be carried by the idle whim of a bag filled with hot air and no visible means of support. But Buddy Pepper was not the sort of fellow to stand idly by while disaster overtook him, and his family of friends were waiting to be saved.

"Quick, everybody!" he shouted, taking command as the senior officer of a troubled vessel should. "Jettison all ballast!"

Everyone unhooked a sandbag and dropped it over the side. The bags fell like lead weights to the ground, some of them almost but not quite managing to strike Nate Seeger's truck.

"Careful, you'll hit Cupid!" Opal cried as the basket floated closer to earth. Hearing the cries from the back of the truck, Cupid looked up at the sky and was thrown into a state of panic. Though she was fettered by stout chains and hawsers, she began to pull and strain at her bonds, determined to break free. So violent, in fact, were her movements that the truck was in danger of being overturned, and Bendix, a maniac behind the wheel, had considerable difficulty maintaining control over his vehicle.

The only part of Cupid's anatomy that had not been secured, her trunk, was being flung wildly about, and her pitiful cries shattered the air. Never had she trumpeted so loudly, letting Opal know she was aware of the danger she was in and would help out if only she could find a way.

The balloon, however, freed of its ballast, began rising again, despite its puncture wound, and as it floated upward, Opal watched with a sinking heart as Seeger's truck receded into the distance. With the Dented Dragon and the circus posse steadily losing ground, it seemed that unless there was a miracle she might never see her friend again.

Buffetted by the wind, the balloon drifted limply off over a farmer's meadow, casting a large shadow across the landscape, which seemed now to be rising up to meet them as they began to fall again. Lower and lower the balloon dropped as more air

166

escaped its silken envelope, until, with a mighty *splash!* the basket hit the limpid surface of a cow pond, followed by the large, by now airless, balloon which, like a big striped circus tent, billowed, then settled gently around them.

Instead of sinking, however, the wicker basket remained afloat, with all its passengers safely intact, while the balloon itself sank into the water and disappeared from sight.

"We is surely gonna sink next," Banjo moaned, "and I can't swim a lick."

"That's all right, I'll look after you," said the resolute Betty, as the water began to seep into the basket. "I'm a good swimmer—Buddy, as well."

"And you can count on me and Pickles, too," Opal added reassuringly.

With these words Banjo took heart, and he helped the others as they leaned way over the side of the basket and paddled with their hands toward the shore of the small pond. It wasn't very long before they grazed bottom and Buddy quickly lifted the two females and carried them to safe ground, while Banjo, clutching Pickles in his arms, came wading behind them. Once safely ashore, he knelt and kissed the ground, then Pickles, declaring his gratitude, first for having the good fortune to fall on a farmer's pond instead of Mother Earth, and then for not having sunk to the bottom and drowned.

All in all, except for the food that Betty had thoughtfully brought along, all now soggy and inedible (including Opal's birthday cake), they had ended up with only a damaged ballon. Who knew what amount of time and trouble would be needed to repair it. But at least they were all safe and sound, with no broken bones, and that was more than enough to be thankful for.

After talking over matters, it was decided that Buddy and Betty must stay with their injured balloon, while Banjo and Opal carried on with the most important mission, which was to get to town as quickly as possible in the hope that the trail of the kidnappers would not be cold.

The sun was setting behind pink and gold clouds in the west, and the land was darkening as the friends said good-bye. Buddy and Betty remained to guard their property; they would all meet up later in Countytown, where they'd get the law on their side. Banjo, Opal, and Pickles stood on the highway shoulder where Banjo stuck out his trusty thumb. It wasn't entirely their unlucky day, for soon they were able to hitch a ride on a farmer's hay-wagon, and so in this comfortable manner they made their way along the same road Nate Seeger and his contraband had taken an hour before. And if anyone had looked, he would have seen fire in Opal's eyes, enough to set fire to any plans Nate Seeger had for her stolen elephant.

Chapter Fifteen

In the Toils of the Law

FOR ALL THAT THEY MIGHT HAVE SUFFERED, A FATAL accident in Buddy Pepper's hot-air balloon, the trip to County-town proved a pleasant interlude as they rolled in comfort along green shaded roads—Opal loved the smell of fresh-cut hay—and it wasn't very long before they arrived at the town square in front of the courthouse. Opal recognized the imposing bronze statue of Major General Bolivar Wilson Pickett Primrose, the Colonel's famous great-grandfather, which graced the square. She noted that the Major General's plumed hat and gilded epaulets had become a local hangout for a flock of pigeons, whose drop-pings had turned the poor man's head and shoulders chalk white.

Banjo had just helped Opal down from the farmer's wagon and she was pulling stray wisps of hay from her skirt, when suddenly her heart quailed. She was staring head-on at a living reminder of the Primroses: the Rolls-Royce, with Jekyll in his olive-drab livery, bending down to inspect a bad dent in the left front fender.

But where were the Primroses? And what were they doing in Countytown?

"Whoo-ee," said Banjo, "I wonder who hit Miss 'Gusta's car? I bet she gave him Hail Columbia for that dent."

Pickles evidently agreed, because she trotted right up to the chauffeur and began yapping noisily and snapping at his leg. Jekyll took one look at the dog, another at the dog's master, then hotfooted it inside the hotel, reappearing momentarily with his mistress and the Colonel and followed by Miss Blossom, who was the only one to exhibit pleasure at the sight of the errant Opal Thigpen.

"*There* you are, you naughty truant," exclaimed Augusta, shaking her gloved finger under Opal's nose. "What have you to say for yourself?" she demanded.

Even Blossom wore an anxious expression, and Opal could think of nothing to say, so she simply kept silent. Not so Banjo, however, who jutted out his jaw and spoke right up. "You don't have no call to go namin' no one some naughty truant when she ain't been naughty."

"Not naughty? To run away and worry us sick unto death, wondering if the girl hadn't fallen among brigands or thieves? Which appears to be precisely the case. Why, you're that dreadful show-business person," sniffed Augusta, now eyeing Banjo with haughty disdain. "A thoroughly disreputable character, if I do say so. Goodson," she said, turning to address her husband. "Goodson, what have you to say in this matter?"

"Eh? Why, uh, quite right, my dear," Goodson agreed. "Thoroughly disreputable. One might even say reprehensible." It was then brought out that the Primroses had booked into a suite at the Dixie Hotel overnight for the reason that the Colonel was meeting with the state highway commission regarding the new road that was to run through Peavine Hollow (which was why Granny Bid's little house would be torn down).

As friendly as ever to Opal's cause, Miss Blossom made a soft cooing sound. "Oh, I wouldn't call Mr. Bailey *that.* How are you, Mr. Bailey?" she inquired. "It's nice to see you again."

"Well as kin be expected when a man has been dispossessed of his rightful property," Banjo confessed glumly.

"Really? Robbed, do you mean?"

"That's 'zackly what I mean. This young lady done had her elephant stolen right out from under her!"

"Goodness, was she riding it?"

"No, she was riding the balloon, the kidnappers was down below. Now they've run off with Cupid the Lord only knows where. I aim to get 'em jailed."

"Rubbish!" boomed Augusta. "She has no legal right to that elephant. Her trainer, Mr. Seeger—such a kindhearted individual—was merely taking what is rightfully his, and good riddance say I."

Banjo cocked a suspicious eye at Augusta. "How's come you know it was that varlet Nate Seeger who done run off wid Opal's elephant?"

"Not that it is any of *your* affair, but I shall enlighten you anyway. The fact is, our vehicles collided on the square, his Mack truck, our Rolls-Royce. May I say it was our auto that caught the brunt of the collision, the truck wasn't even scratched. However, being aware of our good connections, the worthy Mr. Seeger was at pains to make quite satisfactory reparation, thank you, *and* to inform us of how you bilked him out of his property."

"*Bilked* him?" The outraged Banjo was sputtering everywhere. "Are you sayin' we'uns stole that elephant from him?"

"I am indeed. You exchanged a fake gold watch for the beast.

And if there is any justice in the world, you shall go to jail for your thievery."

Banjo chuckled wryly. "Well, I guess we're safe there, all right. Since there ain't no justice nowhere in the world, I reckon we'll keep free of jail."

Miss Augusta pushed her nose into the air. "You should have thought of that before you allowed this misguided child to run off with another man's property."

"But that's not true, Augusta!" Blossom exclaimed, in an uncommon show of spunk. "That man didn't want Cupid. He was going to shoot her! He had a shotgun to Cupid's head. Isn't that so, Opal?"

Opal nodded eagerly. "He told me to take Cupid and never bring her back again. He even signed a paper. And now . . . and now . . ." She burst into tears, and the sound of her distress urged Banjo on.

"Now see whatcha gone 'n' done, making the poor li'l bug cry."

Augusta was her most prideful. "I may tell *you*, Mr. Bailey, I have seen a child cry before. It is nothing new to me, I promise you. It would be far better if those were tears of repentance," she added, with another sniff and a reproachful glance at Opal. "Just look at the girl, she appears to have been lolling in a haystack. You come along with us, now, Opal Thigpen. We'll put you in a decent frock and send you along to Mrs. Vermilyea and see if she can't yet do something with you."

"Oh, please—don't make me," Opal pleaded. "I can't leave. Banjo, help me."

Banjo and Augusta both made a hasty grab for Opal. Augusta pulled in one direction, Banjo tugged in the other, and Opal felt herself stretched to her limits in the middle. As a crowd of rubberneckers gathered around the fracas, Goodson decided it was time to step in. Banjo, who was resolved not to let go of Opal, stuck out his foot and tripped the Colonel, sending him sprawling on the sidewalk in his good Sunday suit, his landing cushioned somewhat by his panama hat.

Meanwhile, Augusta, impervious to the pleadings of Miss Blossom, had dispatched Jekyll for the sheriff, and in due course he appeared, hot and sweating, his tin badge glinting on his chest and his trusty .45 occupying room on his hip.

"What seems to be the trouble here?" he demanded.

"Sheriff Bledsoe," Augusta began, "I am Augusta Primrose, and this"—pointing at the somewhat disheveled Colonel—"is my husband, Colonel Goodson Primrose. And *that*"—pointing at the statue in the square—"is our ancestor, General Pickett Primrose."

The sheriff whipped off his hat and used his shirt cuff to further brighten up his five-pointed badge. "What kin I do fer you folks?" he asked solicitously.

Augusta now pointed at Banjo. "We wish this man charged with felonious assault and locked up where he can do no further harm."

"*And*," added the blustering Colonel Primrose, "we wish a front-page story released to all the news periodicals stating the true facts in this case, that my wife and I have been wrongfully attacked, that my glasses have been broken and my good panama hat sat upon!"

Everyone knew there was only one newspaper, the *Peavine Daily Clarion*, and that since a Primrose relation was the managing editor, the likelihood of the "true facts" seeing print seemed slim at best.

"But what's going to happen to Banjo?" Opal wanted to know.

"What is going to happen to him?" replied Augusta. "I shall tell you. He will be tried and convicted and sent to work on the chain gang, which is a just and fitting punishment. Breaking rocks helps build character. I read it in the *Reader's Digest*."

"The chain gang!" Opal's heart froze at the thought of poor

Banjo swinging a sledgehammer on a rock pile. And in stripes!

"Here now, m'man, no need for any rough stuff," said Banjo as the sheriff's deputy tried to hustle him through the crowd that had gathered. "I'll go quietly." He called over his shoulder as he was marched off to jail. "Opie, look after Pickles, y'hear?"

Pickles!

Where was she? Opal hadn't seen her since she'd tried to bite Jekyll's leg.

Augusta and the Colonel charged Miss Blossom to keep an eye on "that girl," then marched back into the hotel, and as the two set about looking for Pickles, Opal quickly filled Miss Blossom in on life along the Sawdust Trail until Nate Seeger showed up, then asked if anything had been heard from Daddy up in New York. Miss Blossom reported that there had been no reply as yet, but that she was sure her daddy's postal card—if not Daddy himself—was on its way.

Somewhat consoled by this, Opal agreed that their most important mission now was to find Pickles and then try to figure out how to get Banjo released from jail.

"Gracious, what a situation," Miss Blossom said, looking around, then calling after the little dog. "Here, Pickles, here, Pickles. Pickles!" She called so loudly that some people thought she was a pickle vendor and tried to buy some dills from her.

Just then, who should appear but Sister Eclipse, behind the wheel of the Dented Dragon. Having left the mounted posse to help Buddy and Betty retrieve their drowned balloon, Eclipse had continued on to Countytown, hoping she might stray across Seeger's truck and its stolen cargo. As ever, Eclipse was pretty good with her hunches. She was greatly put out to learn that, thanks to the Primroses, her Banjo was being put behind bars, and that Augusta and the Colonel had sided with that "no-'count crook" Seeger and his confederate.

"Justice is blind!" Sister went on, quoting in her loud, deep voice. "But by Jove here's one lady's goin' to take off that blindfold or know the reason why! Where's that meddlin' fool, 'Gusta? An' where's that dimplin' boob she's hitched to? Lemme at 'em, by golly. I'll give 'em justice, I will."

Sister was already rolling up her sleeves, spoiling for a fight. Blossom suggested she calm herself and help out in the search for Banjo's dog.

On the other side of the square, Opal continued to call and look, for at all costs the dog must not be lost; it was quite sufficient to be missing both a banjo player and an animal seven feet tall.

Despite their efforts, it was Pickles who found them, reappearing out of nowhere, her eyes bright with knowledge, her pink tongue hanging out. She began prancing on her hind legs and waving her front paws, just as she had when she first met Opal along the Old Cotton Road. But there was a difference: Now she would prance around some, run off a ways, then come running back, barking furiously as she did her little dance again.

"What is it, Pickles?" asked Miss Blossom. "Why, I believe she's trying to tell us something."

Opal stooped to pet and stroke the little dog's ears. "I think she wants us to follow her," she said. "In fact, I'm sure of it!" Then, as the dog dashed off again, Opal grabbed Miss Blossom's hand, and they all jumped into the Dented Dragon, which clattered off down the street.

With Pickles guiding them, the truck chugged up one street and down the next, to the point that Opal began to wonder if Pickles hadn't lost her mind and was leading them on a wild goose chase. Yet, so persistent was the animal that Opal felt sure an answer would soon appear. And very soon it did.

At the end of a dark street in a deserted part of town, Pickles came to the end of her journey in front of a low, grim-looking building with a sign reading: THE ACME AUTO REPAIR GARAGE.

Sister Eclipse was speeding along at a good clip as they came down the street, and when she put her foot on the brake pedal she hit the gas pedal instead. In consequence of this the truck rushed on, and rather than stopping, it crashed right through the front of the building. The noise was deafening and they all covered their ears from the sound of falling bricks and mortar. Pickles, who'd had to move fast to make way for the truck, trotted over to Sister Eclipse and gave her a reproachful look.

"Accidents *will* happen!" Eclipse declared, prying herself from the truck and adjusting her hat, which had slipped over one eye.

As they all looked around the dim and dusty garage, they wondered why Pickles had brought them here of all places. There was nothing they could do just then about the Dented Dragon— though it was handy that they'd landed in an auto repair shop— so they decided to explore a bit.

There must be some reason Pickles had led them here to this deserted place, Opal thought. Only one bare light bulb glowed in the cavernous room, and, holding each other by the hand, she, Sister, and Miss Blossom peered about in the gloom, looking for Pickles, who had disappeared again. What had become of her this time? By now it seemed apparent that this was where the kidnapped Cupid had been hidden away by Nate Seeger. It certainly was a big enough hideout for her. With this in mind, they began looking everywhere they could think of for the elephant. Once they thought they spotted her, a dark hulking shape tucked away in a corner, but it turned out to be only an old wreck of an oil truck.

Just then Pickles reappeared, and by her clever signals she hurried the rescuers from the front part of the building clear to the rear. And there they found Cupid! Oh, but what a cruel, pitiful sight. The poor creature had been chained by each of her legs to the steel tracks of the hydraulic autocar lift, and there she stood, twelve feet in the air, peering down at them with a frightened, doleful expression on her face. The minute she saw Opal in the doorway she began to whimper, waving her trunk weakly, and striving against her chains.

"Oh Cupid, honey, what have those nasty men done to you?" cried Opal. The sight was enough to break her heart. "Quickly, we must get her down."

"Never fear," declared Miss Blossom, "we'll soon have her free."

"How we gonna bust them chains?" Sister Eclipse asked. "They's fit to hold down a World War tank."

Once again, Miss Blossom proved her mettle, thin and fluttery spinster though she was. Quickly she located the electrical switch that operated the hydraulic lift. Set in motion, the apparatus smoothly lowered Cupid to floor level again; such a joyful look of relief flooded into the elephant's eyes and her trunk slipped trembling around Opal's waist. She lifted her up and hugged her close to her body. Oh, thought Opal, how good it felt, how wonderful to have her elephant restored to her and safe once more.

But no—not safe yet, for there was still the matter of the chains. Sister was right: The links were thick and strong, and there were padlocks on them and no keys in sight. Miss Blossom found a hammer and cold chisel and she and Sister Eclipse took turns trying to smash the chains, but they held fast. No amount of human endeavor, it seemed, was going to sunder Cupid's bonds, and the tools were abandoned in frustration.

"I guess it's up to you, Cupid," Opal said into the elephant's ear. Cupid flapped her ears and looked at Opal as if to say, "Are you crazy? Me bust those chains?"

"You can do it," Opal said firmly. "I know you can. Just make up your mind to it. Just say 'I can do it' and you will. Because you can if you think you can. That's how it's been since time began. No, don't give me that woebegone look of yours, you just give a good yank and then we'll see what happens."

So Cupid stiffened her legs and pulled back as hard as she could. She strained and strained, but nothing happened.

"It's no use," said Miss Blossom. "The chains are too thick and strong."

"No, I'm sure she can do it," Opal declared firmly. "I know she can. *Think*, Cupid, use all your brute strength and force, but use your brain, too. Elephants have very keen brains. Yours is particularly superior. Think positively and it will happen. It's the only way you'll ever get free. Otherwise we won't be able to help you, and you'll be stuck here. And when that mean old Nate Seeger comes back, he'll take you away someplace, and we'll never see each other again."

Opal was weeping, and Cupid used the tip of her trunk to wipe away her tears. Then a strange thing happened, glorious to see. The elephant's face took on a tight, frozen expression, her eyes grew wide, and her whole body seemed to expand with energy and purpose. Her four legs locked as she strained with all her might and main, and then the chains began to pop, first one, then the next was torn asunder against the enormous force being applied to them. But it wasn't just pure physical power; Cupid was "thinking it," too, you could see in her intent, resolute expression how hard she was thinking. "I can do it, I can do it, I-I-I can do-o-o it-t-t-t!" Opal was so proud of her she was beaming.

Then—*pop! pop! pop!* and *ping!*—the work was done. Cupid was free at last, and she hobbled awkwardly off the hydraulic lift, for her exertions had made her ankles sore. But, oh, what a wonderful feeling! She waved her trunk ecstatically and in a single spectacular movement wound it around Opal's waist and carried her up to

178

the place where she always sat. Then, rapturously tossing her head and opening her mouth, she let out an earth-shattering roar of triumph and joy.

Now they moved quickly. Making their way out of the garage to the curb where they stood under the streetlight—it had grown full dark while they were inside. They planned what their next move was to be. The Dented Dragon had given up the ghost; its motor simply refused to turn over again, so, leaving a note for the garage owners (the fair thing to do in such a case), they decided that the best plan was to make their way together back to the town square. But no, something was wrong!

"Wait up, folks!" cried Eclipse. "We done forgot Banjo! We got to get him outta that jail 'fore they sends him off t'the chain gang in stripey pajamas!"

"Gracious me!" exclaimed Miss Blossom. "Sister is absolutely right. We must hurry at once to the jail and see what can be done to free Banjo. Let's find a taxi." She started out the door, but hadn't got more than three steps when she felt Cupid's trunk encircle her waist and she too was lifted from the ground onto the elephant's back.

"Goodness," tittered Miss Blossom, as she settled into place behind Opal and put her arms around her waist. "I always wanted to do this when I watched you children at play." She smiled happily at Opal, who now sat with Pickles clutched in her arms. Next to be picked up was Sister Eclipse, whose width and weight had no effect on Cupid's considerable powers. Then, when all three females and Pickles were safely stowed up top in this peculiar but practical manner, with no other mode of transportation required, they hurried down the dark street.

By the sheerest good fortune they managed to attract no undue attention as they made their way to the jail. They did not go directly up to the main entrance, however, but crept by stealth

179

through an alley filled with banged-up trash cans and piles of rubbish, moving along a red brick wall and peering into each of the iron-barred windows of the building.

"Banjo—where are you? Banjo?" Opal called out in her best stage whisper. No answer came, until the very last window, where they heard a feeble reply.

"Opie? That you, honey?"

It was Banjo, all right.

"It's us. Sister Eclipse and Cousin Blossom are here, too. And Cupid. We've come to get you out," Opal whispered. She peered through the iron bars to find her friend much the worse for wear. He had a nasty bump on his head where the jailer had given him a mean rap with his nightstick.

"We is gonna get you out of there fast as ever we can," said Sister Eclipse. Sister made a fist and gave the brick wall a hefty sock, as though to test its strength. A jail is supposed to be sound, but not all of them are. Still, the wall failed to give. Opal darted a knowing look to her elephant, who nodded gravely, then frowned as she gathered her mental and physical powers again for the coming onslaught.

She knew what to do. She took the tip of her trunk and wrapped it around one of the bars and began to pull. As Eclipse had suspected, the building was an old one, the bricks and mortar crumbling, and shortly the bar began to loosen. The second bar was easier to budge, the third easier yet and before long Banjo was crawling through the opening Cupid had made. He had not got very far, however, when he got stuck, his hips wedged both right and left, and could go no farther.

So Cupid went to work again. She inserted her trunk between Banjo and the stonework, and by twisting and turning it like a drill she enlarged the hole. Then she seized Banjo hard around the chest and began to pull. She pulled and she pulled until, with a noisy crack, the entire wall gave way, loosened bricks falling into the alley in a heap, dust rising all around, while the newly dislodged Banjo dangled in midair. It was, Opal decided, rather like a tooth extraction without the dentist.

"C'mon, quickly now!" urged Sister Eclipse as Cupid set Banjo on his feet and he shook the plaster off his clothes.

"Yes," said Miss Blossom, "there's not a moment to be lost."

In no time at all Banjo had joined the three ladies seated on Cupid's back, taking Pickles onto his lap and exercising care not to let her fall off, and with this oddly assorted quartet hanging on for dear life, the elephant, taking long, resolute steps, lumbered away toward the center of town.

Chapter Sixteen

A Fire and a Rescue!

AS THEY HURRIED ALONG THE DARKENED STREETS aboard the elephant, they could feel Cupid's entire body trembling with anticipation. She was sensing something that she alone could feel but couldn't see, and Opal knew it didn't bode well. Then, as they neared the town square again, the source of Cupid's fear became more apparent. The rising wail of a siren could now be heard, and as they proceeded farther up the street a large crowd of people could be seen hurrying frantically toward the center of town. And so caught up were they in their frenzy that no one took any notice of the exotic jungle beast pushing its way among them with three females, plus Banjo and Pickles, astride its back. Why, it wasn't every day you came across an elephant strolling the streets of Countytown!

Then Opal saw it, the cause of all the excitement: the ugly red wash in the sky, bleeding across the undersides of the clouds, turning them an ominous crimson color. A fire! And a good-sized one at that, judging from the tips of the flames that leapt hungrily up against the night sky.

"Holy maloley," cried Banjo. "What d'ya s'pose could be burning like that?"

As if impelled by some inner voice, Cupid lengthened her pace, moving as fast as Opal had ever seen her move, striding with nimble feet toward the scene of the blaze.

Up ahead the park was jam-packed with excited people. Half a dozen boys had climbed the statue of General Primrose for a handier view, and vehicles were parked at various angles on the street and all over the square's large green lawn. Due to the seething crowd, the fire trucks, sirens blaring, were forced to slow down as they arrived at their destination: the Dixie Hotel, which was going up in flames!

"Oh, horrors!" cried Miss Blossom, peering around in all directions as they reached the scene of the fire. "What an inferno. I certainly hope Augusta and Goodson aren't still inside!"

From their vantage point atop Cupid's back, they had a good view of all the turmoil and the drama unfolding around them. The hardworking firemen in their crested, wide-brimmed steel hats were running out their canvas hoses and connecting them to the nearby hydrants. Others were hauling sets of ladders and leaning them against the walls, and already handfuls of brave men were scaling the extensions trying to reach the upper stories, where hotel guests huddled at the windows, screaming in terror and shouting for help.

Meanwhile, still other fire fighters were on the run, carrying big round safety nets for those trapped guests to jump into. And supervising all this activity was the stalwart chief himself. Wearing a dark rubber slicker, Fred Fitzgerald shouted orders through a large brass megaphone, his grizzled features half-hidden under his hat, his badge proclaiming FIRE CHIEF—COM-PANY 3 for all to see.

"Men, move that crowd back before someone gets hurt!" Fred commanded. "Number one net, hold 'er steady!" High above, a woman screamed in fright, then jumped out of her window. A hearty cheer went up as she dropped into the safety ring and was helped gently to her feet.

Still astride Cupid's back, Opal, Miss Blossom, and Banjo, hugging tight to Eclipse, watched helplessly. Like bright silken banners, orange flames poured through the windows of the hotel, and blinding clouds of smoke billowed forth. Surely those trapped on the middle floors were in serious danger of losing their lives.

"Hey, you'd better get that elephant out of the way," called Fred the fire chief, and Cupid didn't have to wait to be told twice—she knew when she was blocking a fire truck.

Just then, pushing his way through the crowd, a disheveled and fearful sight appeared: Colonel Primrose, his eyes frantically swiveling in his head, his hair sticking out in all directions.

"Cousin Blossie, thank goodness I've found you!" he shouted above the tumult. "Are you all right?"

"Yes, we're all fine."

"What the devil are you doing up on that elephant?" he demanded, as if forgetting there was a fire going on.

"Never mind, Goodson, there's no time to explain. Where is Augusta?"

"I don't know," the Colonel wailed. "I came downstairs to buy some cigars at the hotel smoke shop, and suddenly the fire broke out. I haven't seen her and I'm terribly worried."

Of course he was, the poor man! Losing your composure was one thing; quite another to lose your spouse in the middle of a conflagration like this one. Who could tell what might have happened to poor Augusta?

Miss Blossom's face paled. "You don't mean to say she's still inside! In the fire?"

The Colonel's features crumpled and he looked as woebegone as any man ever did.

"I really don't know," he confessed helplessly. "I've looked and looked. If she is . . ."

He didn't finish his sentence, but everyone knew what he meant. Their rooms were up there on the burning floor; if trapped there Miss Augusta would surely suffer a terrible fate, and though terrified guests were dashing pell-mell from the hotel in their nightclothes, it was plain to see that none of them was Augusta Primrose.

"Look!" shouted Banjo, pointing toward the alley at the side of the building. A crowd of frightened people in their pajamas and bathrobes was huddled on the fire escape, hemmed in by spitting flames and unable to make it down because the badly rusted escape ladder was discombobulated and refused to function properly. Straining to see, Opal thought she could make out a familiar face among them. Was it—could it be—yes! One of the women there on the fire escape was Augusta Primrose!

"Miss 'Gusta!" Opal called, waving her arms, but the frantic woman didn't hear her. "Miss 'Gusta, over here!" Opal called again, but it was no use. In the din and confusion Opal's calls and signals were lost. There was only one thing to do.

Assessing the dangerous situation, she leaned over and whispered into Cupid's ear. The elephant listened with a charged expression, then, giving her head an affirmative nod, she bent one knee and deposited Opal and her friends safely onto the ground. Saving precious time, she headed off in an instant toward the alley, where the first thing she did was stop at the rain barrel at the corner of the blazing building to fill up her trunk with as much water as she could carry. Then, approaching the hotel, she pointed her trunk toward the flames that threatened to engulf the unfortunate souls quivering with fear on the fire escape, and sprayed with all her might. When her trunk was empty she hurried back to the barrel for a refill, then another, employing it like a regular fire hose.

With the flames in the area sufficiently quenched, and the terrified crowd calmed a bit, Cupid went to work with a will, standing on her hind legs and extending her trunk up toward the landing of the fire escape. Her supple appendage wreathed a waist, gathered a desperately waiting form into the air, and amid all the screams and cheers, one by one, silently, carefully, and methodically, she transported the frightened victims down to the alleyway and to safety.

Then it was Augusta Primrose's turn. Trembling with gratitude and relief, she set her feet on "terra cotta," and the Colonel rushed to his wife's side and wrapped her in his comforting arms.

Another woman rescued by Cupid threw her arms around the animal's big gray trunk and kissed it many times. "Oh, merciful heavens, thank you, Mr. Elephant!" cried the distracted woman, her hair half done up in rag curlers. Banjo, standing by helping out, had a laugh.

"That ain't no 'mister,' lady," he said. "That there's a *miss*."

"Well, whatever," said the woman. "I must certainly look a fright," she added, tugging the curlers from her hair, while another woman rushed up to Cupid and planted a grateful kiss on her savior's leathery cheek.

As Cupid carried the last hotel guest to safety, her bravery did not write an end to the story of the fire. Cheers turned to groans as yet another figure appeared out of the smoke on the useless

186

fire escape—a young woman, and clutched in her arms, an infant! Unfortunately, it was at this very moment that the iron staircase began to give way. The weight of so many people having taken its toll, the structure had pulled away from the masonry and, with the woman and her baby still aboard, swung dangerously above the alley.

Everyone stared, horror-struck, as she bravely made her way down the rickety stairs, clutching her infant to her bosom with one hand, gripping the rail with the other.

With each downward faltering step she took, the structure pulled farther away from the wall of the building until the bolts tore free, causing the entire staircase to swing out into the air and threatening to pitch the terrified mother and child down into the alleyway. Opal's heart went out to the poor woman, whose ashen face and wide eyes expressed such terror, and to the innocent babe, whose furious squalls could be heard above the tumult.

"Somebody save my baby!" cried the imperiled mother as the fire escape began to pitch and sway violently, and again it was Cupid who came to the rescue. Positioning herself under the swaying iron staircase, she stood on her hind legs once more and stretched her trunk to its utmost length. Ever so gently she lifted the child in its blanket out of the mother's arms, then, curling her trunk downward, she placed the baby in her mouth.

"Hey, that critter done et that baby!" shouted a red-faced man in the crowd. "She done swallered it whole! That elephant ain't nuthin' but a big ol' cannibal!"

"Not so, m'good man," said Banjo, hastening to reassure him. "There ain't no cannibals in these parts. I guarantee that baby's sound as the day it was born."

Which was perfectly true, because they all could see how lightly and gently Cupid held the baby between her lips. Already the trunk was wafting upward again, this time to girdle the mother's waist and lift her free from the swinging stairs. And not a moment too soon, for the instant Cupid carried her off, the fire escape tore loose altogether and tumbled toward the alley.

"Look out! Here she comes!" shouted the crowd, and with that the entire twisted iron structure came crashing to the pavement, missing the courageous elephant by inches.

Now, having backed away to a safer position, Cupid wheeled with both mother and child, while the crowd scattered with cries of alarm. "Quick, folks, run for your lives!" shouted a man in the crowd. "Afore you all gets tromped on by that big old hairy beast."

Once again Banjo came to Cupid's defense. "Here, here, m'man," he cautioned, "don't go calling her 'hairy,' she's a lady, that elephant. And lemme tell you, ain't no one goin' t'be tromped on by *that* elephant. That's a very sensitive animal. She only tromps when the trompin's called for."

Hearing these words, Cupid slipped Banjo an appreciative look as she set the distraught mother onto the pavement and carefully placed the baby in her arms.

"Oh, how can I ever repay you?" the woman cried. "Thank you, thank you, thank you!"

Though these expressions of gratitude were warm and heartfelt, they obviously embarrassed Cupid, whose cheeks blushed with modesty, not an easy feat for an elephant.

There was ample cause for rejoicing in that part of the square, and three cheers went up for Cupid. Not only had the mother and child been saved from the flames along with a dozen other hotel guests, but Augusta Primrose had been returned to the Colonel in near perfect condition. Elsewhere, ignorant of the sensational heroics that had taken place in the alley, the city firemen had done their jobs well and had put out the flames. The two middle floors of the hotel had been pretty well burned out, and from the scorched and charred window frames Opal could tell that a considerable amount of damage had been done.

But because Fire Chief Fred Fitzgerald was an intrepid fellow and a man of great merit—and thanks to Cupid's rescue efforts— not a single human being had suffered major injury. Doffing his wet gear and removing his heavy steel hat, Fred used his red bandanna to wipe away the sweat that bathed his brow, glad that all had ended well. Colonel Primrose and Miss Blossom had taken the tired and spent Augusta over to the statue of his illustrious forebear, where they sat down on a bench, drinking the hot cocoa that Miss Blossom had thoughtfully fetched for them, and together they talked about how lucky they were to have escaped with their lives.

Not long afterward, rescuers and refugees found themselves all together again, being put up for the night at the Wishing Well Motel out on the main road, where they had baths and fresh beds and downy pillows on which to rest their weary heads, and where Cupid would sleep on a bed of fresh straw in the owners' garage. Everyone was there: the Primroses, Miss Blossom, Banjo and Sister Eclipse, Pickles; even Buddy and Betty had shown up, their balloon already in the repair shop, to be ready for the next show.

Before Opal went to say good night to Cupid, there was a knock on the door of the room she was sharing with Miss Blossom. When she opened it she was surprised at the sight of all her friends gathered outside in the motor court. There were new friends, too, like Fred Fitzgerald and his team of firemen, and they were all singing "Happy Birthday!" to her.

"Better late than never," Banjo added when the chorus ended, and everyone laughed and agreed that while it had not been the most conventional of birthdays, it certainly had been an eventful and interesting one.

And best of all was Opal's birthday present, for behind all her friends stood Cupid, safe and sound, her head lowered shyly, though Opal could tell she was pleased about something and she immediately saw the reason why. Around Cupid's neck hung a large red ribbon with a big shiny gold medal for bravery hanging from it, an honor that Fred Fitzgerald and his boys had stopped by to award her with for a job well done. And there were three more cheers for Cupid before Opal took her off to bed and everyone retired for a much needed rest.

To be sure, after saying her prayers, Opal slept long and well that night, and she dreamed dreams that were soon to come true.

Chapter Seventeen

The Grand Tour

A NEW DAWN BROUGHT CHANGES OF VARYING SORTS, all of them beneficial to Opal and her friends. Before Jekyll drove the Rolls around to carry his master and mistress back to Peavine, both Augusta and the Colonel had one or two important pronouncements to make. So grateful were they for Cupid's daring rescue of Augusta and the other unfortunates trapped in the fire that all the wild charges that had been flung about regarding Seeger's recapture of Cupid were withdrawn. Having thought matters over further, the Primroses found they were perfectly able to believe Opal and Banjo's version of the story after all, and that Nate Seeger was decidedly in the wrong.

Now Sheriff Bledsoe was dispatched to place Nate and his henchman Bendix under arrest on elephant-napping charges, and the men would be placed behind bars for the rest of their days if Miss Augusta had anything to do with it. Good riddance, she said, and then some!

Opal wondered if the dread Nate Seeger would ever learn the error of his ways, prison or not, but Augusta Primrose had, and if she could, then maybe Nate Seeger could, too. Augusta was so contrite, in fact, for her share in the mishaps that Opal and Cupid had endured that she shed copious amounts of tears, using up one handkerchief after the other and asking herself aloud what could possibly have made her say and do such bad things. The Colonel was also sorry for his own wrongdoings, and things were nicely rounded off when both he and Augusta arranged for the mayor of Countytown (an old family friend) to present Opal and Cupid with the keys to the city on the front steps of his office, before cheering fans. Then Miss Augusta offered a public apology in front of Miss Blossom, Banjo, Sister Eclipse, Buddy and Betty, and all Opal's traveling show friends, confessing that she and Goodson had been in grievous and wrongful error to try to tell Opal what she ought and ought not to do with her life. Those were things people had to find out for themsleves and not be told by others. Too bad, but Amelia Vermilyea would just have to look elsewhere for someone to dust her bric-a-brac. Opal had other fish to fry!

"I cannot believe," a contrite Augusta went on, "that both the Colonel and I allowed ourselves to be so dreadfully misled, and by two such odious men." She made a face to show just how odious she now found Seeger and Bendix to be. "Henceforward we shall be more careful about those in whom we place our trust." She smiled hopefully and took the liberty of pressing Opal to her bosom. Her pin grazed the girl's cheek, but no scratch appeared.

At least Miss Augusta had admitted her mistakes, which is what people always ought to do, Opal thought, providing they recognized them as mistakes.

"Now we must be off and away to home," Augusta added with

a great show of elation, slipping her arm through her husband's and carrying him off like a parcel. "Come visit us," she cried from the window of the Rolls as Jekyll, with Miss Blossom in the front seat beside him, drove them away. "Come stay at Primrose Hill. The doors are always open to you and yours." She of course included Cupid in her remarks. "And never forget Peavine," she added, "for I am sure Peavine will not forget you!"

The Colonel waved his new panama hat in agreement, and off they all went, up hill and down dale along the dusty red road that headed south. Opal wiped away a furtive tear, for she was truly sorry to see Augusta and the Colonel leave. It just went to show, you never could tell about people, could you? Sometimes they just weren't as bad as they made themselves out to be. She went and stroked the gray wrinkled trunk of her elephant, for Cupid was feeling a bit melancholy, too.

But Opal knew it wouldn't do to dwell on sad things; it was necessary to look ahead, to see what lay beyond the next bend. And this was true enough, for other events of great importance were to follow the farewells taken that day on the Countytown Square. No sooner had they returned to the circus grounds than they were greeted with exciting news. With all the publicity from the elephant-napping and the hotel fire rescue, Sam 'n' Tam were throwing caution to the wind. They were going on a Grand Tour! That was the phrase they used, and a highfalutin phrase it was. Furthermore, Buddy and Betty, who were still waiting for their Hollywood movie contract to come through, had agreed to sign on for another six weeks.

Naturally both Opal and Cupid were thrilled that their friends were staying on, and at the prospect of the new tour, and it seemed that as life took yet another turn, there was much to look forward to.

"Just think of it, li'l Bug," said Banjo. "No mo' Croker Corners and Suet City; no mo' Porkville and Peanut Town; none of them hick places. From now on it's Kankakee and Oshkosh and Rapid City, and Cincinnatah and Akron and Toledo." Then, Opal knew, they were going to Washington and Philadelphia, and finally Boston, the end of the line for the season.

But, Cupid wanted to know, would the show be traveling to New York? It was the question everyone was asking, not just the elephant. Boston and Philly were fine, of course, but you really weren't in the Big Time unless you played New York, like the Ringling Brothers and Barnum & Bailey shows did each spring.

While Opal and Cupid pondered this question and set to the hard work ahead, preparing for their introduction into those exalted spheres of glorious fame and fortune, their friend Banjo got on with his own plans, of a decidedly more personal nature. Because Sister Eclipse had agreed to waste no more time in becoming Mrs. Banjo B. Bailey, and since this remained the gentleman's most cherished dream, he proceeded accordingly. A married man he wished to be; a married man he soon would be.

And so it was that Banjo and Sister Eclipse were joined in holy wedlock by a justice of the peace in the city of Indianapolis in the state of Indiana. Opal and Cupid were both witnesses, as well as Buddy Pepper and Betty Buckeye, and after the ceremony there was a reception at a downtown hotel, to which all the other show folk were invited.

It was in the Hyacinth Room, after the three-tiered wedding cake had been cut and the bride and groom had been toasted, that, with everyone on hand, the Solo Brothers made another of their thrilling announcements. They stood up on little gold chairs, side by side, cigars in hand, to tell the assemblage that they had made a booking for an appearance in New York City after all! The deal had just been set, and when the Boston playdate was over, they would shut down for a period of two weeks, in order for their star attraction, Opal and Cupid, to make a special guest appearance run at the famous Radio City Music Hall!

What? How's that again? Had Opal heard right? She could hardly believe her ears. Radio City was where her daddy worked! She looked at Cupid, then back at Sam 'n' Tam again, making sure they weren't kidding. But it was no joke, it was the real McCoy, all right. And two weeks at the Music Hall wasn't hay! Opal was beside herself with joy, and there were shouts and applause in the low-ceilinged room as Cupid wrapped her trunk around her and hugged her tight. Fortunately for the hotel management, Cupid resisted the temptation to hoist Opal high into the air as she often liked to do when she was elated, for this would no doubt have caused some damage to the Hyacinth Room's crystal chandelier, not to mention what it might do to Opal herself.

In a toast to the stars and to Sam 'n' Tam's stupendous news, everyone raised a glass, followed by three cheers—hip-hip-hooray! Banjo, with his new bride at his side, stood grinning from ear to ear, for as everyone knew, aside from it being the happy day of his nuptials, the Big Time had been Banjo's dream as much as it was Opal's. Then everyone crowded around, oohing and aahing about how Radio City Music Hall was the most important playdate in the country, and saying how happy they were for Opal and Cupid.

"Who knows," said Buddy Pepper, "there might even be a Hollywood talent scout in the audience." And Betty added that there could be a movie contract in the offing as well. They might *all* end up in Hollywood!

Opal's heart leapt with excitement. At last—just like Cupid had said, all her dreams were coming true, and, most important of all, she was going to get to see her daddy! She shed tears of joy at the thought of it, and Cupid was not afraid also to shed a tear or two (being larger, her tears were naturally bigger than Opal's, but they were shed in a good cause). Before long it seemed as if everyone in the Hyacinth Room was crying over the thought of Opal and Cupid playing the Big Time and being reunited with Jimmy-Jack Thigpen.

Opal and Cupid had never been happier, and they turned to each other with love and appreciation for what each had brought to the other over the past months, reaffirming the depths of their feelings for one another. And as she always did, Cupid listened with all seriousness and a look of hope in her eye as Opal described what it would be like when they got to the Big Apple and the great theater where they were to appear, the greatest theater in the world!

Banjo and Sister Eclipse had planned to make the Grand Tour their own honeymoon, and so off they all went, slapping new labels on their trunks in every city they played. The weeks sped by, each day bringing Opal closer to the moment she would see her daddy again. She knew she would recognize that flash of white teeth that was so characteristic of Jimmy-Jack, and she thought she could even smell a whiff of Daddy's favorite shaving lotion already.

Meanwhile, Miss Blossom, stalwart soul that she was, had proved a faithful correspondent since she and Opal had parted in Countytown, and at each stop on the tour there was bound to be a few carefully penned pages giving the latest Peavine news, which Opal would dutifully read to Cupid. Miss Blossom's first letter was the most important, for she had enclosed a postal card from Opal's daddy that she'd received upon her return home. The sad news of Granny Bid's death had reached Jimmy-Jack at last, and he hoped that Opal was being well taken care of until such time as he could come south for her. Opal smiled at Cupid. Wouldn't Daddy be surprised when they jumped the gun on him and showed up on his doorstep. (Or would that be his stage doorstep?)

More news from Miss Blossom over the weeks told about Miss Augusta, who seemed quite a changed character, given to humorous sallies and mirthful asides these days, while the Colonel, amazingly, had golfed a hole in one. Augusta had even spared Granny Bid's old place, rerouting the new road, and the Cumberpatches had shown uncommon enterprise in setting up a roadside stand on the spanking new motorway, vending Opal and Cupid souvenirs, and were realizing a healthy profit conducting tours of Granny Bid's one-room shack and selling pennants printed: BIRTHPLACE OF THE FAMOUS OPAL AND HER ELEPHANT CUPID!

All this proved interesting to Opal. It was nice to be appreciated at last by the Cumberpatches, she told Cupid, even if they were making money off them. And the alterations in Miss Augusta's character only went to prove that contrary to popular belief the leopard could change his spots, and there was hope for everyone.

In return, Opal had written to Miss Blossom the minute they'd received the announcement in Indianapolis about going to New York and the Radio City Music Hall. It was the most she'd ever written to anyone, but thanks to all the time she'd put in at her schoolwork between rehearsals and performances, her penmanship had improved by leaps and bounds. Besides, she had big news for Miss Blossom, and an invitation of the utmost importance that only she herself could deliver:

> Dear Miss Blossom,
>
> Thank you for your letter with the postal from my daddy and all the letters after that with all the nice news from Peavine about Miss Augusta, the Colonel, and the Cumberpatches. I have a big sur-

prise for you, and Cupid and I hope it will be a big surprise for Daddy, too, so don't write and tell him anything. It looks like we are going to be hitting the Big Time soon. Sam 'n' Tam are taking us to New York to play at the Radio City Music Hall!!!!! and I am writing to ask if you can come north on the train to see us there. With Granny Bid watching from the Pearly Gates, Cupid and I can't think of anyone from Peavine that we would like to have come visit us more, outside of my daddy, but he'll be there anyway, tapping right along with all those big city folks in his flashy red costume with the brass buttons. And there's more news. Since Banjo and Sister Eclipse just got hitched, Buddy and Betty have decided to tie the knot, too. And when we go to New York they are leaving for Hollywood to be in a movie with Shirley Temple. Imagine that!

Well, that's all for now. I hope you can come up to visit and we can surprise Daddy together. Please say hello from Cupid and me to Miss Augusta and the Colonel. Oh yes—and the Cumberpatches, too.

Love and kisses,

Opal

P.S. Tell Henhouse for me that since Cupid was so brave and fearless during the hotel fire in County-town, she got over her fear of mice, too. Didn't I say she was a special elephant?

P.P.S. See you in the Big Time!

Chapter Eighteen

The Big Time—At Last

ON A FINE SPRING MORNING, AS THE LONG SHINY
black limousine that Sam 'n' Tam had hired to transport them to
Manhattan from Boston came over a rise along the parkway,
Opal's heart did a giant flip-flop. There in the hazy blue distance
lay the magical city of New York, to Opal's mind a city every
bit as enchanted as the Emerald City in *The Wizard of Oz*. But
without the emeralds. This city was all lustrous gold and shining
silver, with its tall, slender towers and rooftops brightly gleaming
in the June sunlight. She could even make out the taller-than-
all-the-others spire of the Empire State Building, looking even
grander than it had on her daddy's postcard.

As they passed onto a silver bridge that was like a giant Erector
Set, the traffic whizzing by the window in both directions, Opal
gazed down at the sparkling river. Just one more river to cross
and they'd be on Manhattan Island. She felt an uncontrollable
excitement run through her body, and with this thrilling feeling

came the realization of her fondest dream: The circus was coming to town, and Opal and Cupid were its stars! And tonight they would be with Opal's daddy on the great stage of Radio City Music Hall.

Being on the verge of seeing her daddy again after all these years, Opal could hardly contain herself, and it was such heartening thoughts as these that wafted her into the city on a pink cloud. And suddenly there they were in the crowded, busy streets so jam-packed with people rushing everywhere, with such wonderful sights to see: big, fat yellow taxicabs with black and white checkered stripes on them; neon signs the size of buildings flashing with all the colors of the rainbow; policemen with long nightsticks mounted on real live horses like Colonel Eddy's Wild West Cowboys; electric trains that went whizzing by on overhead tracks (the trains were called the "el" for "elevated"); a man on stilts sporting a top hat and tailcoat and striped pants, and carrying what Sam 'n' Tam called sandwich-boards on his front and his back. The advertisement on the front board read:

SEE THE BIG MOVIE HIT

Top Hat

STARRING

FRED ASTAIRE AND GINGER ROGERS

AT THE

WORLD FAMOUS

RADIO CITY MUSIC HALL!!!

while the back part of the sandwich-board read:

AND

SEE THE LIVE STAGE SHOW

Spring Circus Extravaganza

STARRING

OPAL AND CUPID

ON THE GREAT STAGE

WITH THE ROCKETTES!

Opal's heart leapt. She knew the Rockettes were the famous line of dancing chorines that did precision tap dancing and high kicks, and she couldn't wait to see them.

Then there they were pulling up in front of Grand Central Station, where Sam 'n' Tam had instructed the driver to stop so they could meet Miss Blossom, who was arriving on the one o'clock train from Peavine. Banjo and Sister Eclipse would be arriving from Boston with Cupid and Pickles in a specially designed flat-bed truck, for even the clever Banjo hadn't been able to figure out how to limousine an elephant and her family of friends from one city to the other.

Opal spotted Miss Blossom standing on the big train station platform, peering all about her as if she, too, had just arrived in Oz itself. Opal and Sam 'n' Tam welcomed her after her long trip north and, thoughtful as ever, Sam 'n' Tam had brought a bouquet of flowers. Miss Blossom cooed to beat the band at having such a fuss made over her. Before long they were all seated comfortably in the long black limousine and heading uptown.

When they rolled up in front of their hotel on a busy corner by a large, leafy park with a lake—Central Park it was called— a smartly uniformed doorman assisted them from the car and escorted them up a flight of marble stairs and into the grand lobby. Opal and Miss Blossom were wide-eyed as they looked around, drinking it all in. Then another smartly dressed young man brought their luggage on a brass cart and accompanied them on the elevator all the way up to their beautiful pink and white room, which overlooked the vast green park, stretching below them almost as far as the eye could see.

"Oh, if only they'd allow elephants in hotels so that Cupid could see all this," Opal said to Miss Blossom. "She'd remember Central Park—I know she would—from the picture Daddy sent."

Even before Opal had removed her coat and hat, bellboys were arriving with messages and gifts of welcome: a basket of fruit and cheese in red cellophane with a big satin bow, and a card that read "Compliments of the Management." Then there was a telegram from Buddy and Betty out in Hollywood:

SORRY WE CAN'T BE WITH YOU AND CUPID ON YOUR NIGHT OF
NIGHTS. WE LOVE YOU. THE MOVIE IS GOING VERY WELL AND
SHIRLEY SENDS A SPECIAL HELLO.

Opal hugged the telegram to her chest; an opening night telegram with a special hello from Shirley Temple!

"How thoughtful of Buddy and Betty to have sent it," Miss Blossom said, as giddy with delight as Opal.

And last but not least, another telegram read:

BREAK A LEG TONIGHT, KIDS
LOVE, BANJO AND ECLIPSE

Break a leg, kids? What could that mean, Opal wondered? For her or Opal to break a leg onstage would be the worst thing imaginable. But Sam 'n' Tam explained that "break a leg" was just a show business expression wishing you good luck. Then, checking their watches, the two brothers said it was time for them to go over to Radio City and make sure that Cupid had arrived safely.

"Oh, yes," Opal cried as they reached the door, "surely they must all be here by now. Tell Cupie I'll see her very soon."

No sooner had they left than Opal and Miss Blossom hurried

to get themselves ready for the big night ahead. They were due at the theater at six o'clock, when, during the intermission between the showing of the movie and the stage show, Opal and Cupid would be taken out onto the great stage to say hello to the audience and to remind them that the Spring Circus Extravaganza, of which they were the star attraction, was about to begin.

As Opal arrived with Miss Blossom at the Music Hall, the thrill of seeing her name in lights on the nearly block-long marquee was overwhelming. It was one thing, she thought, to see your name printed in the morning paper, or even plastered on a billboard or a sandwich-board carried by a man on stilts. But seeing the names Opal and Cupid up there over the theater doors, picked out in bright, twinkling lights, was the kind of experience that anybody who ever wanted to be in show business longed for.

As the car pulled up outside the stage door, the friendly stage doorman, Pop, was there to greet them.

"Happy to see you, Miss Opal," he said, "and to have you in our show."

"Happy to be here, Pop," Opal replied. "This is my friend, Miss Blossom, and she's come all the way from Peavine Hollow to see us," she added. Then, as Pop tipped his hat, Miss Blossom cooed for the hundredth time since she'd arrived in New York.

Pop helped them through the crowds queuing up along Fifty-first Street, waiting to get into the great big theater to see the Spring Circus Extravaganza.

"Hey, Opal," one man in the crowd called out, "where's Cupid?"

"Yeah, where's your elephant, Opal? We can't wait to see her," shouted another.

"Neither can I," Opal answered, then Pop ushered them into the stage door, past the little mailboxes and the dressing room keyboard and into the backstage area of the theater.

What an exciting place it was! Opal could hardly take it all in; Miss Blossom, too. Over the loudspeakers they could hear the soundtrack of the movie playing. Fred was talking to Ginger about "running down to Venice for the weekend." Wasn't that glamorous! Then, a group of tall dancing girls came over to say hello. (The Rockettes! Opal's heart leapt—and they were all so friendly, too.) As they gathered around her, chattering excitedly, Miss Blossom, in a dither, excused herself, saying she must find Jimmy-Jack Thigpen and tell him that someone special had arrived—a surprise!—and was waiting to see him.

There were lots of interesting performers backstage: a dog act, a troupe of bicycle aerialists, a ventriloquist, a family of Swiss bellringers as well as a family of trained seals, and a Venetian troubadour with a mandolin. But Daddy, where was he? Opal wondered. This was such a large place that Miss Blossom was probably having trouble finding his dressing room, where no doubt he would be putting on his makeup and getting ready for the show. Opal couldn't wait to see him in his flashy red dancing costume, not to mention the look of surprise on his face when he realized that Opal of *Opal and Cupid* fame was his very own little girl, and that they were going to be in the same show together.

As the Rockettes went off to get ready, telling Opal to "break a leg," which fortunately she understood by now, Miss Blossom reappeared with the news that Cupid had arrived safely with Banjo and Sister Eclipse. Sam 'n' Tam were helping them load Cupid onto the freight elevator for the trip to the stage-level floor. Unfortunately, Miss Blossom had not been able to locate Daddy, but she was sure that if Opal didn't find him, Daddy would find her, for Miss Blossom had left a special message with Pop, the stage doorman, saying it was very important that he get it to Jimmy-Jack Thigpen.

Meanwhile, Opal must get herself ready, for the show would be starting very soon. As Miss Blossom was escorted by an usher in a red uniform to her seat in the audience, Opal followed a woman in a crisp white uniform to a dressing room with two stars and the names OPAL and CUPID emblazoned on the door. The nice woman carefully applied Opal's show makeup (everybody was so friendly in the Big Time, Opal thought), after which the wardrobe mistress arrived with Opal's freshly pressed costume of pink satin and tulle with sequins all over it, as well as her tap shoes, gold to match her wand and tiara.

Then, when all was in readiness, Opal was escorted to the stage wings, and there, waiting patiently between Banjo and his bride, stood her elephant.

"Cupid!" cried Opal, hurrying to embrace her friend. Cupid had been well cared for during their separation; her skin was washed and she'd been refreshed with her favorite toilet water, *eau de jungle*. Her toenails were buffed, and she had a lively gleam to her eye. On her head she wore a silver harness studded with rhinestones and a golden crown decorated with tall pink ostrich plumes. How glamorous she looked; Opal was so proud of her.

"Oh, Cupid," she whispered ecstatically, "isn't it all wonderful? Are you enjoying it?"

Cupid nodded to both questions. She *was* enjoying it, every bit of it. "And why shouldn't she?" put in Banjo. "It isn't everybody who gets to play the Radio City Music Hall. Especially an elephant." At this Cupid ruffled her ears and tossed her trunk, as if to say she thought elephants should be allowed at the Music Hall just like everybody else.

The movie was ending, and Opal knew that she and Cupid would soon be making their entrance onto the great stage. But still no sign of Daddy. Opal's happiness would be complete at this moment if only . . .

205

Banjo and Sister Eclipse hastened to assure her that her daddy was there in the theater and that they had seen him on their way in. Cupid had met him, too, and once he'd gotten over the surprise of it all, he had said he couldn't wait to see his little girl. But he had his hands full with everything he had to do before the show began, and he said to tell Opal he would see her out there on the great stage in just a few minutes. Opal looked at Cupid, in whose eyes she saw something that she had never seen before, and she had a sudden premonition; something was wrong. But what could it be?

Suddenly the organist struck up "The Continental," a melody from the *Top Hat* movie. As they stood there in the wings, bathed by the dim stage light, Opal could feel her heart pounding. She looked again at Cupid and laid her cheek against the gray trunk and whispered. "What is it, Cupid? Tell me."

But Cupid lifted her head and turned away, as if she hadn't heard or didn't want to hear, and she steadfastly refused to answer. Opal stared hard, trying to think. Plainly, Cupid was on to something Opal wasn't aware of, something having to do with Daddy. A secret of some sort. But being as tactful as she was, she wasn't telling. Neither was Sister or Banjo. Was it because they didn't want to upset Opal just before going onstage? But what could be so upsetting? They had seen Daddy. He was right there in the theater and Opal would be seeing him any minute!

But there was no time now for further puzzlement. Suddenly, the master of ceremonies, wearing a suit like a penguin's, was introducing them, and it was their cue to go on. Cupid hoisted Opal into position on her back, Opal raised her wand with the golden star at its tip, then before she knew it they were out there on the great stage in a brilliant blaze of lights, gazing out at the vast auditorium, the biggest room Opal had ever seen, where

206

every seat was filled, and thousands and thousands of eyes were staring right at them. And as the warm waves of applause washed over them, Cupid, Queen of the Tanbark, took center stage, while riding high atop her, smiling and waving at the cheering crowd, was Opal Thigpen from Peavine Hollow—in the Big Time, at last!

Chapter Nineteen

The Night of Nights

AS THE WAVES OF APPLAUSE SETTLED DOWN, CUPID curtsied as daintily as an elephant can and placed Opal's feet gently onto the great stage of the Radio City Music Hall so she could say a few words to all their fans. Opal wasn't used to talking into a microphone in front of so many people, and she was suffering a bout of stage fright that made her hands tremble and her throat choke up. This was one of the pitfalls of the business of performing, and she knew she had to get over it somehow. The master of ceremonies was helpful: Perceiving her jittery state, he took her hand and squeezed it hard as he admired her costume extravagantly, and he was complimentary in the extreme about Cupid's brightly spangled outfit. When he had gotten Opal to relax a bit, he gave her a genial smile and said into the microphone in his deep, baritone voice, "I know one of our stars here would like to say a few words into our microphone, wouldn't you, Opal?"

His smile frozen on his face now, he moved Opal closer to the microphone and nodded for her to begin.

"Hello, everybody," Opal said timidly. "We're very happy to be here this evening. I hope you'll like us."

"Heck, we don't like you!" shouted a loud voice, giving Opal a start and causing Cupid to draw back in affront. "We *loves* ya!" finished the same voice, and both Opal and Cupid breathed sighs of relief.

Enjoying this bit of ad-libbing, the audience laughed and applauded its agreement, which gave Opal some confidence at a time she needed it desperately. Then Cupid slipped the tip of her trunk into Opal's sweating palm as the master of ceremonies took the microphone again.

"Now, ladies and gentlemen here in the Music Hall and out there in Radioland as well," he began, "this evening we have a special surprise for you." He turned to look at Opal, who stood quietly clutching Cupid's trunk, trying her best to calm down. "Like most little girls in the world," he went on, "*this* little girl here has a daddy. But, unlike most other daddies, Opal's daddy happens to work right here in Radio City Music Hall. That's right, ladies and gentlemen, *right in this very theater!*" The master of ceremonies slipped an arm around Opal's shoulders and, drawing her closer, gave her a friendly hug. "Now, Opal," he said, "you haven't seen your daddy for a long, long time, isn't that so?"

"Yes . . ."

"I thought so. But you'd *like* to see him, wouldn't you?"

"Oh, yes."

" 'Oh, yes' she says, ha-ha." The man used both hands to make encouraging signs to the audience, and a barrage of applause followed, urging the appearance of Opal's father as if he might come flying onstage at any minute on a highwire.

"Now, Opal, tell me something," said the master of ceremonies in a confidential tone, "would you like to see your daddy? That is, see him *right now?*"

"Oh, *yes!* I sure would!" Opal felt a growing excitement. Instead of surprising her daddy it looked like her daddy was going to surprise her.

Her toes and fingers began to tingle. Was this the moment, then? She looked around, back into the wings to the left and right of her, straining for a glimpse of bright red that would be Daddy in his costume, waiting with the chorus to go on. But she didn't see hide nor hair of anyone who might be Jimmy-Jack Thigpen.

"Well, Opal," the master of ceremonies went on smoothly, "since you've worked so hard and have waited for such a long time, and since you've given so much enjoyment to so many people, we Music Hall folks—with a little help from Mr. Banjo B. Bailey and the rest of your friends standing back there in the wings—thought we'd hand you back a little of that enjoyment."

Cupid tightened her grip on Opal's hand and was looking nervous again; downcast, even. What could be the matter now? Opal wondered. She held her breath, lost in thought, and scarcely listening to the master of ceremonies' words as he continued.

"So, Opal Thigpen, every single last person here in this theater tonight wants to see you meet your daddy again after so many years, and we're going to have that wonderful meeting right here on the great stage of the Radio City Music Hall, and it is being broadcast at this very moment all across the country on the Red Network. And so, ladies and gentlemen, without further ado, it gives me the greatest pleasure to present to you Opal's one and only, true and real-life father—Mister Jimmy-Jack Thigpen!"

The crowd started applauding again like crazy, and bright follow spots darted all about the great hall as the sixty-piece orchestra struck up "The Stars and Stripes Forever." Out in the auditorium the ushers did nothing to quiet the crowd, but ran up and down the aisles in their red uniforms with their flashlights shouting *Hooray!* and *Bravo!* enjoying what was to come just as much as everyone else.

Opal stood tiptoe to look past the announcer's shoulder for another peek into the wings, breathless with anticipation. And suddenly—there he was!

Opal's daddy, Jimmy-Jack Thigpen!

The only thing was, Opal hardly recognized him, he was so much older looking. But then, she was older, too, wasn't she? He also looked tired, even though he was dressed in his natty red costume with the brass buttons. And more than that—and this really confused her—instead of coming out from the wings where all the other performers were standing, he was coming out of the audience, walking up the steps at the side of the stage, and behind him, all the Music Hall ushers had gathered at the foot of the stairs and were applauding and urging him on, all wearing the same red costume as Daddy!

Opal was still trying to piece it all together when Jimmy-Jack made his way slowly toward center stage, shading his eyes and squinting against the glare of the follow spot.

"And here he is, Opal," the master of ceremonies announced, "your own true-life daddy, come to greet his Opie, who he has not set eyes on for mmmthfrrrpfmph years."

No one had bothered telling the announcer how many years, so he sort of covered his lips with his palm and said "mmmthfrrrpfmph" instead.

Opal was stunned. But this couldn't be her daddy coming toward her, she thought. If it was, why hadn't he come out of the wings instead of the audience? And furthermore, why was he dressed like all the theater ushers? There must be some mistake;

this man was an impostor, not Jimmy-Jack Thigpen. Why, he didn't even have his tap shoes on. She was so confused and bewildered she didn't know what to think. She fought down the impulse to run and hide somewhere and cry, and as she stood there, her feet stuck to the stage, Jimmy-Jack began to speak in a husky voice that Opal instantly recognized.

"Hi, Opal, honey," he said, and put his arms around her, and in that moment, as he smiled down at her and his smile lit up his whole face the way Opal remembered it used to, and she caught the scent of his cologne, something wonderful happened: Opal knew there had been no mistake; this was her daddy—she was sure of it—and at last she was in her daddy's arms!

"Oh, it is you, Daddy," she cried. "It's really you!"

"Sure 'nuff, honey, it's your old dad, Jimmy-Jack," he said shyly. "Guess you didn't recognize me at first. But you do now, don'tcha?"

Oh, yes, she recognized him all right. The audience was applauding again to beat the band, and Opal could see Banjo and Sister Eclipse standing in the wings, a look of relief on their faces, and Cupid, right there behind her, the tip of her trunk in the small of Opal's back for moral support.

Then the master of ceremonies invited Daddy to say a few words into the microphone. Turning to the audience and getting a grip on the microphone stand, Jimmy-Jack began.

"Ladies and gentlemen, I've been working here at Radio City for quite a few years now. I ran off from Peavine Hollow some years ago, leaving this dear little girl to be brought up by her Great-Granny Bid, who died a little while back at the ripe old age of one hundred and three—"

Opal interrupted to whisper in her daddy's ear.

"Sorry, folks, my little girl here says not a hundred and three, but a hundred-and-two and nine months." The audience laughed.

"Well, I guess that's right if Opie says it is. Anyhow, Old Biddy never got to see her little great-granddaughter become such a big star in the circus, but if she had she'd have been right proud, I know. Just like her Jimmy-Jack. That's me, folks. I'm not a star, though I sure wanted to be. I thought when I got a job here, the next thing I knew I'd be up here on this big stage dancin' my feet off. Well, you know how it goes, I guess. I never did get to dance, 'cept out there in the lobby between shows. Now, I reckon you're asking yourselves, what's Jimmy-Jack doing tapping to an empty room? Well, I'll tell you. It's 'cause that's the only stage I've got. It's true; Jimmy-Jack Thigpen is an usher here at the Radio City Music Hall." He held up his flashlight and displayed it as his badge of office.

Opal looked up at him, puzzlement in her eyes. "It's true, Opie honey," he said, "your daddy's just one big fraud. Y'see, folks," he went on explaining, "it not bein' my chosen profession, I was ashamed of getting people to their seats when I should have been tappin' my feet off on the stage, so I had my picture taken in my red uniform one day and sent it to Opie, letting her think I was hot stuff up here in New York, dancin' in the chorus and playin' in the Big Time. I guess that's the kind of sharpie guy I am."

Jimmy-Jack Thigpen's voice had gone all shaky, and he had tears in his eyes, and the hand that held onto the microphone trembled. The audience hushed to utter silence now; not a sound was heard as they sat wondering what would happen next. Over the loudspeaker the master of ceremonies was saying for the radio audience that there had been an unexpected hitch in the proceedings, and he would give further announcements as details became available.

Opal stood in a daze, aware that every eye in the great big auditorium was on her. Once more, she didn't know what to do or what to think. How could her daddy have fibbed to her like

213

that? One of the things he had taught her was always to tell the truth, and all these years he had been doing just what he'd taught her *not* to do. She felt betrayed, and by the most important person in the world to her. Not even Cupid could help her now. Suddenly, standing there in the silence, on the biggest stage in the world, with hundreds and hundreds of people watching, and thousands more listening to their radios at home, she felt all alone and more terrified than before. She burst into tears and turned and ran into the wings, past the stagehands, past the Rockettes and all the other performers waiting for the show to begin and wondering as much as Opal why all this was happening. She ran as far away as she could, looking for somewhere to hide— anywhere! In a dark corner of the wings she spotted a large black wardrobe trunk and quickly slipped inside it, pulling the doors shut.

Though she was scarcely thinking when she pulled the two halves of the trunk together, the sound of the lock snapping into place brought her to. She was locked inside! Instantly her need to hide herself changed to fear, for she must breathe the air in the trunk and she realized that when that air was all used up she wouldn't get any more and that would be that. And no one knew where she was, so they couldn't come rescue her!

But Cupid did. She had followed Opal offstage and had seen her sneak into the trunk, and when Jimmy-Jack came after her, joining Banjo and Sister Eclipse in the search, Cupid used her own trunk to point out the one where Opal was hiding. Banjo went straight to it and leaned close.

"Opie honey, you okay?" he asked, and put his ear against the lock. He heard some muffled sounds from inside, but no word from Opal.

Sister stood beside Jimmy-Jack, waiting, then she whispered into his ear. "Go talk to her."

"I'm so ashamed, I wouldn't know what to say."

"Sure you do," Eclipse reassured him. "Just say what's in your heart. That's bound to do the trick." She gave him a friendly shove, then pulled Banjo aside, and Jimmy-Jack went and talked to the big black trunk like it was a person.

"Opie, honey? This here's Jimmy-Jack, your daddy. I feel just terrible that I've upset you this way. I wouldn't have hurt you for anything in the world. You're my li'l Opie and I love you with all my heart. I know I've done wrong, fibbin' to you like that after all I tried to teach you, but, you know, grown-ups can make mistakes, too. You see—I reckoned it was all in a good cause. I figured if you thought I was up here in New York bein' hot stuff you'd be able to stand it better down in Peavine with your momma gone, till I could make a success of myself and have some money to be able to send for you. I've been plannin' to do that for the longest time, honest I have. Nothin' in the world would give me more pleasure than havin' my Opie right here with me in New York. But, well—it's been rough." He sighed and shook his head. "I confess it, hon, we've been havin' this doggone Depression, and folks aren't so inclined to be generous when it comes to handin' out tips for a theater seat. But I guess you know that."

"Yes, Daddy, I know," came Opal's voice from inside the trunk.

"Then maybe you can understand why I did what I did. I just wanted you to be proud of me. I wanted you to be as proud as proud can be, and it was the only way I knew how."

"But you could have told me the truth," came Opal's voice through the trunk. "The truth wouldn't have hurt any. It's always the best thing in the long run. You always said that. And I wouldn't have minded that you were an usher. Somebody has to do it."

"You're right there, honey lamb," said Banjo, getting down on his knees beside Jimmy-Jack. "Somebody's got to do it is right, and they tell me that around here your papa-daddy is the A-one top drawer best doggone usher in the whole city of New York!"

"Amen," said Sister Eclipse fervently. She kept her fingers crossed in the hope that Opal would come out before she ran out of air. There was a silence in the trunk while Opal mulled things over.

"Opie, it was partly for Granny Bid, too," Jimmy-Jack went on. "She was more like a momma to me than a granny, you know that. And a boy's momma always wants to be proud of her son. Now she's dead and gone and I guess maybe she's looking down from heaven, and she knows what an all-fired phoney-baloney her Jimmy-Jack is. So, you see, honey, your daddy's got himself a double burden to carry, a heavy load to tote around with him." He sighed and cracked his knuckles, then patted the side of the trunk where a label read:

THE PEORIA HOTEL

BEST LITTLE HOTEL THIS SIDE OF DULUTH

PEORIA, ILL.

"Opie, honey, it's awful hard talkin' to you with you all shut up inside this trunk. Besides, you're liable to suffocate in there. Won'tcha open up just a teeny bit so you can breathe and your daddy can see you when he's talkin' to you?"

There was another silence, followed by sounds of movement from inside.

"Daddy?"

"Yes, honey?"

"Unlock the lock, please."

Luckily the key was in the lock, and when Jimmy-Jack turned it the trunk opened a crack. Peering through it, he could make out Opal's big shiny eyes.

"That's my girl," he said, offering encouragement. "How about a teensy bit more?"

The trunk opened two more inches and presently he could see Opal hiding behind some clothes. To make herself smaller she had folded herself up like a jack knife.

"I reckon your joints must be gettin' stiff along about now, Opie," her daddy said.

Opal allowed as how he was right. She did have some annoying cricks in her knees and elbows, and Sister Eclipse was quick to suggest a rubdown with eucalyptus oil before the night was out.

At last Jimmy-Jack was able to coax his daughter from the trunk altogether, and he helped her to her feet. Then he took her over by one of the stage curtains where it wasn't so dark and put his arms around her. "Now you've found out the truth, Opie. Your daddy's nothin' but a phony. And, honey, all I can say is I'm real ashamed of myself. I don't know how you can ever forgive me."

"Oh, Daddy, you don't have to apologize," said Opal, looking up at him. "I understand, I really do. You know I forgive you." She threw her arms around his waist.

"That's real good of you," he said, and hugged her back, tight enough to hold back all those lost years. In the meantime, Radio City Music Hall's Spring Circus Extravaganza had begun, and Jimmy-Jack knew that despite what had occurred, in the tradition of "the show must go on" Opal had a very important cue coming up. "Now, Opie," he began, "since you're not still mad at your daddy, maybe we can talk some more later and you should go get fixed up so you'll be ready for your big show."

Opal's expression became grave and she frowned. "Oh, I couldn't do that, Daddy. I really couldn't."

"But why not?" Jimmy-Jack looked over to where Banjo and Sister Eclipse stood, listening to every word.

Tears had welled in Opal's eyes, and she began to sob. "I just

don't think I can. I was so afraid out there, and now all this—
please don't ask me. . . ."

Jimmy-Jack took his daughter on his knee and smiled his
hundred-watt smile. "Opie, honey, you are the very best daughter
any daddy could hope to have. Little did I dream that that tiny
mite of a baby would grow up to be a big star in the circus and
a Music Hall headliner to boot. Something tells me you're the
one in the family with all the talent, after all, and I'm so proud
my buttons are fit to bust." As Opal turned away in confusion,
her daddy took her chin gently and made her look into his eyes.
"Opie, this is your big chance. You've worked so hard for this.
Why, I even heard there was a Hollywood movie scout for Mr.
Zanuck out there in the audience tonight. He might put you and
Cupid into the movies. How would you like that?"

Opal hardly knew what to think. It was odd how the brain
could fail in those moments when it was most needed. Of course,
she'd like to be in the movies—like Buddy and Betty were. And
look at Shirley Temple! But all that now seemed like a dream of
long ago.

Then Daddy took her hands and pressed them warmly. "Opie,
honey, I know I ain't done right by you. I know I haven't been
a good daddy."

"Oh, Daddy, don't say that, *please* don't!" Opal exclaimed.

"But it's true, honey," Daddy went on. "You know it and I know
it. But look here, now—here's the thing. I want you to do something for your daddy."

Opal looked at him, uncertain as to what he was going to ask.
"What is it?" she asked meekly.

"I want you to just go on into that dressing room over there
and fix yourself up all pretty again. Then I want you to go and
tell Cupid it's all okay and everything's goin' to be all right and
that you and she are going on with your show tonight."

Opal stared at him as another wave of panic overtook her. The whole idea of going out again on that stage in front of all those people, despite all her dreams, now gave her a sinking feeling in the pit of her stomach. But Daddy wasn't alone in his persuasions. Banjo came forward again and added his own coaxing words to those of Jimmy-Jack, and then Sister Eclipse got into the act, and she talked a lot (as Opal had reason to know she often did), and then they were all talking, trying to persuade Opal to go on.

But they were only words, and Opal was surer than ever that she wouldn't be able to face the crowd again—that great smiling, applauding crowd that she always loved to perform for, but that now seemed like some great big monster, ready to gobble her up.

She trembled at the thought as she tried to make up her mind what to do. But time was growing shorter. Act after act of the stage show had gone on to perform, but you could hear it: The audience was getting restless and impatient, and had begun to stamp their feet and chant loudly.

> *We want Opal,*
> *We want Cupid,*
> *We want some dancin',*
> *So don't act stupid.*

Opal was struck by these words; even though her mind was a a blur, she found it interesting how the entire house could chant in rhyming couplets. But still she couldn't find it in herself to take the fatal step back onto that great big stage.

"I'm sorry," she said apologetically, "but that's my decision, and I intend sticking by it."

Everyone was speechless. It just didn't seem possible. Opal glanced from face to face; they were drawn and defeated. Then she looked at Cupid, whose expression was more morose and downcast than it had ever been, as if Cupid knew from the beginning how badly Opal's surprise would turn out, and how little Cupid herself could do about it. Cupid blinked her eyelids and two big tears slipped from her eyes and ran down her gray cheeks. She gave a halfhearted gesture with her trunk and turned away. Then her large gray shoulders lifted and fell in a mighty sigh, her knees gave way, and she fell to the ground and rolled over right there in the darkened wings while out on the great stage the family of Swiss bellringers were in the middle of their act.

"My garsh," said an awed stagehand, "that elephant just expired."

"Somebody call the wagon," said his pal. "We better embalm her quick before she gets stiff and we can't get her through the door."

"You'll do no such thing," said Opal sharply. "Cupid's not dead. I know her tricks, and this is one of her oldest."

She got down on her knees, and, lifting her elephant's ear, she began whispering into it. "Cupid, honey, this is Opie. I'm right here beside you, and I'd be awful worried if I really thought you were going to die, but I know you're just funnin' the way you like to do. I know it's because you're mad at me for saying I couldn't go on. And I couldn't—before; I was too upset. But now I can see things in a different light, and I really do want to get out there and have us strut our stuff like we've talked about for so long. Truly I do. So if you'll get onto your feet and let me get you fixed up I'll go get ready, too. And, listen . . ." Opal leaned closer and whispered in Cupid's ear so no one could hear. Cupid listened with a wrinkled brow, then smiled and nodded and tossed her trunk high in the air.

"Good, I'm glad you agree," said Opal. "I'll arrange it, wait and see."

220

So saying, she turned and headed for her dressing room with the two gold stars and their names on the door. Cupid nodded sagely as she watched Opal go, knowing what her friend was about to do. Meanwhile, all the backstage crew and performers were in a state of high excitement:

"Yes, yes," said the stagehands, pulling ropes and throwing switches to work the scenery and elevators, "the show must go on!"

And, "Yes, yes, we want to dance with Opal and Cupid," said all of the Rockettes, eagerly queuing up in the wings for their big entrance.

And suddenly the master of ceremonies was striding out onto the stage carrying his microphone, holding his hand up to the audience and interrupting one of the trained seals, who at that moment sat atop a colorfully painted platform with a red rubber ball balanced on the tip of its nose.

"One moment, ladies and gentlemen, please," the master of ceremonies began, "I have good news for you. I have just been reliably informed that moments from now Opal and Cupid *will* appear again!"

With these words the audience applauded, then began to stamp and cheer and shout and holler. Hooray! They were going to get what they had paid to see!

Taking his cue, the orchestra conductor raised his long, slender baton and alerted his musicians. Then he gave the downbeat, and the music began. It was "Puttin' on the Ritz," and the crowd applauded even more in anticipation of what was about to come. Every eye was riveted on the great stage, ablaze with color and light, as one by one, starting with the most petite, tipping their top hats and fingering their canes, the Rockettes toe-stepped their way onto the great stage. The audience oohed and aahed as they watched, and when all the dancers were lined up across the stage from right to left, graduating in size from shorter girls at the ends to taller girls in the middle, their rhinestone-studded costumes and tights shimmering in the dazzling lights, they began the series of precision maneuvers and high kicks for which they were famous the world over.

Then the line divided down the middle into two sections, and as the Rockettes fanned out in perfect formation toward the sides of the stage, the floor of the giant stage, as if by some feat of magic, opened up—as big as the Grand Canyon—and a large subterranean elevator began to rise slowly into view. The audience aahed again and applauded, for on the rising platform, standing completely still in an array of poses, was a spectacular line of thirty elephants! Yes, thirty big, gray, wrinkled pachyderms, and all wearing top hats!

When the platform reached the stage level and stopped, the elephants took their cue to break their formation. In synchronized movements they fanned out like the Rockettes before them had done, onto the apron of the stage, where they proceeded to wrap their trunks around the waists of the dancing girls, hoisting them high into the air and setting them onto their backs. At this point the elephants and the Rockettes atop them began to move and sway to the rhythm of the crescendoing music, and standing in the wings, Opal knew the time had come. But where was Daddy?

Then, as Opal looked around, there he came, striding toward them, all decked out in a silk top hat and a suit of tails and carrying a black walking stick with a gleaming gold top. Behind him stood Banjo and Sister Eclipse, beaming, and Miss Blossom, who had returned backstage during all the commotion earlier to make sure Opal was all right.

And, boy, was she all right. "Oh, Daddy!" she cried, hugging him like she never wanted to let go. "Don't you look wonderful!"

Jimmy-Jack tipped his hat back off his face with a swing of his cane and smiled. "Yes, Opie, it's you 'n' your daddy now, it's the Big Time for sure."

Her heart bursting with happiness, Opal slipped a wink over at Banjo, Sister Eclipse, and Miss Blossom, then nodded at Cupid, whose trunk curled and swung her up to her accustomed place behind her ears. Then Jimmy-Jack held out his arms and Cupid wrapped her trunk around his waist, too, and lifted him up and set him down behind Opal on her big broad shoulders. With two such important personages sitting atop her, Cupid raised her trunk into the air as high as it would go and trumpeted a call of such glee that it could be heard all the way to the back row of the topmost balcony in the Music Hall. And Opal alone knew the depths of Cupid's feelings; for them both, this moment was wishes and dreams come true.

"Smile, hon—*smile!*" cried Banjo from behind them. "Let the customers see the ivories!"

"*Cue Opal! Cue Cupid!*" called the stage manager as a little red light flashed from the orchestra pit.

In a split second's worth of time Opal glanced over her shoulder at Daddy, then over to where Banjo and Sister Eclipse and Miss Blossom stood, all bursting with pride. It was a look back, not just at her daddy and her friends, but at the childhood she was leaving behind, at little Peavine Hollow and Primrose Hill, at Lucerne and Lola and Zephyr, and the Old Cotton Road and Old Man Cumberpatch and all his crazy tribe, and at the waving fields of corn and the red, dusty roads of Mississippi.

Then, straightening, she looked ahead again, out to where the lights shone so brightly and thirty elephants were waiting to dance.

"This is it, Cupid," whispered Opal, "let's go strut our stuff!"

There was one last pang of momentary stage fright as she waited for the conductor's cue, but in another moment that fear fled as she was squeezing her daddy's hand and Cupid was carrying them out onto the great stage. Suddenly they were bathed in the welcome glow of those wonderful warm pink lights, and the music rose to greet them, and with the music, the sound of six thousand clapping hands washed over them like a warm friendly shower, and Opal forgot about everything but being in the light and hearing the music and the applause. It was all for her—for her and Cupid—and for Daddy, too. She could feel the waves of love coming at them from everyone in the audience, and as she smiled and waved her golden wand, she gave that love back to them, for as she began to sing, her heart went out to them, to each and every one of them.

On that night of nights, on the great stage of the Radio City Music Hall, Opal sang the best she ever had. And they liked it.

And when she danced with her daddy in his tails and his top hat, Jimmy-Jack was a dancing fool; and they liked him, too.

But most of all they loved Cupid.

But then, so did Opal.

The following week, the first week of June, Opal and Cupid, with Banjo and Sister Eclipse and Jimmy-Jack Thigpen, boarded the *Super Chief* Express. They were going far beyond the Sawdust Trail, even beyond the great stage at the Radio City Music Hall— all the way to Hollywood. And when they arrived the big studio chief, Mr. Zanuck himself, was on the platform waiting for them, with Buddy and Betty—and Shirley, too—and a great big banner welcoming the new stars to a new adventure in Movieland.

About the Author

After a notable career as an actor on the stage, in television, and in films, climaxed by his award-winning performance in *The Cardinal*, Thomas Tryon retired from acting to concentrate on writing. His first novel, *The Other*, published in 1971, became a huge best-seller, was made into a movie, and is now taught in high schools and colleges across the country. Six other novels followed: *Harvest Home, Lady, Crowned Heads, All That Glitters, Night of the Moonbow*, and *The Wings of the Morning. The Adventures of Opal and Cupid* is his only novel for young readers. Mr. Tryon died in 1991.